LET THE DARK FLOWER BLOSSOM

LET THE DARK FLOWER BLOSSOM

A NOVEL

Norah Labiner

COFFEE HOUSE PRESS
MINNEAPOLIS
2013

COPYRIGHT © 2013 Norah Labiner
COVER & BOOK DESIGN Linda S. Koutsky
COVER PHOTOGRAPH PinkBadger, iStockphoto

Coffee House Press books are available to the trade through our primary distributor, Consortium Book Sales & Distribution, cbsd.com or (800) 283-3572. For personal orders, catalogs, or other information, write to: info@coffeehousepress.org.
   Coffee House Press is a nonprofit literary publishing house. Support from private foundations, corporate giving programs, government programs, and generous individuals helps make the publication of our books possible. We gratefully acknowledge their support in detail in the back of this book.
   Good books are brewing at coffeehousepress.org

LIBRARY OF CONGRESS CATALOGING-IN-PUBLICATION DATA
Labiner, Norah, 1967–
Let the dark flower blossom : a novel / by Norah Labiner.
p. cm.
ISBN 978-1-56689-320-6 (pbk.)
I. Title.
PS3562.A2328L48 2013
813'.54—DC23
2012036525

FIRST EDITION | FIRST PRINTING
PRINTED IN MINNESOTA

ACKNOWLEDGMENTS
Lines of poetry are taken from the following: "Sweeney among the Nightingales," by T. S. Eliot; "Ode to Broken Things," by Pablo Neruda; "The River Merchant's Wife: A Letter" and "Hugh Selwyn Mauberly," by Ezra Pound; and "Leda and the Swan," by W. B. Yeats.

You be the judges
Between Me and My vineyard:
What more could have been done for My vineyard?
That I failed to do in it?
Why, when I hoped it would yield grapes,
Did it yield wild grapes?

—ISAIAH 5:3

CHAPTER 1

Susu breaks the first rule of storytelling

HE ONLY SAID HER NAME TO ME ONCE. It was a hot dull morning. We had coffee and oranges on the balcony. He stood at the crumbling stone peeling an orange. He looked down at the street below. He said, "I saw you once years ago." I came to the edge, the stone, a balustrade, he called it; and stood next to him, holding my cup, a demitasse. The coffee was bitter black boiled through with cardamom and sweetened with honey. "It was snowing," he said. "I called after you," he said. He looked at me in the sun, and I pitied him, but didn't want him to know this. He put a hand to my face, and I knew that he wasn't really talking to me, that he was talking to her. He said, "I saw you in a coat with a fur collar." And then he broke the orange into two, and he handed half to me. He said, "I'm sorry." He said, "I'm sorry about the world. I'm sorry that this is all that is left for you, just bones and rotten broken things." He looked down at the street. This was the last morning, wasn't it? of coffee and oranges and green birds. It was morning, and he talked, as he watched the girls on their bicycles, as we stood on the balcony. He waited. He waited. A bird flew low to him. I said, I asked him, "How does the story begin?" He picked up from his plate a heel of bread, buttered. He broke the hard floury crust to bits and scattered it for the birds. He licked the butter from his fingers. He did not answer. He turned. He went from the sun of the balcony back into the room all shadow. There was a box on the table. Each morning I opened the box. Each morning I asked him the same question. And he would not, he would never answer. I should have hated him, but I did not. I collected my things for the seaside: postcards; licorice; a mystery novel. He sat at the table. I was at the door. I looked back. I had a terrible feeling. I felt, I thought that I might never see him again. I was going to leave and then, I did not leave, because I was young and I thought that I would never see him again, because the green birds and bread and oranges prophesied, promised omens, and that the foreign sky was too old, too hot, too ancient for me; I went back to him. I waited. I waited. In a vase on the table there were dark flowers. In the lobby of the hotel there was a statue of a goddess. And everyone said that she was a saint. There was sun from the balcony, but he sat in shadow. He took his manuscript from the table. The pages were tied around and knotted with string. He untied the knot. A sheet of paper fell to the floor. And he said, "The story begins with a rock and ends with a scissor."

CHAPTER 2

Sheldon finds no justice in poetry

ROMAN STONE IS DEAD. I read about it in the newspaper. His obituary ran in the *New York Times* with that picture of him from the jacket of his first book: twenty years old, smiling, fair-haired, and careless. He was never one to put on the serious face of the tortured artist for a press photo. He was never the intellectual caught in deep contemplation of the human soul. No, you'd find him grinning as though the photographer captured him just at a dirty joke's obscene one-two punch. He exemplified that rule so beloved by English professors, myself once included: he wrote from experience. Herein was— or *is*—the danger. He was a storyteller. His life was his logos. And his death—his murder—was only the second-best story that he never told.

I live on an island. Nothing goes to waste here. The apples are sweet. The grapes are sour. I have a hatchet and a shovel. Newspapers come to my box at the postal station. I save the old papers for kindling. This morning when I lit the stove, I found myself burning Roman's picture. I tried to get the page back from the fire, but I was too late.

What could I do but let it burn?

I have never found any justice in poetry.

He died six months ago in Virgil's Grove, Iowa, while watching a baseball game on television. He was discovered by a delivery girl bringing his dinner: two cheeseburgers, onion rings, and chocolate cake. She said that the door was open; that she heard the cheering crowd.

He wrote of fate and then fell to it.

The obit called him a provocateur.

The police called his death the result of a robbery gone wrong.

Anaxagoras said: *The descent to hell is the same from every place,* but it was my sister Eloise who pronounced on the day—or maybe it was night—she met him: *Roman Stone was born to be murdered.* She wasn't joking. Eloise, who is the younger twin by a matter of minutes, felt—or feels—an absolute narrative honesty that I myself have never quite been able to evince.

If there is a god who winds watches; if there is a destiny that shapes our ends; then Roman was lucky. He was lucky right up until the moment that he wasn't. His father was a Nobel Prize winner; his mother, an actress turned political activist. He was big and brash and relevant as hell. Even his death was relevant. America's literary zeitgeist cut down in the heartland? What did it mean? Was it a metaphor? Or a symbol? It was more than an ending; it alluded to godlessness and dark times ahead.

Roman's widow, Dibby, wore to his funeral a black dress made by some certain in-demand designer; and his mournful readers wondered, without guile or accusation, only curiosity, about how much such a garment must have cost. Roman's two sons, in Eton suits with short pants and kneesocks, sat one on either side of their spectacularly pretty nanny. Dibby Stone sat further down the aisle—disconsolate; crying into a black lace handkerchief—propped between a foreign diplomat and a film star, both of them dear acquaintances of her late husband.

The eulogy began with a question.

Who was Roman Magnus Stone?

The question sounds like a quiz show answer. I remember suddenly a winter afternoon years ago. Nothing brings out nostalgia—even for the rotten times—like loss.

Who was Roman Stone?

I am Sheldon Schell.

I was once his sidekick. Back in the days when we were young, when the paparazzi loved nothing more than to catch a close-up candid of Roman—the loudmouth, the lothario—getting into trouble. Remember the time he threw that pompous actor into a swimming pool? Or how he smashed up his Porsche but walked away from the wreckage without a scratch? What about that award ceremony where he fell off the stage? You may not have noticed me in the photographs, but there I am nonetheless, lurking behind Ro or half-dissected—an arm or shoulder only—in the frame. There is one particular shot of us—; it was snapped at a Hollywood premiere. This was 1983. Roman's first novel had just been adapted into a film. He could do no wrong. He was romancing a starlet. His name was inscribed in the gossip columns. The photo appeared in a glossy magazine known for tracking the comings and goings of the latest glitterati. The girl, Roman, and I stand before an absurdly flowing champagne fountain. I am scowling. Roman has his arm around the girl. She is fawnish and fragile. He appears like a golden good-humored satyr at her side. The caption reads: *Harlow Jamison and Roman Stone, with unidentified friend, also a novelist.* Soon after this, the girl made a splash by very publicly breaking up with Roman and then checking herself into rehab. I don't know to what substance exactly she was addicted, but she had a complete break-down. I heard that she never quite recovered her mind. This is not said as an indictment of the poor girl's character; she was delicate. Soulful, even. I always liked her. I offer this detail as a testament to how difficult it was for the rest of us to keep up with Roman.

I am S. Z. Schell.

I am also a novelist.

This is not a novel. It is a memoir; it is a memoir by way of being a compendium of memories. It is a true story, even if the truth that I supply is based on nothing more tangible or less axiomatic than my capacity for remembrance itself.

I am a hermit, sure—a misanthrope, maybe. I won't attempt to provide some simulacrum of the past. I won't go about arranging memories into an orderly line of time—simply for the sake of read-ers. Readers; oh! was Ro ever mad for them. Pleasing an audience was only his second-favorite perversion. No one could toss the coin, knot the noose, or beat the clock as he could. When he had a girl tied to the chair, you always turned the page a little more quickly. Poor rotten Ro—the book club heartthrob. He was admired and annotated. He was born to be explicated. Who could deny him this rite of final exegesis?

I was born in Omena, Michigan, in 1960. I was named after my father. My sister was named for my mother. Twins ran in our fam-ily; and it was said that of the two children, one would be good and the other bad. A twisting dirt road led to us. Our house bordered a salt creek. We crossed the creek to get to the woods beyond. We had a garden with an apple tree, with plums, and roses, and white flowers climbing a wooden fence. The fence was meant to keep the deer out, but it did not. They were drawn to the salt. The flowers must have tasted of it. The white flowers opened at night. The apples were sweet for only a short time before the snow fell.

My father saw the world in terms of right and wrong, and this caused him unbearable pain. He was prone to headaches. He had fits of despair. He slept by day; was wary of sunlight. My mother gave him medicine. Sometimes he wept. And his face would go ghostly white. At night he descended the staircase. He looked then as Moses must have when he came down from the mountain. We whispered, so as not to disturb the substance of his suffering. We were in awe of him, of his agonies. He built wooden toys: little ships, mazes, tops, dollhouses, and boxes. By trade, he was a casket-maker; by philosophical bent, a phenomenologist; by way of Medieval humor, melancholic. My sister and I called his dark moods: the crazies.

I spent hours in escape at the library. I read books filled with strange acts: bravery, sacrifice, love, unspeakable emotions. I fought bulls and fished with Hemingway. I walked the Liffey's banks with Joyce. Flaubert unbuttoned Emma's blouse. Fitzgerald took me for riotous excursions in his Stutz Bearcat. I hopped trains with Kerouac and shared a prison cell with Koestler. I went underground. I lighted out for the territories. I lost myself in Faulkner's wisteria-scented twilight. I lost track of time idling along Swann's Way. I learned. I dreamed. I knew what I wanted to do with my life. I wanted to write novels. It was with great adolescent and egomaniacal pleasure that I wandered the fiction stacks alphabet-wise—moving slowly, running my fingers along the spines—coming to a halt—finding the place where one day my own book would sit. I knew words. I had dreams. What did I lack? I lacked only experience.

I longed for experience. And then I went to college.

And I met Roman Stone.

Sheldon, I was named. Shelly, I was called. Or Shel.

I preferred to see my name in initials.

Eloise and I won scholarships to Illyria College. We traveled from Michigan to Iowa on a Greyhound bus. We took turns at the window seat. She read *The White Goddess*. I scribbled colossal thoughts in my notebook. I was anxious to begin my life. I had a portable typewriter; a box packed full of paperback editions of modernist classics; and a dossier file of letters of reference from former English teachers. I was, they agreed: a real writer.

Roman came from the East. He had been kicked out of any number of prep schools. His father was an economist, an expert in monetary theory. He played golf with the president and racquetball with Kissinger. He collected pop art, vintage pornography, young wives, and murder weapons from famous crimes. He was a nut, sure, but even he had limits to luxury; he was unhappy with his son's antics. He wanted Roman to take college seriously. Milton Stone exiled his only son to Illyria in hopes that Ro would get into less trouble out in Iowa than he had in Maine, in Vermont, in Massachusetts, and New Hampshire. What did Ro's mother think about all this? She couldn't be concerned with something as effete as her son's academic mishaps. She was a knockout Swedish girl who had appeared in one or two Bergman films in the late fifties. His parents met at a Nobel ceremony; their marriage—a brief ill-fit union of buttondown capitalism and sans-brassiere socialism that produced one singularly amoral child—didn't last long. Astrid, his mother, left Roman with his father in New York, while she went off and worked in refugee camps in various war- and disease-ravaged places across the globe. When Roman was sixteen his father married again; this time to a nineteen-year-old piano prodigy. If I inherited from my father his mercurial moods, Roman got from Milton Stone the hapless ability to accumulate cash and appreciate spectacular girls. *Appreciate* is too politic a word. To hear Roman tell: he really fell for his stepmother. He said that he seduced the poor girl, while his father in the next room was on the telephone explaining risk aversion to the president. All this: the family yarns, the tangle of fame and sex and money and genius, made up the substance of *Babylon Must Fall,* Roman's blockbuster first novel.

We were an unlikely pair, Stone & Schell, like an old vaudeville team, the suave straight man and the goofy fall guy. It was the luck of the draw that brought us together; we were assigned as roommates at Illyria in September 1978. He had spent that summer slumming around London. I had been stocking shelves at the Ben Franklin. We got on as only opposites do. I was serious, and he was a showman. I was anxious, and he was an exhibitionist. He was a Yankees fan; his father had season tickets. I followed the travails of the Tigers on a transistor radio. If you want to be high-minded about it: he was Dionysian, and I was Apollonian. We were eighteen. I was a slow learner; he was a quick study. I was dark. He was blonde and blue-eyed; when he was drunk or otherwise inspired his high forehead glowed pink, damp, and radiant. He carried his weight well; he was broad and easy and affable. I was too tall and tended to stoop, hunch, and mumble. I had in me more of my father's crazies than I then dared to admit.

I never minded that Roman took center stage—or center field—and he, for his part, loved an audience. He was elegiac on the topic of baseball; in the truest degenerate crypto-Byronic sense, he was romantic. And this drove girls mad for him. He dated Eloise. He broke her heart, though she readily and repeatedly forgave him.

Girls always forgave him. His cruelty seemed, at least to them, unintentional.

He wrote the book in one draft on my typewriter. I should have taken this as a symbolic or territorial affront, as bad as, or worse than his mistreatment of my twin. But I was silent. *Babylon Must Fall* was published in our senior year of college. And it was a hit. The world was ripe and ready for Roman. He arrived on the scene at the age of twenty, just when readers needed him most. They were tired of important books: of morality tales, politics, the past, the 1970s; war and peace and psychedelia; of hullabaloo, hippies, and beatniks; historical epics; manifestos and feminism; radical chic and issue art; of intellectual games, puzzlers, and poetic one-upmanship. They wanted flat-out fun. They wanted stories about beautiful young people with money doing wicked things. This, Roman could and did provide. He wrote the perfect contemporary novel. It was sweet and sharp and smart and salty and melt-in-your-mouth at the shopping mall sordid.

The book was destined for Hollywood.

And we followed not far behind.

After graduation Roman went out to California. And I, with no plans of my own, and swept up in the maelstrom of his literary success, tagged along. In L.A. Roman fit right in. He was fair-haired and tan. He bought a Porsche convertible. He wore linen suits and sneakers. He turned up his collar and never turned down an invitation. I was adrift. I was aimless. I was no good at sunshine. I was— everyone in Roman's hip new entourage agreed—a real buzzkill. We went to discos, to parties, to private after-hours clubs where uninhibited rich kids shed the last of their inhibitions. I couldn't get troubled thoughts out of my head: my father's moral questions; Moses coming down the mountain; the image of Lot's wife—casting one last longing glance over her shoulder—harrowed me. Sure,

I swam in the ocean. I gazed at palm trees. I ate oranges. Sodom was sensational. Gomorrah was great. Roman was in his element. But I was lousy at the lewd life. So what did I do? I retreated from California in despair. My quest for experience was a gold-rush bust. I went back to the Midwest.

Roman left soon after. He headed for New York, where he got caught up in the cocaine, irony, and high-fashion crowd. He wore black and championed l'art brut. I buried myself in graduate school in Wisconsin. Ro sent me postcards. In Las Vegas gambling fascinated him. In Lake Tahoe he learned to ski moguls; he broke his leg and discovered the joys of Demerol. Paris was a blur. Rome was a riot. I took a teaching job at Lindbergh College in Minnesota. I married a girl named Pru. She was an art department beauty, a painter of abstract self-portraits. In brief: we were young. We were happy and unhappy by turns. I complained about my students. Pru colored her hair—pink, blue, violet. I never liked teaching, never had the knack for it. In New Orleans Roman got fat on deep-fried beignets and teacup bourbon. He leaned left—or right—depending on who was buying the drinks—in Miami with the expat intelligentsia. From Seattle, Ro wrote that kids were wearing torn flannel, shooting up heroin, and playing dark music down in basements. I couldn't have cared less. I stopped opening his letters. I barely glanced at the pictures—the Space Needle, the Eiffel Tower—on his postcards. I was getting on with my life.

I lost track of Roman over the years. At least, I tried to lose track of him. Just when I thought that he was gone, he would resurface with a new skill, a new interest, a new book. He was a great success at absolutely everything in general and nothing in particular. He hobnobbed. He gobbled. He got around. He dined at the White House. He met Princess Di; she was rumored to be a big fan. Roman became a celebrity. He was a natural. People liked him.

They bought his books; went to his lectures; laughed at his jokes; liked to know what he was wearing; where he ate and drank; what drugs he was doing or from which he was being rehabilitated. They followed his romances, indiscretions, his fetishes and bad breakups. And when he gave up his enfant terrible antics—married an honest-to-god Southern belle and finally, it seemed, traded his cosmopolitan perversions for suburban bliss—his readers breathed a collective sigh of relief. His readers wanted the best for him. For some strange reason, it seemed to be in America's best interest to see Roman Stone happy.

I never wanted to tell this story.

I wouldn't have considered it, but—

This morning Beatrice picked up my mail for me. I remember. I remember this. Her face in the cold morning. As though she had run all the way through the woods. I was lighting a fire in the stove when she came in through the kitchen door. Beatrice held a letter out to me—and for a moment I could not take it from her. I had a terrible feeling. I felt as though someone had begun to dig my grave. When I looked back at the stove, I saw the newsprint photograph of Roman burning.

I took the letter from her hand.

I opened the envelope.

It held a thin sheet of paper.

I unfolded it. And read it while standing before the fire.

S. Z. Schell:

> *I know who killed Roman Stone.*
>
> *If you want to know about his death, answer three questions about his life.*
>
> *I will come to collect.*

And here he had signed his name.

The way that my cat will present me with a mouse whose neck he has just snapped.

Benjamin Salt—

His name should have meant something.

And, of course; it did. It does.

No one could have expected this turn of events.

Roman Stone is dead.

And I am living on an island.

Benjamin Salt is coming to visit.

He has questions. He wants a story.

I must ready the guest room.

2.

Mrs. Sarasine found herself, on a Sunday morning in November, entirely alone. If it had not happened by plan or design, this solitude was still not unwanted. Quiet hushed throughout her elegantly appointed rooms. The early snow had brought about the cancellation of this month's meeting of her baking club; and now the ingredient evidence of the proposed chess tartlets: the organic buckwheat flour and free-range eggs, the brown sugar, the bourbon vanilla, the hand-ground China cinnamon, the fat golden raisins and blanched pecans, the butter and fleur de sel, the slivered almonds, pistachios, and walnuts occupied her kitchen. Her husband's return home from that interminable murder trial (where Louis Sarasine, counsel for the defense, had entered a plea of *not guilty* and had gone on to destroy the lone witness with a charge of false memory syndrome) had been delayed. The jury was—indecipherable, he said. Or was it enigmatic? It was hard to read a jury. They might be kind; they could be cruel, but Louis said that in the end they would follow the rules. He believed this: in the innate logic of an argument. Or rather, in the innate logic of his own arguments. She had a brief image, an idea: a bird flying, an airplane crashing. She saw herself a widow in a black dress; she knew just the one—and then, no, no. Don't think it. Don't dream it. Don't imagine it, and it won't happen. What one dreams is always possible. Louis was an expert in possibility. He called every day to tell her stories of dead girls. He wouldn't be in to O'Hare until who knows when. And her daughter was traveling abroad: vaguely and euphemistically abroad; and not due back anytime soon; so had said the scrawled hand on a postcard of a ruined amphora dated five months ago. Even the French bulldog, Zola, was spending the day at the groomer's being shampooed, clipped, and—oh, undergoing some new eucalyptus aromatherapy treatment meant to alleviate canine ennui. All the girls in her book club were raving about it. Snow was falling over Lake Michigan. And Mrs. Sarasine, a woman who never let a moment idle by, who kept herself from certain dark thoughts and uncertain realities by keeping busy, sat before the window, staring out at wintry Chicago, still in her silk-trimmed cashmere robe. There were any number of ways that she could have put her time to use. At her escritoire (*oh Moth-er,* her daughter used to say, *call it a desk for Christ's sake*) a stack of cards awaited her, with thank-yous, and how-are-yous, with regrets to extend and envelopes to address; there were phone calls to return. She could have gone to the gym (forty laps four times a week in the heated Olympic-size pool); she could have attempted a batch of those chess tartlets. There was that black dress (hadn't it looked good in the mirror?) to return to the store. No, no: even if the snow would let up, she didn't feel like braving the first rush of the season downtown; though, usually the holiday shoppers, the displays in the windows, the Salvation Army kettle ringers, put her in a pleasant frame of mind. It made her think that perhaps there was hope for civilization.

Should she go to the bookstore and find a new pick for the book club? It was again her turn to choose. The telephone rang, but she did not answer. She studied her fingernail polish. The color was called Shell. And this, whether the delicacy of the pale lacquer or the recollection of the word, caused her almost but not quite beautiful face to soften.

3.

My island is called on old maps—*L'Île-du-Père,* but that name has long since fallen away and now it is known as Pear Island. French missionaries settled here three hundred years ago. They brought evangelical dreams. They wanted to speak the word; but, instead of divinity, they spread disease: smallpox, typhus, plague, influenza, measles. And then having thusly conquered the New World, the missionaries themselves were beset with a mystery ailment. Some died of fevers; others went mad. Those who survived the illness were left lunatics—lunar antic—; they wandered at night along the shore searching for the lost father for whom they had come so far, to such a strange place. Or so goes the legend that the tour guides tell to summer visitors as they show the old houses, the town square, library, the inn, the haunted woods, sandstone bluffs, and spare beaches. In the summer the ferry runs round-trip twice a day—to and from the island to the mainland. Now it is November. The last blackthorn apples have been collected from the trees. The roses have gone to ruin. The days are short and dark. There are few year-round residents. Soon the ferry will cease for the season. This is my world: an island in Lake Superior off Wisconsin's northern peninsula. This is my island—or at least I imagine it as such—. I call my island *Perdu;* I came here a widower wanting to lose my memory, wanting only to forget.

Pear Island is a sanctuary for wild birds.

And there is no small amount of either irony or symbolism in such a statement of fact.

My house is a gateman's cottage. It has two bedrooms, a kitchen, a cellar, and a study that looks out upon the lake. The furnishings were left here, and I have kept them. The walnut chairs are battered but solid. The kitchen table isn't too bad, with a volume of Poe set under the wobbly leg. It is in an aged armchair in the book-cluttered study, that I spend—or waste, that I ravage or run out the clock on—my time.

The walls are covered in faded floral paper. There is a flowery scent, as well, vague—an odor of desire or sickness—. My bed holds the shape of some ghost body. The previous owner was an old man; he died and was buried on the mainland. The cemetery here is full up with the crooked crosses of missionaries and lunatics.

Once on a beach—as a child—I saw a hermit crab take up residence in a tin can.

The old man died and I moved into his shell.

I live alone here.

I fell into habit, in the early years: I woke late in the afternoon; idled over coffee through the pages of Bulfinch's *Mythology;* through Aeschylus, Sophocles, and Eliot. I mourned *Les Fleurs du Mal;* or lingered on *Adonais'* last triumphant stanzas. Maximus of Gloucester longed for blood, jewels, and miracles. Prometheus bound upon the rocks cried out: *I yet have no device / By which to free myself from this my woe.* Oedipus followed the trail of his own footsteps. The mysteries of Eleusis remained so. Have you seen the eternal footman take your coat and snicker? In the margins of every page I found recrimination, accusation. In short: I was afraid. I read until the light waned. And then, as evening fell, I made my way on foot to my nearest neighbor's house. Dr. Lemon is a retired psychiatrist, and we had a standing appointment for dinner and a game of chess. I say *had*—because he is in failing health. Our evenings are abbreviated of argument now. I talk, and he listens. He lives with his daughter, Beatrice. The doctor suffers from a disease that is—in inverse chronological order—destroying his memory. He remembers the far off, but recent events elude him.

He recommended books. He lent me volumes from his library. I was studious. He was sage. And we moved—slowly—our rooks and knights across the black-and-white squares; our games carried on for days.

Dr. Lemon would sigh and announce his move: *Queen takes pawn, my friend. And this is as it should be; all is right in the universe.* And he would offer me, poured out with his trembling hands, a glass of plum brandy.

I would walk home late in the darkness.

The first year passed into the second; the second into the third.

Twelve years on an island.

When first I began to visit the doctor, his daughter was no more than a girl.

Beatrice was born on the island. She never went to school. She ran wild through the raspberry brambles. She read every book in her father's library. Her mother died in childbirth. Her mother was a descendent of the original mad settlers.

Beatrice knows the plants and trees. Knows her birds by genus and species; by habit and habitat; and has given names to her favorites. She can find her way by the stars. Her dogs follow her through the woods. Her father taught her French and Latin. Her father taught her all that he imagined she would need to know. Lately, Beatrice has been concerned with survival in case of nuclear attack, avian flu, or any otherwise doomsday scenario. She has been ordering gear from catalogs: hurricane lanterns, a camp stove, water purification tablets, and paraffin candles. She cares for her father through his illness. She visits me in the afternoon, after she has given her father a medicine that lets him sleep. She likes to sit at my kitchen table, watching *Tomorrow's Edge* on the little black-and-white TV.

I told Beatrice that I was expecting a guest.

"What kind of cake would he like?" she asked.

She was hoping to bake a Santa Fe sugar cake. She said that she had never tried to make one before. But she had read about it in a story. And then she was silent. And her gray eyes darkened—so like her father's—and I knew just what she was thinking. She was wondering: —what would happen if she baked this Santa Fe sugar cake and the real, that is, the actual cake, did not please her quite so much as the idea of the cake?

Beatrice has short dark hair. She is slight and slim. This description does not tell too much about her. It would be better to say: Beatrice Lemon likes it when late at night the radio picks up faraway stations. Or: she has always wanted to bake a Santa Fe sugar cake, but she has been awaiting the opportunity that has now presented itself in the imminent arrival of Benjamin Salt to do so.

Yes, I am awaiting Salt.

He knows who killed Stone.

It was Roman who told me about Salt.

Benjamin Salt published, at the tender age of twenty-six, his first novel, a tome, a Herculean hurly-burly of literary ephemera called, *Here Comes Everyone.*

There was a photo of a typewriter on the jacket.

And the title was spelled out across the keys.

Critics doted on him. His success was swift and astonishing, though not absolute. As it always goes: a few reviews were less than good. Not bad—worse than bad—they were indifferent. They were tepid. This tepidity—this lukewarmedness—affronted Salt. He was outraged. Never one to sit back, he acted. He started his own literary magazine, *Cogito.* He wrote a manifesto. He opposed irony. He decried criticism. He cried out for miracles. He demanded symbolism over subtext. He put a voluptuous young starlet—wearing only eyeglasses and a strategically placed dictionary—on the cover of the premier issue. He championed passion. He called for an end to *the pervading pessimism of our time.* He sparked debate. In cafés and chatrooms people were discussing important issues; thanks be to Benjamin Salt. He had an office full of unshaven men in flip-flops and straight-haired serious Scandinavian-seeming girls who wrote upbeat articles and relentlessly positive plot summaries. He had apostles and disciples. Their office motto was: *Be positive or get the fuck out of here.*

He hit the college lecture-hall circuit. He packed auditoriums. He told stories. He preached from his podium a message of obliterating hope. He was mobbed by autograph seekers. Kids crushed to get seats up front. Girls fainted and boys raised fists. It was pandemonium when Salt pounded the dais and proclaimed—*We are history! We are everyone!*

And in Hollywood the book was already being made into a film.

Of course, you could see why this was interesting to Roman. Ro was reputedly clean, sidesplittingly sober; he had settled down into domesticity, into lo-cal and low-impact adulthood. He and his wife Dibby, the beauty queen, had two young sons; and they were living on a horse farm in Connecticut. Ro didn't begrudge Salt his newfound fame. He only wondered—as we all do at the beginning of a story—what would happen next?

I couldn't open a newspaper without reading about Salt.

And so I learned about Benjamin Salt; he collected antique keys, postcards, wristwatches, and typewriters; his Brooklyn brownstone was haunted; his wife was a novelist named Elizabeth

Weiss; he had a son, Bruno; his dog was a long-haired dachshund called Kafka.

Salt believed in the principles of a cruelty-free existence.

The absurdity of such a belief had not yet occurred to him.

In photographs—I saw Ben and Liz at a cocktail party fundraiser with the lit it crowd; she in a black dress leaning full cleavage-wise toward Ben; he whispering in her ear.

Here they are strolling down the street on a lazy Saturday: Ben in his peacoat side by side with Liz, in high boots and a newsboy cap, pushing Bruno in the baby carriage.

I soon wearied of his happy life. I tired of his nonstop self-reflexive ubiquity. Of his mysterious lack of mystery. If a tree fell in the forest would Salt hear it? How had I ever lived without the knowledge of what he ate at breakfast? How had I existed without knowing about his fascination with ships in a bottle, with lucha libre wrestling, or his guilty pleasure of Black Jack chewing gum? Week by week, the evidence against him collected in my box at the postal station.

Babylon Must Fall was Benjamin Salt's favorite novel. It had inspired him. Ro was his hero. After reading the book the boy knew that he was meant to be a writer. When he took the book from the shelf—he felt as though he had pulled the sword from the stone.

What has any of this to do with me?

Or my island? Or the habits of a hermit crab?

Scuttling across a sea of floors?

I grew to hate Salt.

I have grown to hate Salt.

He seems to rise up out of my nightmares—

Is he real? Is there—in reality, in italics; with quotation marks or sugared like a Santa Fe cake—a living breathing being named Benjamin Salt?

Who could create such a monster?

It's rumored that he is rewriting the Old Testament. That he's adapting Heidegger's *Time and Being* as a buddy film. That he's going to be the Mets' new starting shortstop. That he does riotous stand-up comedy at Laffers in Hoboken.

The two a.m. set really kills.

Please remember to tip your waiter.

I'll be here all week folks.

I'll be waiting out eternity.

I'll be waiting for Salt.

With my camp stove, tinned meat, and paraffin candles.

With the peregrine falcons and double-crested cormorants.

With the wood warblers, bittern, grackle, rock doves, and red-winged blackbirds.

It is now dark. I do not pull the chain on the lamp to banish the darkness. I have sat for a long time between this sentence and the last. Like Dr. Lemon with his trembling hand upon the carved-ivory queen.

Out the window—

I see Beatrice walking along the water's edge with the dogs in the dusk.

4.

Eloise Sarasine sat upon the velvet sofa reading *Babylon Must Fall*.

5.

"Be true," my father told me.

This is the first rule of storytelling.

6.

Her book fell to the floor.

Evening fell against the rich tones of the room: the velvet sofa; the crème de cassis draperies; the forest green *this;* the jacquard *that;* the jade leaf and plum japonica; the scarlet vine; the sage in jardinières arabesque and mosaic; the story in morocco; she in cashmere; and oh oh oh that Shakespeherian rug down onto which the book tumbled, losing its page and her place in it. Remember that chimpanzee who wrote poetry for tossed coins and wrapped toffee in a Paris train station? What had become of him? In Hollywood a boy in a Frankenstein mask once asked for her autograph; he had mistaken her for a movie star. It was not entirely wrong, was it? that she had signed his paper with someone else's name? Each thing became the next thing. The dinosaurs had turned to oil. Ink was made of burnt bones, pitch, and tar. The bones of the children of the czar were lost in the woods. Birds carried twigs and seeds. Birds flew from bough to branch. Children turned to monsters. Eloise rested her cheek against a velvet cushion. Her memories, her moods, her maudlin inclinations were muted by pomegranate miniatures and majolica teapots. Her house was quiet. The rooms were ornamented with oddities and keepsakes from curio shops and her travels with her husband: the plaster parrot they called Flaubert; a ballet-class photograph of her daughter in black leotard and pink tights; a grinning cupid statuette with arrow pointed upward; a green-patinaed bronze figurine of ravished Leda; and oh, the Persian rosette that they had discovered in that market stall in Marrakech. Upon the mantel over the fireplace rested a row of antique clocks, none of which worked: an ironic pursuit, her collection of lost time.

In the violet hour, between despondency and decadence, she considered bathing; then she decided against it. The feminine rituals meant to be luxuries had turned into chores. Things for which one felt an obligation. One had to exfoliate; one had to clarify. One had to keep up. It wasn't a matter of vanity. It—this perpetual obligatory self-clarification—was part of something greater: a narrative of one's life. You were the story of your life. And a story could—and would—take an unforeseen twist or turn just when one was feeling utterly expendable. This was called drama—wasn't it? The expectation, not of the future in the abstract, but of one's own future and what will happen tomorrow. Though some might have the vulgarity to call it *hope*—

The clocks on the mantel had no claim to chronology.

A cedar box, a cloisonné egg, a footed vase.

An orange, a postcard, a mystery novel.

She liked stories in which the good were rewarded and the bad were punished.

Languid, long-armed, she lifted from the table the ovoid Etruscan vase. A museum piece; a find; a relic.

She gave a sudden laugh—

At the idea of herself as the only real historical inevitability.

And what next?

What *now* and *now* and *now?*

The vase was beautiful.

No, the thing was ugly.

What if she smashed it?

She set the vase back upon the table.

And wondered if the walls could do with a coat of paint?

Was she weary of the marbled warmth of ambergris? Had she lost her fondness for aubergine? Should she have the place redone in stark unblemished white? Retro-minimalism was the rage, but, no, the bleached-bones concept of cleanliness being next to stylistic godliness was just too too too exhaustingly fascistic—

One could suffer only so much less-is-more symbolism.

The inevitabilities had turned into luxuries; the luxuries had turned into necessities; and the necessities were utterly expendable.

She needed—depended on—her cell phone, but she didn't answer its questioning ring. She supposed that she could live without it. She had no feeling for plastic. When offered the option, she chose paper. She was, of course, of course, concerned with the ozone layer, the oceans, the melting polar ice caps, and her carbon footprint. She recycled. A satellite in space could find her anywhere on the planet. Wasn't this the point? One had to be a citizen of the eternal-now. Or else risk being outpaced and outmoded. She knew which hand-bag was the must-have of the moment, and she had it. She replaced each thing with the next: apricot for apple; pica for elite; ash for candle; sign for symbol; the myth of Sisyphus for the fact of gravity. Each season brought a new vicissitude in the height of hemlines and heels. If she didn't keep up she might fall out of the world. And once out; how would she get back in?

Her cashmere robe was chocolate brown; beneath it, her silk nightdress was patterned in black-and-white William Tell toile. She had stainless steel countertops, Italian tile, and an authentic eigh-teenth-century executioner's table in her kitchen. Her affection for an object did not rise in proportion to the expense of that thing's acquisition. She had no love, or hate either, for her cast-iron enam-eled cookware. She had no sentiment for her ornate silver espresso machine; not even half so much as she did for a chipped pink seashell painted garishly with the words in carnival script, *I hear the mermaids calling!* Mrs. Sarasine's eyes were seaside blue. Her hair was a color called Caramel. Each year her stylist took it a gradual con-fectionary shade lighter. She had gone from Licorice to Cocoa to Truffle to Toffee to Caramel, and imagined that when they lowered her down in the ground she would be wrapped in a linen shroud to match exactly her Dulce de Leche up-done chignon.

Oh well, it was all right to think about such things in November; wasn't it? *How death is that remedy all poets dream of?*

About a plague on the other side of the world? About the messages that birds carry from one place to the next? About apes swapping their sticks for pens and inkpots? About Saul becoming Paul on the Damascus road? About the rain-weary commuters in Paris teeming the Gare du Nord with black umbrellas? And the mud and blood-ied white dress of the blindfolded czarina as she fell in the woods? Or the velocity of a four-seamed fastball as it speeds to its fate? About Charon rowing his passengers across the waters of forgetful-ness; what a joke, she sighed. Keep a coin for the ferryman. He demands payment. He will have his due. It happens whether you like it or no; and what you like is of little consequence.

In the kitchen, Mrs. Sarasine poured a cup of coffee and at her executioner's table (well, that's what it was—) prepared a spare evening meal of a cold hard-boiled egg. If the comedies were not so funny as they once were, neither were the tragedies as sad. Her hands were small. Her shoulders were narrow. She was very nearly an anatomy lesson: the bones of clavicle and hip; the slender fingers, those expressive metacarpals; the long femur and lengthy shin were elegantly formed and entirely visible. Her hair was Caramel. Her rooms were quiet. In her coffee, she stirred cream and spooned sugar. Snow fell and was falling. She knew noble accents and lucid inescapable rhythms. She knew that just as she had been hated she had been loved. And though she had certain theories about why the caged bird sings, she was undecided as to whether existence pre-ceded essence. Or why it so happened that year by year, as there was more *to* her; there was less and less *of* her.

Mrs. Sarasine, hair unwashed, mysteries insolvent, ablutions unaccomplished, skeleton unadorned, white skin unannointed, in her flowing robe and flowered gown, with cup and plate in hand, with nothing behind her and nothing before her, sat at her escritoire. Atop her stack of cards lay an envelope, addressed in a familiar hand. It had arrived yesterday. She hadn't yet opened it. Something about it had struck her as ominous. It troubled her from the first. Perhaps she had hoped it would simply disappear. Of course, it did not. And now the continued presence of this envelope, unopened, was darkening her mood. It seemed to be the thing that was coloring the walls gloomy; that was making her feel ossuary-weary; that was causing her to ponder graveyard poetics. She took her pearl-handled letter-knife and cut open the envelope.

CHAPTER 3

Susu wonders what it would be like to sleep with him

HE HAD ALREADY BEGUN. He talked about television. He made us, made everyone in the auditorium feel smart, because he was smart, and he was talking about television. He talked about things that people liked. Things like celebrities and baseball and murder. He used the words *algorithm* and *lacunae*. He said, "We all have a homesickness for the generation in which we were born." And I wondered what it would be like to sleep with him. After the lecture there was a reception in a room with high old windows, and girls poured wine and lighted candles. He was signing books. It was evening. It was summer. I was wearing a black dress. Girls carried trays of grapes and chocolates and dark little espresso cakes. He took a chocolate from the tray. He took my hand. He called me the day after the lecture. He was at his hotel. He had missed his flight out. He had overslept. The heat made him lazy. He wanted me to meet him at his hotel. He asked me if I knew where it was? He always stayed at the place when he was in Chicago. I heard the sound of ice in a glass. "Do you know the place?" he said. He said, "I want to tell you a story." The afternoon was hot. The heat had turned thick and gloomy. I found him in the hotel bar. He was at a table in the corner. He ordered a drink for me. We sat in silence. He drank whiskey. He flipped a coin on the table. He asked me, "Do you like tragedy? or comedy?" He asked me did I like the place? He said, "Do you want to know the beginning of the story or hear the ending first?" He covered the coin with his hand. When he lifted his hand the coin was gone. He said that he liked this old ruined monument of a hotel, where once years ago he saw a ghost pass him in the hallway so close that she might have been a hand touching his sleeve. "Of all the gods nailed to the cross," he said, "Discord was the most beautiful." He drank his whiskey and ordered with a gesture of two fingers to the barman another. He liked basements and places without windows, because he didn't have to try to remember where he was. At any moment he was, he could be, he could have been—anywhere in the world. "And I won't fall out," he said. "Of what?" I said. "The world," he said. I didn't understand, and I wasn't used to drinking in the afternoon. I placed my hands flat, palms down on the table against the white cloth. He looked at my hands. He took my hand in his. He slipped the ring from my finger. I let him. He held the ring in his palm, jokingly weighing, appraising the diamond. He said that I could get a lot for it. The ring rolled across the table. He was playing the magician, shifting the ring from palm to palm. It appeared in his empty glass. It spun. It was spinning on the white cloth. He held it between his teeth. It disappeared under a linen napkin. In its place the coin appeared. The ring was gone. And suddenly though I don't know how—it was back on my finger. I was drinking plum brandy. He had ordered it for me. I thought that it would be sweet, but it was not. It was thick like the afternoon. I said then, I told him that I had been here in this place when

I was a girl and there had been a lady sitting, I pointed, over there right over there, with a little dog. I knew the place. I did. I had gone there long ago with my mother. In winter. I remember that it was snowing. My mother had promised me cake. Whatever kind I liked, she had said. My mother had a coat with a faux fur collar and her hair fell against it. She had sat with her dark hair in the dark room. She held a china cup with roses, at the table with a white cloth, upon which was set a dish of sugar cubes, the silver, a pitcher of cream, and we had little iced violet cakes. There was an old lady wearing a velvet beret sitting with a tiny dog on her lap, and she fed the dog now and again a rolled bit of bread and butter. I didn't tell him about my mother. I told him how I had had chocolate in a cup with roses on it. And that there were violet cakes on a plate. They were violet cakes, but they tasted like licorice. "Isn't that funny," I said, "how everything that one so longs for tastes of licorice?" He looked at me. It occurred to me that maybe I looked too much like my mother. That we had read too many of the same books. Or not read enough of them. I did not know what to do. I looked around for the lady with the little dog or or or for hills like white elephants. He drank. He said nothing. He finished his glass. Outside it began to rain, but I did not yet know this. I was wearing a brown dress. He told me that I was beautiful, that maybe I was the most beautiful girl he had ever seen. It was raining. When did I realize that it had been raining? It wasn't as we walked from the darkness of the bar to the lobby to the elevator. It wasn't in the elevator. Or in his room where the curtains were drawn against the heat. The elevator door opened. We walked down the hallway. On the flowers, the black roses, on the carpet. We were in his room. He closed the door. There was a table, on it: a bottle, a glass, an overflowing ashtray, his latest book. He took off his jacket. He saw me looking at the book. He asked me if I had read his books. I said, "I'm tired of books where one thing happens and then another and then a girl is naked." I said, "I hate it in the movies when the girl takes off her dress, and and a man is sitting on the bed looking just just just gazing at her. I hate that," I said. He said, "It's supposed to make you envious." I asked him, "Envious of the girl? I just feel bad for the actress," I said. He said, he unbuttoned a cuff of his sleeve, "Not the girl," he said. "The man," he said. His arm bent at the elbow; he fumbled with the other sleeve. He couldn't get the button. He held his arm, his sleeve out to me, the way a child will. I undid the button. He said, "Do you want to be an actress?" I said, "No." I said, "I don't want to be an actress or write a book or be on television or or dance or sing or or or." I was drunk. I had never been drunk before at four in the afternoon. It was raining, but I did not know that it was raining or that the heat had broken and shattered and smashed, that it was raining all over the city, raining on the pigeons and bricks and flowers and dirt and on gardens and graves and shops and cars and umbrellas and children and dogs and cats in doorways. I did not know so many things. He looked at me. I sat on the bed. I fell back against the bed. I said, "I have to tell you something." He said, "What? a confession?" He said, "Already?" He said, "Could you wait? I have the confession scene planned for the last chapter." He loosened his tie. He undid his collar. He took off his wristwatch and set it on the table. I looked around the room. His jacket was thrown over a chair. His jacket fell, had fallen to the floor. I saw the bottle and glass, a chocolate bar wrapper, a newspaper and ashtray, a pen and books, the mirror. I saw his face in the mirror. I said, "I've never read any of your books, but I saw the movie. The one with the blonde girl. The movie with the blonde girl. I cried at the ending," I said. I said, "Why did the girl have to die in the end? Why'd you have to go and kill the girl?" He lighted a cigarette and sat beside me on the bed. He said that I didn't look well. He asked did I want anything from room service? He said we could order anything we liked. What did I like? Did I like marshmallow? Did I like caramel? It was absurd the things that they would bring you. It didn't have to be on the menu. He said that sometimes people could be unreasonably kind. He ashed his cigarette. Did it bother me, he asked, his smoking? "Vulgar habit," he said; his wife hated it. He looked at me. He asked me if I was ill? The day was hot thick oppressive. I wished that it would rain. It was already raining. I did not know yet that it was raining. It would have been nice to know that it was raining on the flowers and the dogs, on the houses and the windows. He pulled the chain on the lamp. The room was dark. He said, "Close your eyes." He sat beside me, his shirt cuffs undone. Then he lay back, one hand under his head the other holding the cigarette. He lay on his back on the bed beside me, smoking. It was quiet. It was dark. He said, "You have a very silly name. Are you ever called anything else?" I said that he could call me what he liked. I said that I liked marshmallow and caramel and that I had never been drunk in the afternoon, and that the smoke of cigarettes did not bother me, and that I liked television. That I was not afraid of snakes or spiders. That I liked dogs. That I was named after my mother who was named after her mother. That one day I would live by the sea. That I liked cheeseburgers and chocolate cake. That I was vengeful. That I was true. That I liked movies in which the good were rewarded and the bad were punished. That whatever it was that he wanted from me, he only had to ask. That he had only to ask. And not even. That he did not need to ask. That he did not even have to ask. That I would do whatever he wanted me to do. I said that my ring was a diamond. I said that a diamond was only a rock. I said that I had a white dress with a black shadow on it. I said, "Tomorrow I'm going to be married." It was dark and quiet and raining. He said that the girl had died at the end of the book because that was how the story went. It was only a book. And he had written it a long time ago. Perhaps if he wrote it now it would end differently, but it was hard to know a thing like that, and what difference did it make? He said that he killed the girl because that was how the story had to go.

CHAPTER 4
Sheldon mythologizes the past

A WEEK HAS PASSED. My pen never touched paper. I wanted only to watch the winter birds test the reality of branch and bough with their questionings. Do you doubt me? How can I, without benefit of wing or claw—with nothing more than ink— attempt to journey back into the past?

Today: I collected my mail from the island's postal station. I admit, I felt a strange sense admixed of dread and anticipation. The afternoon was gray. The damp-eyed and ancient postmistress was lonely. She gave me my letters, but she held one back. She commented on its far-away postmark. She noted the looping girlish hand of the sender. And said how she had once been to New York City herself, when she was a girl; could I believe it? and she had gone all the way up to the top of the Statue of Liberty. Finally, wistfully, she relinquished the letter.

I walked home through the woods.

It is only now—as I sit at my desk that I open the envelope.

I unfold the page.

To find only one sentence:

How does the story begin?

Beneath his words, a stain, a sticky thumbprint of raspberry jam.

2.

Now and again, Eloise thought about murder.

3.

I am witness and widower. I was a student. I have been a teacher. I
have professed. I took the podium. I have taught, corrected, consoled,
passed and failed; pitied. I am a hypocrite. I offered hope where there
was none. I took the arm of the grieving. I grieved; took the shovel;
took my turn; took my share; turned away. I grew rich through mis-
fortune. I grew up. I grow old. I get gloomy. I hide out. I hid, too. I
keep my own counsel, as the ancients used to say. I've kept silent.
Now I am no longer silent. I am forty-eight years old. Roman Stone
preceded my arrival into the world by four months; my sister followed me by barely eighteen minutes. There are things that I wish
that I had not seen. I will confess to acts that I have committed, no
less terrible for having been done in the name of kindness. No less
kind for being terrible. Philosophers and criminals agree at least
upon one thing: guilt and innocence are relative terms.

Is this how I am to begin?

I write longhand on unlined paper.

4.

Eloise opened her book.

The story was dark and terrifying.

5.

September 1978, Illyria College in Virgil's Grove, Iowa. On a day all
of sun. From the brightness into the dark hall of the dormitory; up
the stairs to find my room I went. I opened the door; I stood for a
moment in the doorway. Roman sat at the window. He was smoking
a cigarette. He wore a white shirt and madras trousers. I remember this—

because I had just come from the Greyhound station, from that interminable trip from Michigan. I was tired and dirty; had slept little on the bus, and little in the days that preceded it. Hungry too. El and I, we had peanut butter sandwiches in Fort Wayne; coffee and Hostess Snowballs from a vending machine at a stop in Moline; in Cedar Falls at a fruit stand, Eloise bought a sack of yellow apples. She took one out of the sack, and she made a show of shining it on her blouse before she handed it to me. "What did Eve say to the asp?" she asked. And she paused, waiting. "This bites," she said. She did not laugh. I did not laugh. She shrugged her shoulders. She pitied me, but she did not want me to know this. We had left nothing behind; a fire had burned down our house the year before. Eloise still imagined the smoke caught in her hair. And I suppose that I too invest more symbolism than I should in the fact of the doorway in which I stood, when I saw Roman. I was soggy and sweat-stained. I had a suitcase and my typewriter, a green Baby Hermes. Ro sat with his back to me. I didn't know what to make of him. He had pulled the desk chair over to the window. He had his feet up on the window ledge. A paperback—that account of the Andes plane crash in which a soccer team resorts to cannibalism—was on his knee. He wasn't reading. He stared out the window toward the courtyard where, moments before, my sister and I had parted ways. A large black trunk with shined metal fixtures sat on the floor. He smoked in silence. He turned; sized me up; knew in an instant what I was and what I was not. He produced a key and unlocked the trunk. He took out a bottle of whiskey; opened it; drank, and handed the bottle to me. I was exhausted from the long bus ride. I drank. I got drunk that day, really and thoroughly tight, for the first time in my life. While he talked and I listened.

He told me about his famous father and his young stepmother. About getting kicked out of school. And his summer kicking around London. He had nothing, it seemed, to hide.

He unpacked his trunk. I recall: he had stashed booze and dope, Gauloise cigarettes, chocolate bars, detective novels, dirty playing cards, pills and toffee and caramels, binoculars, a Bible, a blindfold, and a baseball bat. God knows Roman must have thought Iowa was the end of the world. Last exit on the train to purgatory. All that his trunk lacked in the substance of temptation was Mephistopheles, a handgun, fireworks, and real live naked girl. I should have seen Roman for what he was: a bright brilliant magician. He pulled sleight of hand over fist, his tricks; his ropes and rabbits—every experience for which I so yearned—out of a silk top hat.

In asking for this story, in putting forth the command: tell! Salt is asking me to mythologize the past. To find something remarkable in a random meeting between two teenagers, who had by luck or lack thereof, been thrown together as roommates.

Stone & Schell, read an index card taped to the door.

Is Salt to haunt every page as I write this?

Does he need to know—what it is like in September in Iowa? The color of the leaves; the angle of the sun? Am I expected to recall what was served for dinner—that first night and all the nights after? Such things are lost to me. What happened? There was a get-to-know-ya cookout in the courtyard. We drank Goody soda pop, sugary orange and spiked with Everclear. We talked about god. A couple of girls were sitting by us. Ro charmed the hell out of them. We rolled joints and ranted about revolution. We smoked dope and waited for Godot. Did this happen on that first day? Perhaps. It might have. I can't say that it didn't. It happened so many times over the next four years that I couldn't say to a high degree of certainty that it did not happen that first day, as well as every day thereafter.

Does Salt need to be acquainted with the geography of small liberal arts colleges in the Midwest? We were surrounded by woods, by thousand-year-old oaks and impassive pines.

We were up to our necks in Gothic gloom.

The dark ivy-covered brick buildings were ominous. The trees added shade to shadow. We crossed the stone-paved courtyard to get to the dining hall. Ro used to put hard-boiled eggs in his pockets; though I can't remember why. What else? The professors lived in professorial misery in bungalows on a willow-lined lane called *the ghost walk*. Everyone said it was haunted. Here I add a fact, perhaps prematurely: it was in one of these nutshells—a guesthouse for distinguished visitors, no less—that Ro's own story will end. While I continue to begin—

Our room was small and dark.

I set my typewriter upon the desk.

Ro set his fingers to the keys.

"What the hell?" he said.

He looked down at the keys. As people who don't know how to type will do. And he saw that the letters on the keys were blacked out. Or rather, each key had been carefully covered with a perfectly-sized square of black tape. This is how my father had taught me to type.

This is how my father trained me in the art of memory through absence.

Never look down, my father told me, when you are crossing a bridge, climbing a mountain, or telling a story. My father was funny like that. What mountains had he climbed? What bridges had he crossed? What stories did he leave untold?

In the dining hall—the next day—Eloise brought her tray and sat down beside us.

Ro said, "Hey, you two look exactly alike."

Eloise said, "We're twins, you idiot."

And Ro burst out laughing.

He didn't like it when girls gave in too quickly.

He liked it when a girl would put up a fight.

I either remember or I do not remember.

I am either or I am not.

One day I will burn every piece of paper upon which I have written a word, and take my possessions—the cracked cups and kettles and keys and rotten apples, the bells and books and clocks and candles, the spoons and knives, the ink pens and plates and pictures, the bones and bottles—down to the water and throw them into the dark waves. What good does it do to incinerate or to drown? This I have learned through repetition; this I have learned by rote: nothing disappears. Even ashes have a name.

CHAPTER 5

Susu decides to go away with him

H E WAS ON THE PHONE ORDERING BREAKFAST from room service. It was morning. He ate a chocolate bar. He lighted a cigarette. I was watching television. Workers draining a pond found a lost girl packed into a suitcase. In home video footage she was shown reciting a poem in a leotard and pink tights. He took the remote and went through the stations: a talk show host had the blackened sole for dinner last night, and wasn't it to die for? The Yankees won; a dog chasing a cat; an infomercial for knives; Miss Marple solving a murder, teacup in hand; an airplane crashing into a rolling blue ocean; the girl again, running; the funeral of a dictator; scenes of an old war; a cat chasing a mouse; a beauty pageant; a black-and-white horror movie: two boys and a girl walking in the woods; a tree falling in a forest; a game show with questions as answers; girls going wild; a divorce court; a burning house. He left it on a soap opera: an elegant widow in a black dress was confessing to a crime. He crumpled the wrapper of the chocolate bar. He handed me his cigarette. I took a drag off it, but coughed. He laughed. He changed the station. The girl again, the poem, the suitcase. The face of a young man. A spoon turning in a mixing bowl. A swimming pool. The Three Stooges. A gardener with a shovel. A cartoon Zeus hurling a lightning bolt. A bikini. A home run. A tour through a vineyard. A bicycle race through the mountains. Teen vampires. Hunters in the snow. A flag unfurled. A chicken roasting on a spit. Cars driving in circles around a track. The dramatic reenactment of the murder of the Romanovs, Anastasia falling in the darkness. I kept thinking about the girl in the suitcase. And the morning, the sun, and the chocolate, and the shadow on my white dress, and the diamond ring, where was it? On my finger. There was a knock on the door. Breakfast arrived. There was coffee with cream and sugar. There was bread and butter; he ate bacon and eggs. He ate in bed. He ate with his fingers. He took a poached egg and put it on his buttered toast. There was a plate of pastries. There were croissants and jam pots. He said, "Do you like gooseberries? I used to have a gooseberry cake every year for my birthday." I said, "That sounds awful." He ate. He said, "It was." He said, "It was awful, but I looked forward to it." He shrugged. He said, "Or maybe it was blackberry." He took a pear tart and set it on a plate. And he put the plate in my hand. He said, "I'm going away soon. I'm going to see the burning king." He set his plate, with its wreckage of crust and jam and egg, on the bedside table. "Who's he?" I said. He said, "It's a carnival." He said the name of a faraway place. I had seen it written in books. "It's the celebration of the fall of a tyrant. He was wicked, this old tyrant. I know, I know, all tyrants are, but this monster married his own daughter. It took a hero to vanquish him. The carnival goes on for three days. The women wear white. The men hang straw effigies of the king. And then at the end of this celebration of the fall, the fate, of the wicked king, children light the straw bodies on fire with torches," he said. "And they sing. They sing a song about murder and hope. It's inspirational in an I'll-grind-your-bones-to-make-my-bread sort of way. You should come with me," he said. He turned to the horror movie. The boys were walking through the woods with an ax. Where was the girl? He smoked in silence. I went to the window. I drew back the curtain and saw that it had rained and that the day was sunny but fine and perfect for a wedding.

CHAPTER 6

Eloise hides the letter

L OUIS SARASINE CAME HOME in a better mood than might have been expected, considering the grisly details of the murder trial, and the delays in both airline transportation and the slow-but-fine grinding wheels of justice. The jury had been deadlocked up until the last, but this he took as no indication of his execution of the defense or his expertise on the topic of Repressed Memory Syndrome. His authority was unquestionable. He had the uncanny ability to separate a sign from a symbol. To see, in this case, brutality as a text-book phenomenon, even when the bloody knife was brandished before him wrapped in a plastic evidence bag. In the muted hues of their living room, they sat: she on the sofa, and he in a leather chair. He brought her—a bracelet, antique—and his stories, which he told. One after the next. Until it was hard for his wife to listen, let alone hear about the girl's body left by the roadside.

Mrs. Sarasine, dressed this evening in dove gray, extended her arm toward her husband and let him fasten the delicate clasp on her emerald bracelet.

2.

So to Iowa then I came, burning, with my bag of Hesperidian apples and the tools of my trade and my twin. I met Ro, and, oh we became the best of buddies. I suffered through his comedies and he laughed at my tragedies. He was polite. He knew how to use a knife and fork. He always said please and thank you. He knew how much a thing should cost. And this had very little to do with what he was willing to pay. El and I made our way at Illyria, scholarship kids that we were. I fell in with Roman, and El came tumbling after.

3.

Louis told his wife the story of the murdered girls.

He yawned, and said then that it was late, and he was going up to bed.

What about her?

She in the lamplight looked up from her book.

She said that she just wanted to finish this page.

4.

Ro and I talked about art. I suppose that we were foolish; but there was grand ambition to our foolishness. We were inventing the world; every idea and whim and want was new. He believed in inspiration. I talked of rules. I told him that a real writer must have three immutable rules of storytelling. Or else how would you know where to begin—? let alone how to end a story? I told him about the cracked kettle, the black flower, the house of fiction. I talked about the destruction of language. I talked about my book. I told him that it was a story about fate. Ro said, "Fate is a girl with scissors. How much damage—really—can one girl do?" I watched Ro pursue Eloise. She struggled at first; then she gave in. What choice did she have? Every story is a story about fate. She said that he was born to be murdered. And he laughed. Ro and Eloise throwing apples at ghosts as they walked the willow lane. Weren't they like the star-crossed lovers in a novel? Or a god and girl on a Grecian urn?

5.

The letter was tucked between the pages of her book.

6.

The summer after our freshman year, Eloise and I went to New York with Ro. We made camp in Milton Stone's Upper West Side apartment. John Lennon and Yoko Ono were reputedly holed up somewhere in the building. Ro said the ghost of Boris Karloff wandered the hallways. Ro's father collected curiosities: art and artifacts; oddities. Ro showed me: laudanum vials, glass syringes, a hair bracelet from a long-dead queen, great silver scissors that—Ro hefted in his hand to dramatize his story—had been the very weapon used by the vengeful seamstress in that famous turn-of-the-century murder. He led us to the liquor: bathtub gin, rye, Siberian vodka. Ro held a bottle of wormwood absinthe. He poured us each a glass. El raised her glass. She drank; she said it tasted like licorice. I was already drunk when I saw the pink-and-orange Andy Warhol rendition of Roman's mother, Astrid. Ro stood beside me and looked up at the picture; he spread his arms in an expansive gesture of mock reverence. "'*And upon her forehead was a name written, Mystery, Babylon the great, the mother of harlots and abominations of the earth,'*" he said. And what can I say? Ro was a relentlessly educated, pretentious bastard; really he was. He could chapter and verse it with the best of them. I was impressed. I saw Central Park from an empyrean height. This was a long time ago. Everything impressed me. Hell, even the air-conditioning impressed me. It was a miserably hot summer. We lived in cool and rarified absurdity. While down below:

the hoi polloi, the riffraff, the real citizens of the real world went about their sweat-soaked lives.

I found a part-time job at an antiquarian bookstore. O.K., Ro got me the job. His father was a friend of the owner. I spent my afternoons sitting at the front desk reading leather-bound editions of Swift and Dickens and dutifully snubbing the few customers who ventured into that dark literary sanctum. Eloise had an internship at a fashion magazine. Ro used to crank-call her at work; drive her nuts, things like that. Except for the poor put-upon maid, who arrived in her black uniform to clean up whatever mess we had made the night before, we had the apartment blissfully to ourselves. Ro's stepmother, Mary Clare, was in Milan. And Milton Stone was in London. So we drank his antique booze. Spun his jazz records. Had Chinese food delivered at two in the morning, whatta life! Moo Goo Gai Pan, Thelonious Monk, Coca-Cola, and crème de cassis, in our pajamas. Ro and El took over the master bedroom. Ro told me to take whatever I liked. And though I was impressed, I was still defensive about such things. About my relative poverty, my sudden dependence on Roman. I never took, honestly, more than I needed; nor took for the sake of taking. I knew, instinctively, that I did not want to be in his debt. That sounds odd, I know; considering that I was living it up so freely, so famillionairly, in his realm. I kept my eyes open. I wanted to see, to know. I wanted to learn about the world without being harmed or hurt or even hungered by its lessons.

I told myself that I was only a spectator. An observer. Not really a participant.

I could justify anything then, just as I can rationalize everything now.

Ro slept through the days of that summer on Egyptian cotton sheets and swansdown pillows in his father's monumental bed; while Eloise edited copy at the short-lived *Pout,* which taught teenage girls the latest in starvation and sex tips; I wandered Greenwich Village, toasting literary ghosts at the White Horse Tavern. I saw the haunts of Henry James and the streets that Whitman sauntered, pondering. But Ro liked Rabelais. More than once we took the train to Coney Island. The boardwalk, the Ferris wheel, the fortune-tellers, the Cyclone, the sea? Eloise had a sunscreen that smelled of oranges. We ate hotdogs and drank red grape Mad Dog from the bottle; in the sand laughing at the tourists, we vowed to spend every holiday together.

The night that Eloise and I turned nineteen, Ro took us out on the town. He was in a grand and infectious good mood. We met up with a couple of his former prep school buddies. They had taken the train down from New Haven. We had dinner at a posh French restaurant. We drank. We ate. We smoked cigars. We were the picture of youthful dissipation. We were served bavette de boeuf au buerre d'escargot by waiters in white jackets. Then for dessert: gâteau de Marie Antoinette. Ro and his buddies (whose names I can't recall; something like Brett and Donny) bellowed the birthday song, while El blew out the candles as though facing the guillotine. We had champagne and strawberries. And when there was no more food to be found or drinks to be drunk, the waiter brought the bill on a silver tray. Ro didn't even look at it. He just paid up. He impressed me with his apathy. I saw the generous tip that he left for the waiter. Yes, that night Ro was buying. After dinner, Eloise begged off with a headache and took a taxi back to the apartment. While Roman, Brett, Donny, and I continued on.

There were bars, bright lights, booze, dirty picture houses, pinball arcades, dark alleys, fateful choices, sudden vicissitudes. The world was a Hollywood backlot. The world was ready; but it could wait. Ro wanted ice cream. I found myself sitting between Brett and Donny in a basement cafe on Mulberry Street drinking espresso, while Ro spooned up spumoni and regaled us with the story of his seduction of his stepmother.

I had heard the story before.

This did not matter.

Each time that he told it, he changed it.

In this version of the story: Mary Clare and Milton Stone had just come home from a night at the theater. Ro's father took a telephone call in his study.

And there was Mary Clare in her black dress on the velvet sofa—

On her hip, explaining the plot of the tragedy that she had just seen.

Mary Clare explained tragedy to Ro.

Clytemnestra slaughtered Agamemnon.

All that terror and pity.

Mary Clare unpinned her hair.

She said that it had been so so so very damned cathartic.

That it had left her wanting more.

The waitress came by.

The drink of the day was called la Mela del Peccato.

Did I want to try it?

I ordered another coffee.

Brett leaned forward in his chair.

Donny drank.

He was drinking Campari and soda.

His mouth was stained red.

The basement was dark with smoke and licorice.

Ro had Mary Clare on the floor.

Her stockings—

Her dress was torn.

She begged Ro for more.

That's how Ro told it anyway.

He lifted his spoon.

He ate, while we waited.

While I waited, young and eager.

Ro may have been a romantic, but fate was an ironist.

His spumoni had the look of a bowl of cherries.

"And then what happened?" I said.

The waitress came by with my coffee. Brett grabbed her by the arm. The white cup fell to the floor and smashed. The waitress slapped Brett. Donny, in a show of solidarity to his friend, or just for the hell of it, overturned our table.

Ro laughed, but he knew it was time to go.

He threw a heap of money on the bar. And we beat it. We stumbled up the basement steps with the waitress chasing after us with a broom. That's how the night ended. Ro decided—instead of putting up his buddies in the apartment—to drive them back to Connecticut. His father had bought him a new car that summer, a Range Rover. Brett and Donny passed out in the backseat. Outside of the city we stopped at a sad shack of a gas station. This was past four in the morning and there was a girl working alone at the cash register. I was getting some coffee. Ro—he was buying cigarettes—and when the girl turned to get the cigarettes from the shelf, he boosted a twenty-five cent pack of Juicy Fruit chewing gum from the counter.

I never knew a rich kid who wasn't a thief.

As I saw him slip the gum into his pocket and give the girl a bit of his big-city bluster, it seemed that I also saw the events of that evening suddenly—clearly—with clarity. What had really happened? The wine was bitter. The food was salty. The cigars were wretched. The waiters rolled their eyes. Didn't I catch a glimpse of the sommelier spitting into a bottle? The Yalies were boorish and foul-mouthed.

Eloise choked back tears from the cigar smoke. Marie Antoinette herself, a cake of white buttercream, bore a suspicious resemblance to Betty Crocker. And bavette de boeuf? It was gristle and garden snails. When Ro told his story of seduction, I admit; I listened. I thought he was brash. I thought he was joking. I was charmed; I was too eager. The more I thought about it: —the black dress, the torn stockings, the smoke, the licorice, the stifled pleas, the very apple of sin—the more it mystified me. At least Eloise missed that part of the night. As she got into the taxi she fell and twisted her ankle. Back in the apartment with only the lonely ghost of Boris Karloff to keep her company, she took a handful of Valium and passed out on the velvet sofa.

Ro and I drove on to New Haven in the dawn.

I felt betrayed, not so much by Roman, but by my judgment. I fell for his generosity without understanding—or acknowledging—that repayment for such largesse would certainly come later, and at an impossible cost.

I was young and later was a long time off.

7.

Eloise Sarasine née Schell folded the letter in half.

She had read it several times since its arrival.

8.

Ro and I lived in an apartment our sophomore year. My type-writer sat on the kitchen table. The light was good in there, or maybe the thin wall that separated my bedroom from Ro's afforded me too much knowledge of what went on in there with my sister. He had a crowd of carousing pals to whom he could tell his stories. He kept late nights. I had morning classes. We left notes shift-locked in all caps on the typewriter: WHO IS THE GIRL? he

wrote. WHAT GIRL? I answered. And he typed back: THERE IS ALWAYS
A GIRL.

He was right, of course. There is always a girl. This one was
called Wren. We met in a class called the Politics of Liberation. She
loaned me her Marx, and I lent her my Lacan. Wren had dark hair
and damp hands; she wore black-rimmed glasses. I talked of objects,
and she, of objectification. She was a militant peacenik in dungarees,
combat boots, and a green army surplus jacket. She rhapsodized
about the rights of workers. About her dreams of a utopian society.
And sexual liberation: she was big on that one.

Kill your television! Keep your laws off my body! I'd rather be
smashing imperialism! She was sloganeering, soapboxing, intolerant,
and emphatic, but Wren had too the fluttering quality of her name-
sake; those remarkable round little birds whose body temperature
reaches 120 degrees, in a fever of flight. She called me brother. She
called me comrade. She called me S. Z.; and I confess: the slight
bright way she elided the letters of my name caused me to feel the
first raptures of ironic love.

We met in September.

We used to take our books and go into the woods.

She lay back amongst the black flowers, the weeds, the rot and
ruin. She made chains of late violets, nightshade, and dandelions.

Wren unbuttoning her flannel shirt.

It was a burning autumn, a fall of Rousseau and Thoreau.

There were leaves of grass caught in the pages of my Whitman.

Then the rains came.

I read Baudelaire. And she, de Beauvoir.

Wren spoke of the cause of her sisters in struggle.

In my bedroom—

Naked, but for her eyeglasses. Adamant, adamantine—

Ranting about the military industrial complex.

She loved peace. She hated hatred.

And she hated Ro. Other girls were taken in. Other girls fell for him, but not Wren. She was certain that he listened to us, his ear to the bedroom wall. He represented the myriad woes of the world. He was a tyrant. He had driven empires into the dust. He was not simply patriarchal; he was *the* patriarchy. It was as though he had risen from the pages of a history book to taunt her. She talked with a sharp fondness of the guillotine.

There was one thing about Ro that did impress Wren. Not a thing, really, to be fair and grammatically accurate; a person: Ro's mother, the first Mrs. Stone, the brainy Swedish pinup who ditched the glitz and glamour of a film career to dig irrigation ditches with UNICEF. She gave up caring for her own child to care for the children of the world. Wren called Ro's mother an icon. It was true, no one looked more beautiful in the throes of an IRA sympathy hunger strike. Who else had donated her payout for appearing in *Playboy* to the plight of California's migrant grape-pickers? Who but Astrid Stone had made the bandoleer a bold fashion accessory on the Paris catwalks? No one protested with more panache than Ro's mother.

I only met his mother once.

It was that October, in 1979.

The Orioles and Pirates were in the World Series.

Astrid Stone showed up at our apartment. Unexpectedly—for she never announced her travel plans in advance. It was a bright warm autumn day. She was wearing a fur coat. And oversized sunglasses. She came in, looked around our dismal digs. She took off the dark glasses. She took off her fur. She dropped the coat on the floor. She was wearing a leather skirt and black lace blouse with nothing beneath it. She sat on the sofa, crossed and uncrossed her long legs in high black boots.

"Roman," she said in her glacial Nordic drawl. "Baby, you live like a pig."

And she lighted a cigarette.

She didn't like being in the States; it made her edgy. She thought that she had been followed to our apartment. There were important people in the world who wanted to see her shut up. That's what she said anyway. In her see-through blouse. With her face an exquisitely feminine version of her son's face. She had come to raise money for an orphanage in El Salvador. She was on her way to New York to roll Ro's father for some dough. Certainly Roman understood that she had to keep her plans secret? She had to stay one step ahead of her enemies.

Ro made Cuban coffee. She drank it black. She held the cup flat on the palm of her left hand, while grasping the handle with her right.

She lowered her voice into a whisper. She asked Roman to go check the street for suspicious strangers. And while Ro excused himself—he actually went outside to look around—I was left alone with the first Mrs. Stone.

She got up and went to the window.

She drew the curtain aside only slightly and peered out.

She sat back on the sofa.

I was sitting across from her.

She looked at me.

"You're the boy who lost his parents," she said.

"Lost?" I said.

"Not so the right word?" she said.

"Dead?" she said.

"Died, no?" she said.

She set her cup upon the table.

She ran a hand through her hair.

She opened her handbag and found a silver case. She took out a cigarette, offered me one; I declined. She tapped it against the case.

She leaned toward me.

I lighted her cigarette.

She tilted her chin upwards.

Her neck was long and swanlike and white.

She exhaled smoke.

Her eyes narrowed in the smoke.

She told me then how in a church outside Mexico City she had seen a statue of the weeping virgin. She told me that she had seen swarms of locusts descend upon green fields and leave nothing in their wake. She had seen starving children; destruction; war; flood; ruin; and she thought each day would bring the end of the world.

What was I going to do while I waited for the end of the world?

She asked me, "What are you going to do?"

I told her that I was going to write a book.

Smoke spiraled upward in the sunlight.

She laughed.

"When you tell about me," she said, "don't forget to say how beautiful I was."

Ro returned reeking of pot to report no nefarious or likewise shady activity along the quiet streets of Virgil's Grove. Astrid Stone was appeased. They spoke for a while, mostly about Ro's father. And then his mother put on her dark glasses and fur coat and left.

ROMEEN BAYBEE, I typed, WHY YOU LEEEVE LIKA PEEG?

Ro dug out from his secret stash of treasures.

A magazine.

He handed the magazine to me.

Open, pages spread.

I looked.

She was beautiful.

I studied English literature. Eloise took courses in linguistics, and Ro was in economics. I scribbled in my notebook. I went on about art. I used words like *truth* and *beauty*. Eloise talked about signs and signifiers. And Ro was fascinated by currency.

Ro told me about his stepmother. And what they had done. He talked about Mary Clare. How goddamn happy he would be if it were just the two of them; how maybe he would do away with the old man, hunh? Why not? It was just an idea. It was just a goof. It wasn't real. How would you do it? he asked. With a gun, with poison? And there I was. Sitting at the kitchen table with my typewriter. Oh, I was thinking about words, words, words. Ro sat beside me at the table. With a knife jamming the bread. Saying how damn sweet the world was. Wasn't it?

"Would that make a good story, do you think?" he asked me.

A story about a boy and his stepmother plotting to kill the old man?

"It's a little cheap, isn't it?" I said.

"The crowds in the Colosseum had a taste for blood," he said.

"That was a long time ago," I said.

"The world may change," he said. "But not me."

And he was pretty damn happy about it.

As he ate his dark bread.

And stared out the window.

"Want to go to the old farmhouse?" he asked me.

"What old farmhouse?" I said.

"Just a place my father keeps," he said.

He was planning to go over winter break.

"Bring the girl too," he said. "What the hell."

"I can't," I said.

"You can't?" he said.

"Why not?" he said.

He tilted back in his chair.

"Rock, paper, scissors me for it," he said.

"For what?" I said.

He pulled his chair close to the table.

We hit the table, one, two, three.

I was paper.

He was rock.

He lost.

"Is Eloise going?" I asked.

He lighted a cigarette.

Then tipped back in his chair.

And smoked.

While I wrote.

In silence for a while.

Then he said, "So it's yes?"

I said, yes.

"You really can't help yourself, can you?" he said.

"What?" I said.

"From stealing lines," he said.

I told him that I'd rather be a liar than a thief.

He told me to shut the fuck up.

The farmhouse.

The snow.

The winter.

New Year's, 1980.

Ro, Eloise, Wren, and I.

The four of us sat around the fire.

Wren wanted a ghost story.

Ro said that he knew one so terrible—

That the telling of it might curse him forever.

We drank champagne.

And felt a certain terror.

Even with the crackle of wood in the fire.

At each sudden spark or errant burst of flame.

"Should I go on?" said Ro.

Ro began.

Wren sat rapt.

Eloise was eating an orange.

After that holiday something changed. Maybe it was too much booze or too many ghost stories. Wren and I did not fall out of love. How could we? She assured me that we had never been in love. She said that romantic love was a terrorist tactic used by the patriarchy to keep women down.

We were comrades.

It was a wretched winter.

I read *Frankenstein,* and she, *A Vindication of the Rights of Woman.*

What hope was there for us then?

The snow fell.

One day—or maybe it was night—

Wren lay smoking in my bed.

She was naked, reading.

Her book fell to the floor.

She leaned on her elbow.

She turned on her hip, ashed the cigarette.

And she asked me, "Do you believe in monsters?"

Then she dressed.

Wren buttoned her flannel shirt.

She dropped out of school at the end of the term.

And moved to Oregon to join a feminist farm collective.

Her ideology had outpaced her desire.

We vowed to remain brothers.

Scissors cut paper.

Rock smashed scissors.

Ro had a laugh about it.

I spent hours at the library.

Reading Greek tragedies.

Ro and I lived in our apartment on—what was the street name, again?—on Bard Street. Sure. Why not? All the world was a stage. And we defied augury. Or at least, we tried.

One night Ro came home drunk from a party.

I heard him.

A crash, something breaking, falling to the floor.

I found him in the kitchen, sitting at the table.

He sat at my typewriter.

He rolled a sheet of paper into the carriage.

He started banging on the keys.

I stood watching him.

"What are you doing?" I asked him.

"Writing my life story," he said.

In a month the manuscript of his first novel was finished. I have to say this about him: once he started something, he was singularly focused.

He wrote late at night, early into the morning, and then slept through his classes.

Writing made him hungry, he said.

I remember now: this was why he took hard-boiled eggs from the dining hall. He had pilfered a saltshaker as well. He always salted the egg in an absurdly delicate, even continental gesture, before cramming the whole thing into his mouth.

CHAPTER 7

Susu defies augury

HE SAID THE WORD *INSPIRATION*. He said *fate,* and I laughed. He said *time,* and it stopped. I went away with him. He liked a dark place an ancient rundown hotel out of the way on a side street an avenue of twists and turns and insidious intent. He liked it when the night porter's wife brought to him hot almond milk. He liked the chipped bowl and the tarnished spoon. He liked it if the sheets were worn, bleached, and darned. He looked for omens and portents. There was; there had been a shadow on my white dress. There was no wedding. There were signs. There was a carnival, a myth, a murdered king, a teacup, a fluttering bird at a crust of bread. He said, "Truth is an artificial construct." He said, "All the poetry in the world won't save us." He liked salt, and he liked sweet. He liked the old stories. He said, "Many a man has been left hanging because there was no knife to cut him down." I saw ruined palaces. I saw marble gods. I saw dark birds in doorways. He talked of poets and kings. I collected picture postcards. He talked. He told. He taught. I twisted up my hair and tied it with a ribbon. I turned my spoon in my cup. He took my arm. When I could not sleep, when the strangeness of the strange city kept me awake he said, "Imagine that you are sailing on a ship to Byzantium. It is night and you must navigate by the stars." He said, "Imagine that you are winding your way through a labyrinth." And as each night began to lead to the last day and one dark place lost its distinguishing charm from the next place as we wound our way through the streets I began to understand that there was a design a plan a destiny that each avenue was leading us to and toward some inevitable conclusion and I would have to listen I would have to learn or else I would never find my way to the end.

CHAPTER 8

Eloise argues about infinity

AFTER DINNER (at that little Japanese place where they serve warm plum wine and the girl leaves the bottle on the table) and a movie (a restored print of *Masculin Féminin*) and then home looping the loop by midnight for dessert (the remains of a bitter chocolate torte) and an argument (no, no, it was just a discussion) about Goddard (she said: didactic; he said: dogged) and god (she opposed; he supported) over espresso (with lemon rind for him; cream for her) and he said, "Once the girl took the stand, I knew that the jury would come back with a verdict of not guilty," just before she put the cups in the sink, and she said, "Is there a better word for it?"

2.

The second rule of storytelling was explained to me by an elementary school teacher: a dramatic dark-haired girl, just out of college, who one day ran off with the janitor—leaving behind for those of us who so unironically loved her a mysterious message on the blackboard: *Godnight!* She told me after reading my lengthy attempt at a short story, "Shelly, never kill off the main character." I recall that story. I did kill off the main character *(pro-tag-on-ist,* she said, breaking up the syllables like lemon drops), but as, and I explained this to her; the pro-tag-on-ist returned as a ghost, it didn't really count as killing him, did it?

3.

Louie said, "Innocent." Eloise told him that that was not what she meant; not what she meant at all. She said, "Is there a better word for 'girl'?" He said perhaps they could go away in the spring, "Would you like that?" Would she like that? And then it was late. Not too late. Just late. He said that there was no better word for it than girl.

4.

Roman Stone is dead.

I write the sentence easily enough.

It looks on the page like—

A little pawn pushed out alone on the battlefield ahead of an army.

What if I had not started this story with the moment that I met Ro?

And yet now that it has begun: does it matter where it began? I could have started with my childhood. Dug up a first memory or two: sunlight on a windowpane; bread and butter; Mother with a knife in the jam; Father's papers fluttering to the floor. I would if I could push-comes-to-shove the story relentlessly forward through the years—schoolbooks, lessons, silence broken by Mother's laughter.

Snow, sawdust; a hammer, nails; the stairs down to the cellar. El & Shel in the woods. She and me at the salt creek. Eloise and I riding bicycles; from under the apple tree we saw the locked door to the cellar workshop; where father worked on his designs, his puzzles, where he dug his grave ideas and built his great impossible knowledge.

He knew everything. Is this possible?

I seem to recall that he knew all that there was to know.

Father had a sickness that we could not understand.

Mother gave him his medicine.

Eloise and I under the apple tree.

Eloise and I arguing about infinity.

I and El diagramming sentences.

Me and she dividing one number into another.

This is El and Shel. What the hell.

When we were eighteen we went to college.

On the Greyhound Bus.

A little girl and her mother were sitting in the seats in front of us. The girl had her face pressed up against the window. She was licking the glass.

I looked at El. And she at me.

And the girl kept licking the window.

Eloise looked sad, I guess. If that's the word for it.

On the way to Iowa.

All that wheat and corn and wonder.

All we had was each other.

Until we met Ro.

5.

Eloise in her silk nightdress. Louie in his striped pajamas. He said, "Tell me about the box." She pulled the chain on the lamp. In bed. In the darkness. She waited. She waited. When she said, "What box?" he was already asleep. Louie slept, but Eloise did not. She was thinking about a girl lost in the woods. She saw the shadows of trees against the wall. She heard, she seemed to hear the ticking of a clock. It must have been her own heart. She thought she heard, how could she explain this? the sound of a shovel digging in the hard frozen ground.

6.

The day, or maybe it was night, that Ro met my sister, he told me that he was in love with her.

7.

Eloise rose without waking her husband. In the kitchen she put on the teakettle. She was thinking of the house in which she had grown up; thinking of the tangled vines of the garden. Of Mother digging in the garden—pushing back with palm to forehead her dark curls. Of the white faces of moonflowers and lilies. Of Father. And the responsibilities that begin in dreams. Of Shelly cutting in half an apple with his penknife. Saying to her, telling her, *El, it's just us now.*

She turned off the flame on the burner. And poured the water from the kettle into her cup. She was thinking of dancing bears and dark birds. She was thinking of a modern Prometheus. Of signs and symbols: poor Susu! remember how brokenhearted Susu had been, at age six or was it seven? When she had wanted a part in that school play? Was it Aesop's fables? No—it was mythologies, ancient stories, old stories. In the tale of Pandora, Susu had wanted to play Hope, who rises up in the end in her white dress. The dark-haired green-eyed girl was cast instead as Vengeance. Well, she had looked darling in black. It suited her, even then.

Eloise dropped a sugar cube into her tea.

She turned her spoon round in the cup.

A small rock holds back a great wave.

Vengeance is a better role than Hope.

Susu on stage.

Susu in her black leotard coming out of the box.

With hands on her hips saying: take a picture, it'll last longer.

What was *it* and how long would it last?

Eloise in the living room—

She paused before the fireplace.

Took in hand a jade statuette.

Chronos, the great father who ate up his own children.

Time would swallow us all down.

Zola was sleeping on the sofa.

Zola lifted her head from the velvet pillow.

Wait, wait, Susu had played Discord, not Vengeance.

Oh, what did it matter now?

Roman Stone was dead.

That was how the story had to go.

She knew the story of old waxwinged Daedalus and his son.

She knew of Apollo riding his chariot across the sky.

Apollo had a sister. A girl running through the woods.

Eloise knew of Discord and her golden apple.

She knew all that there was to know, and this knowledge was no
consolation.

Eloise stood barefoot on the Persian rug.

Zola watched her.

Stared at her mournfully.

Eloise sat at her writing desk.

She unfolded the letter.

She read the letter again.

It was only a few words.

How could these few words—
Like petals on a wet, black bough—
Hold the possibility to change everything?
She picked up Zola and held her like a fat bullish baby.

8.

"Why do you write in the dark?" Beatrice asks.

Beatrice stands in the doorway, as though to remind me with her slight youthful presence, that the things of which I have written happened a long time ago. That 1979 passed into 1980 with neither too much sturm nor nearly enough drang.

She goes about the room, turning on lamps. And she brings about the illumination of objects. Magic, miracle; magically, miraculously: things appear.

The fear of objects follows the illumination of the thing.

The room suddenly becomes itself.

We become ourselves.

The chairs, the tables—

No longer simply words to replace the real, but *real*.

Where there was darkness there is light.

Beatrice comes to me at the desk. She leans over my shoulder—

Beatrice picks up the pages.

She sits on the sofa and begins reading.

Ro finished his manuscript. He got it to a literary friend of his father, and through a chain of vaguely shrouded and loosely nepotistic associations, the book was published in our senior year. *Newsweek* called Roman Stone: *the face of the 1980s*. And *Time* hailed him as: *the voice of a generation*. It was funny. It was a riot. I didn't take his success very seriously. I had other things on my mind. Like aurochs and prophetic sonnets. Like durable pigments and the immortality of art. Although perhaps the *immorality* might have been more useful in the end. After graduation, Eloise landed a fellowship in Paris studying linguistics with a famous semiotician. I went to California with Ro. He got tan, took pills, tore through actresses. He was Ro, the real thing. I was Shel, the sidekick. We lived in a house on the beach. I set my typewriter on the kitchen table. Do you know the joke: *why did the man throw his clock out the window?* Ro liked that one, but it isn't a joke. It's a riddle. *He wanted to see time fly.* A year later: Eloise found us in our golden state. She brought Ro a tin of hand-fluted madeleines. And she gave me a volume of Balzac.

And, oh, Eloise brought back something else from Paris: her new husband.

He was an actor. His name was Zigouiller. He was called Zig. He had rough leading-man good looks. And he wanted to make it big in Hollywood.

Eloise was bone-skinny. She chain-smoked. Her fingernails were painted black. She had gone from naïf to nihilist. She had been lonely in Paris, so she hid in the darkness of the cinema. She saw *The Amityville Horror* eight times. That was where she met Zigouiller— he ran the projector—or rather, to use his unfortunate and entirely real name: Herman Munster. He had grown up in some snow-globe perfect little mountain town, which was in the news awhile back, when a mass grave was discovered there. That has nothing to do with the story. Neither does this: *Zigouiller* means "to murder," or rather, "to do in," in French.

Harlow Jamison was living with us; she was the actress starring in the movie adaptation of *Babylon Must Fall*. She had been discovered as a teenager in a shopping mall in Lincoln, Nebraska. She had white-blonde hair, a baby-doll face, and a disconcertingly weary voice. She thought that Ro was in love with her. She thought of life as a movie; fate was nothing more than a plot twist. We shared a habit of insomnia. Late at night, in the kitchen, while the clock ticked, and my fingers did not move on keys, she found me at the typewriter.

I used to say that her voice sounded like a graham cracker crumbling into a glass of gin. Back when I said such things.

It too was a long time ago.

Harlow had Ro.

And El had Zig. Sure, he wasn't a big star, but he did all right for himself in the movies. He had a quality, somewhere between menacing and brooding, that lent itself to the role of the sympathetic sadist. He was in such B-screen erotic thrillers as *Nightfall, King Me, Girl in a Maze,* and the soft-core cult classic *Ava and Eva.* In the epic *Fatherland* he played a tortured writer. It's true: he ended up playing one tortured sadist after another. He played sadistic spies, the occasional sadistic cyborg, terrorist, morally bankrupt cat burglar, or in the disturbing and utterly unerotic case of *Ava and Eva,* a sadistic sadist. Zig grew despondent; in France he could have been a hero, but in America he was a villain. He didn't want to be relegated to a lifetime in a black turtleneck and ski mask. He was typecast. He was disillusioned. Zig had El. And El had Ro. Ro did what he wanted. I had my typewriter. And the sun shined every day. It was only right that Zigouiller and Roman became pals: drinking Pernod, swimming in the ocean, getting coked up and ranting about *Cahiers du Cinéma.*

When I left for graduate school in Wisconsin, Ro and Harlow and El and Zig were living together in that house on the beach.

"Is it true?" Beatrice asks.

"Did all these things happen the way you say they did?" she says.

"Does it matter?" I say.

She gets her wide-eyed lost look.

As though she is retreating into some deep feminine hideout in her heart.

And she won't argue the finer irritating points of semantics.

Not tonight anyway.

She wants to finish reading.

Beatrice in the lamplight.

She rests her head on the arm of the sofa.

She reads on.

One by one the pages fall to the floor.

CHAPTER 9

Susu sees the burning king

I LEARNED OF BOILED BEDSHEETS the stains of blood bleach and bodies. I learned of cigarettes sand stars birds with dark wings bells clocks rain mildew mud heat fire flame hope signs salt symbols. He talked. He told. I remember I remember a carnival and we walked away along the water strung with lights. I was walking with him winding our way along a seawall stone steps children lighting our way with candles twined with burning knots of sage lighting the way for us and we went down like we were making a descent down down down to his underworld. Ghosts of straw were strung up all around us. He said, "Be true, be true, be true; show to the world your worst and if not your worst then some token by which the worst can be inferred. Show me the worst," he said. "Fire, flood, locusts, destruction," he said. A girl ran past us. He watched. We stood on the street. He held my face in his hands. A boy bounced a ball against a stone wall. He said, "You would do anything that I asked, wouldn't you? You really aren't afraid, are you?" He took my hand as the narrow walk gave way to a wide esplanade where girls sold flowers and we followed its turns along past the girls holding wreaths of white with petals scattering past little boys throwing balls past the fortune-tellers past orange figs and lemon and licorice past the kings burning in effigy and the children in paper crowns. "I'll do anything," I said.

CHAPTER 10

Eloise turns toward an undeniable conclusion

LOUIS SARASINE, IN CORDUROY AND TWEED, in the car on the drive back from Lake Forest to the city in the darkness of almost winter told his wife Eloise how well she had done, how absolutely beautifully she had soldiered through it. He asked if she needed another one? She said yes. Always answer yes as there is no such word as no in the unconscious. He doled out a pill into her gloved hand. The leather seats were heated; the evening was cold. The day had been cold and bright. If it had snowed, they could have gotten out of it. Thanksgiving at his brother's house? Oh, how could she bear it? The spoiled children, the gossip, the limp crudités and blood-orange cranberry jelly, the electric carving knife, and that sacrificial bird browning in the oven. Even at the front door she had turned to Louie and asked if it was too late to turn around? He didn't need to answer. The door opened. And what could she do? Eloise was divested arm by arm of her marbled faux fawn coat by an eager niece, seized up and borne along by a battalion of perfumed aunts and cousins, into her sister-in-law's kitchen where the congregated Sarasine women were drinking Goody cream soda, grenadine, and apple schnapps (*it's called an Original Sin!*) while whispering about a certain missus who was engaged in an illicit such-and-such with that mister, from you-know-where. The crime was implied. The details went unspoken. Did the little girls, aprons tied over their velvet dresses, licking fingers of whipped cream from the mixing bowl, understand? what about their older sisters placing dessert chocolates on a tray? *Eloise be a dear and*—a crying baby of indeterminate sex was set by a young mother upon Eloise's knee. Amidst the clatter of silver, the distant cheers of boys and men watching a football game; the crash of ice in glasses; the knife cutting flesh from breast and bone. A girl—a newlywed—wanted to hold the baby, and Eloise was happy to relinquish the bundle. Eloise sat with her back to the eggshell white wall. How did one bear it? Louis said, *look at it as an experiment. A social experiment*—It's funny, he said, *if you think about it.* But she endured it, that is, got through it by imagining herself winding a skein through a labyrinth, taking each twist as it came; following the turns toward some undeniable conclusion.

They were driving home.

They drove on.

Louis was talking.

He asked her—

He was asking what she had thought of the—

When she interrupted him.

She said that she just remembered the oddest thing: that once her mother had tried to bake a pie from the green apples—

"From your tree?" he said.

"Yes," she said. "From our apple tree."

"You never said before," he said. "That they were green apples."

"Didn't I?" she said.

"So what happened?" he asked. "With the pie?"

"Oh, I don't know——" she said. "It didn't turn out. We thought it was funny, Shel and I."

"What did your mother do?" he asked. "Was she upset that the pie was ruined?"

"Oh, no, no." said Eloise. "We were singing *Bye Bye Miss American Pie.*"

"And your father?" he asked.

"What about him?" said Eloise.

"Did he think it was funny?" he said.

Eloise looked out the window.

"We didn't tell him. We threw it away, the pie," she said.

"Where was he?" Louis said.

"In the cellar. I think," she said.

"What happened in the cellar?" he said.

"That sounds like a horror movie," she said.

"*What Happened in the Cellar?*" she repeated.

They drove on in the darkness.

"How old were you?" he asked.

"When?" she said.

"The pie——" he said.

"Oh," she said. "Really little. Five or six."

Eloise closed her eyes.

How tired she was——

"That song," Louis said.

"What?" she said.

"It didn't come out until later, did it?" he said.

"We were singing it." she said.

He went on, "Not until the seventies, I'd say——probably '72."

"I was small," she said. "I remember."

"You must have been, what——?" he said.

"We were in the kitchen—" she said.

"About twelve?" he asked.

She knew then that he had trapped her.

Led her to his own undeniable conclusion.

He had unwound the skein and she had followed it.

And she didn't want to talk anymore, but he kept asking her questions: which part of the memory did she have wrong? Could she and her brother have been singing a different song? Or had she been older? Was it an apple cake, not a pie? Or had it happened, really, at all?

She supposed that he doubted her memory.

He said that it wasn't the reality of the memory that was important, it was the fact that her mind wanted to have this image—this idea—within its archives.

She was too tired to disagree.

To tell him that it was *the reality* that mattered.

Chair is a word. It replaces an object, a thing, a concrete utilitarian device that is called also *chair*. One can't sit in *chair-the-word*, but does occupy *chair-the-reality*.

Baby is a word. It replaces a fat little person of indeterminate sex, who is called *baby*. And when one of these creatures is plunked down upon your silk shantung dress as you sit in a chair with your back to the wall in an eggshell white kitchen where the women come and go and do not talk of Michelangelo you realize just how wretched and hopeless the world is.

She rested her head against the leather seat.

Louis turned on the radio.

It was a call-in show about hunting.

Deer hunting season had begun.

"Turn the station," she said. "Will you? Please, for god's sake."

2.

I left California for the Midwest. I went to Wisconsin, and I worked on my PhD in Madison. I taught classes. I lurked in libraries. I fell for the dark romantics: I hid among the hardbound copies of Hawthorne. Ro called me from Paris, where he was eating a Toblerone and reading *Oui* in his hotel room. He called from Rome, where he was romancing a fashion model; he bought postcards, remedies, and black licorice in the botteghe oscure. Ro called me drunk, da Milano; high, from the mountains of Turin, where he searched for the shroud and found instead the dark sweet miracle of ciccolato. He asked, "How's the book?" How did Ro find where I was hiding? The beat beat beating of my telltale heart must have given me away. I laughed, I was bitter, I was broken. I said to him, "What book?"

3.

Mr. & Mrs. Sarasine ate breakfast at their kitchen table.

It was such a beautiful thing, a rare find: an authentic black walnut and ash-inlaid eighteenth-century executioner's table. They had bought it in Prague and had it shipped home.

Louie asked her, what was she going to do today?

He said that if she was going out, she should take a taxi.

It was going to snow, he said.

The streets would be awful.

Are we out of cream?

Eloise looked up from her horoscope in the newspaper.

"Snow is general," she said.

Louie picked up a knife.

Louie took an apple and began to peel it in one long seamless tangle.

4.

I met Pru in Minnesota, in a town called Little America. She was twenty-three. I was twenty-eight. She taught introductory drawing. I taught freshman composition and a survey course of American literature: Melville, Thoreau, Whitman, and Poe in paperback to bright-eyed butter-cheeked blond-haired farm kids. This was at Lindbergh College. The students and professors alike, with an antediluvian lack of irony, called the town *L.A.*

I was caught in the vortex of all symbols.

I became a symbol myself: the dark outsider.

One thing happened and then another.

Eloise and Zigouiller divorced. After the failure of the interminable eroto-historical epic, *Fatherland,* Zigouiller retreated back across the Atlantic. And Eloise was in Chicago, raising their little girl on her own. Ro was as riotous as ever. The last that I heard from him had been a postcard from Copenhagen, with a cryptic note about mermaids and ice skates. I was dispensing doses of literature in Little America. I didn't have the temperament for teaching. I was doused in Dickinson's metaphysical gloom.

It might as well have been gasoline.

Because I could not stop for death; would he kindly stop for me?

That's what I remember about Lindbergh College.

Hester Prynne's lexicographical shame—

Bartleby's polite preferences *not to*—

And lost Lenore—

I found Pru at a faculty art show. She was standing—her back to me—before a canvas. And as if suddenly aware that she was being watched by a lurching stranger, she turned; her face, her face over her shoulder and she gave me a funny half smile.

Pru painted abstract nudes: self-portraits.

"Doesn't that defeat the purpose?" I asked her.

We left the gallery together. I left with her. She with me.

On bicycles, for god's sake.

It was November and cold and the flat dark prairie smelled of burning. She was wearing a plaid coat over her dress; I think it was black, the dress, though it is hard to recall. Yes, that's right. Pru in her black dress and plaid coat and boots riding a bicycle. She rented rooms on the top floor of an old house. I followed her up the staircase. The steps creaked. She clung to the banister. She fumbled for her key. It fell from her hand. She found it on the hallway floor. She unlocked the door. She boiled water for tea. Did I mention her hair was blue? Bicycles, black dress, blue hair, autumn, burning, fallen key, tea in mismatched china cups: we were that innocent. She read my fortune in the tarot. She chose three cards from the pack. She squinted at the symbols. I learned that she was nearly blind and she had that day broken her only pair of eyeglasses. When she had looked across the room at the gallery, she didn't see me. She turned the three cards over, one after the next. She waited for the kettle to boil. Her eyes were bothering her. The weakness of her eyes troubled her; but I admit, I confess; I was relieved that she couldn't really see me.

We sat in the darkness on her second-story porch in our coats.

The tea went cold in our cups.

It began to rain and we went inside.

She was Prudence Goodman from St. Louis, Missouri. A painter of indecipherable and yet impossibly desirable shapes. And I was a promising writer suffering for his art. I told her about my novel. She gave me her blurry-eyed smile and said, *I bet it sucks to be you.*

How could I not fall for her?

Her singularly soft mouth? Her slightly sloping shoulders?

She went in big for fate and destiny and ghosts. She read our horoscopes from the newspaper. *The problem is not in ourselves, but in our stars,* she used to say. She was funny like that. Her skin was white. Her eyes were brown. And her hands smelled like turpentine.

Pru on the porch.

Pru in her plaid coat with a scarf wrapped around her neck—

When did I learn that the burning, which seemed to fill the air, was the acrid bluish smoke coming from a nearby hog rendering plant?

When did the beginning cease to begin?

5.

Eloise Sarasine, in variant shades of gray: Persian-lamb coat, charcoal gloves, and scarf knotted into an ashen knot, wandered a crowded downtown bookstore on a day in December.

It was Eloise's turn to choose for her book club.

Opening a book had a certain secret thrill for her.

It was like standing with one's hand on a doorknob.

It was like untying the string on a box.

A boy was sprawled on the floor reading Beckett. He looked up at her belligerently. And as she passed him, she wondered; she couldn't stop herself from wondering: had he ever murdered anyone? She picked up a book from the end display. There was a typewriter on the cover. The young author stared out at her from the back jacket, as though he had not existed before she imagined him—with his eyeglasses and witty winning face. The critics praised him; they called him *Literature's last best hope*—. Oh well, *hope:* that was something, right?

Mrs. Sarasine, having selected two books with her gray-gloved hands, waited in the line at the cash register. The salesgirl took up the first book; she opened it and she read the first sentence aloud. She closed the book, then asked, "Do you need it wrapped?" Eloise chose a fleur-de-lis paper. Eloise asked the girl if she had read the other book. The girl sighed, her hand on the scissors—and said that she was just *so* tired of bright young men. She preferred the classics. The girl had violet hair, and Eloise felt a bit envious. So she had the book wrapped, for the sake of not disappointing—or courting the displeasure of—this girl whom she wished she knew; a girl who seemed so much like the girls whom Eloise had long ago known and the girl whom she herself used to be, but was no longer.

Mrs. Sarasine thanked the girl, looked at her watch, and then took her shopping bag out the revolving door into the cold afternoon.

She was in luck. She caught a taxi just at the curb.

She got in and directed the driver to take her to the Parliament Hotel.

6.

The day after the night that I met Pru, I went back to look at her house, in the sunlight. In the diffuse damp autumn afternoon. I waited at a distance. Then the door to the house opened. Pru stood in the doorway. She didn't see me. She got on her bicycle. I watched her ride off down the street. I had an image of her. I was already collecting pieces of her. So that if she were broken, I could put her back together. If she were shattered, I could reassemble and save her.

7.

Eloise—gray lamb's wool coat, black boots—strode through the lobby of the Parliament Hotel.

The letter had led her here. The letter contained so few words that it barely seemed to exist. *Meet me at the bar of the Parliament Hotel.* It wasn't signed. Only the hour and date of the proposed assignation. Once she had been called by its sender: *almost beautiful.* What about now? And now? She was walking through the lobby, upon the carpet patterned with crushed roses, into another world:

an underworld; the darkness of the elegant old bar. She went to her fate. She could not stop herself. She went to Zigouiller.

8.

Pru and I lived in a house on a street called Valhalla. She took the sunny back room as her studio. I used to get such an odd feeling— an uneasiness, then a sudden rush of familiarity—to see her bicycle left, unlocked, lying on the grass before our doorstep.

It was July 1989. I was teaching an evening course of Intro to Poetry,—when I came home to find Pru sitting on the front steps with Roman. I hadn't seen him in years. I should have been surprised. And yet I was not. His magical appearances did not astonish me, but I still might marvel at the deftness of his disappearances. Roman was talking. Pru had her face tipped toward him, listening. As I approached, I couldn't hear what he was telling her. Pru was laughing. The hot night. In her thin dress. A strap had slipped down over one shoulder.

Ro was on his way to the Mayo Clinic. His father was there; Milton Stone was dying, but Ro wasn't too broken up about it. "Something's wrong with the old man's heart. That's funny, isn't it? He always thought he'd be murdered," he said. "Milton Stone in the library with the great silver sewing shears," he said. He might not have said *heart*. He might have said *ticker*. He might not have said *shears*. He might have said *scissors*. Pru thought that he was being brave. I knew that he was just being Ro. And we sat outside drinking Grain Belt in the darkness. Ro and Shelly and Pru as though it were the most natural thing in the world.

Pru with pink hair.

She sat listening to Ro.

Ro reached over—

Between one word and the next—

And fixed the fallen strap of Pru's dress.

Yeah, Ro kept us laughing.

Telling his stories.

Stories of ghosts and gods and girls.

Pru in the moonlight shivered.

Ro touched her bare arm.

It grew late.

And then it was late.

Not too late.

Just late.

Pru held her face in her hand.

And looked up at the stars.

Did she mind?

If we went on without her?

Ro had so much to tell me.

Ro and I left Pru behind and we walked to a campus bar.

Ro was the same as ever.

He had put on a bit of fat.

Rather than making him seem soft; this bulk was imposing.

He asked me about my sister.

Two boys were running down the street in the darkness.

They ran past us.

We walked.

He said, "I bet you still believe in talent?"

He went on.

"And the house of fiction?"

He laughed.

"—The golden bowl, and the Grecian urn, the cracked looking glass, the rules of the game, and truth and beauty and all that marble faun bullshit?"

He paused to pull a sprig of blossom from a branch.

"Just give me a shovel," I said. "And tell me where to dig."

"What the fuck does that mean?" he said.

He was wearing khaki trousers and a white Oxford shirt.

He was sweating through his white shirt.

He asked about my book.

Was it finished yet?

I shrugged.

"Do you know what your problem is?" he said.

"Please," I said. "Enlighten me."

"You think," he said, "—that failure is the proof of great art."

We walked.

Past houses and gardens.

A dog barked.

Ro on a roll.

"Who said anything about art?" I said.

I remember saying it.

And thinking that I was being clever.

"Look at this place," he said.

The air was tinged with smoke.

Burnt offerings to an old god.

"Jesus," he said.

A light was extinguished in a window, behind a lace curtain.

"Why are you here?" I said.

He said, "I'm your friend."

He was either so ironic that he had become serious—

Or so serious that he was nothing but ironic.

I couldn't tell.

We walked.

The hot night.

He wiped his brow.

"Don't look so smug," he said. "It wasn't a compliment."

He told me that he was going to a monastery in Tibet.

Or maybe to Barcelona for the winter.

Then on to Delphi.

And Crete to find the ruins of Daedalus's labyrinth.

Why didn't I come with him?

"What the hell," he said. "Bring the girl too."

He liked Pru. He knew that there was something secret and spectacular about her. He just hadn't figured out what it was yet.

We came to the place.

We went in.

We sat at the bar.

Ro lighted a cigarette.

"You'll destroy her," he said.

He shook his head.

He squinted through the smoke.

"A girl like that," he said.

"So now you can tell the future?" I said.

"Not *the* future," he said. "*Your* future. Because it looks just like your past."

After a drink or two, it occurred to him.

"She's got money," he said. "The girl. She's got money, doesn't she?"

He didn't need to hear my answer.

He had a sense about these things.

There was a baseball game on the TV over the bar. The Twins were playing the Mariners, out West. We watched for a while. Ro kept ordering us shots of Maker's Mark. And I remember saying how I still preferred to listen to the games on the radio.

"Same old Sheldon," he sighed. "You stupid sentimental fucked-up motherfucker."

And then he ordered us another round.

He spent the night on my sofa and left the next day.

His father died soon after.

And Pru read about it in the newspaper.

"Your poor friend," she said.

9.

Eloise and Zigouiller had a drink or two.

They drank vodka, warm and neat: a shared peculiarity.

He told her that he was in from L.A.

He was in a movie that was a real hit.

Had she seen it?

She hadn't seen it.

He said no, he supposed that she wouldn't have. He said that it was a movie based on a video game based on the story of the Trojan War. He explained the technical complexities of the movie; that it was some sort of hybrid digital, pixilated, animated, and real three-dimensional version of himself whom he had played. He said that it was big with teenage boys.

He said, "Boys."

To which she laughed.

He laughed too.

As though it meant something; which it did not.

She felt a rush of uncertainty—as though he were a specter, a figment, a phantom; what had he called it? *A hybrid three-dimensional version of himself* containing the past and the present—because it was impossible for her to believe that she was talking about fate with Zigouiller in the dark rose-wreathed gloom of a hotel bar. She touched her hand to her cheek. It was warm and real; she was not a ghost, nor a version of herself; she was only *herself;* and she supposed that she was, after all, real. Or at least real enough.

He said that he would be in town for a while.

He had a part in a play.

He knew that it was fate.

That had brought him here.

He wanted to see her.

He liked this place. Did she?

She said that whether one liked a thing or not mattered so little these days.

He said that it was good to see her.

As she held her glass in both hands.

The inevitability of what would happen next was delayed only by politeness. By decorum; by formalism; by what it meant to be respectively: an almost beautiful woman wearing a large diamond wedding ring and an imposing French actor drinking warm vodka and sharing peculiarities at three in the afternoon in the bar of the grand old Parliament Hotel.

They sat in silence.

And then—with a presumption as absolute as it was accurate—he took her arm.

And she knew that he was real, that he was, in fact, *Zig,* as she had named him.

It was without speaking that they walked together to the elevator.

He hit the button.

They waited to go up.

They waited.

The elevator arrived; the doors opened.

They got in.

The doors closed.

He used to say *lift,* instead of *elevator;* she remembered this.

And when the doors opened again—she saw the plum carpet with the crushed roses.

They continued on down the hallway.

Into his room. With a memory of licorice.

The door closed behind them.

And it wasn't until later, after the afternoon passed into evening—

—that she, wrapped in a sheet—

Remembered to ask him, whom had he played in the movie?

10.

Not all of the memories are my own.

I defer to my sister for a moment. Eloise told me of a winter afternoon when she was nineteen; it is her story. So here I paraphrase—

She and Ro were watching *Jeopardy!* on the little black-and-white TV in her dorm room. There was a snowstorm; classes had been canceled. The two of them had spent the day getting drunk. It was just past four o'clock—outside it was already dark—when Ro decided that he wanted to go sledding. They didn't have a sled. And the snow wasn't stopping. They went out into the woods. Eloise was then deep in her tragic heroine phase; and never very good with liquor. On the narrow path through the pines she fell and twisted her ankle. Roman lifted her up and carried her. She thought Roman was carrying her back toward school. She closed her eyes. She fell asleep in his arms. The thing is: he wasn't heading back— he was taking her out farther; past the sloping hill down which kids used to sled and tumble on makeshift toboggans, past the creek, into the thickening woods. And when Roman was far into the trees, he dropped her. And he walked away. Eloise didn't know how long it was that she lay there—asleep, drunk, dreaming, unconscious—in the woods. When she awoke—cold, lost, and alone—the snow had stopped falling. She cried for a while; then she resolved to find her way home. She said that it was a good thing that Roman cut such a big path. She said that by moonlight, she followed the trail of his footsteps in the snow.

11.

Zigouiller answered her.

He said, "The king."

Priam, Priam O age-worn King—

Zigouiller had his hand on her hip.

Eloise said, "He ignores the prophecies. In the end it destroys him."

Zigouiller said, "Everyone ignores the prophecies."

"I know," she said.

He said, "Everyone is destroyed in the end."

She said, "That doesn't make it any easier. Does it?"

He said that she hadn't changed, had she?

Those whom the Gods would destroy—

They would first make mad.

She supposed that she should hate him.

There was a travel alarm clock on the table.

"When can I see the girl?" he asked.

"You can't," she said.

"El—," he said.

"I'm not being difficult," she said.

"She's gone away," she said.

12.

Roman Stone is dead. He died this summer. In June there was rain. The roses were sick. They caught a blight, a mildew. I cut the branches down to the union bud; in another season they may thrive. Dr. Lemon was in decline. Ro was in Iowa. He had gone back to Virgil's Grove. Ro was to deliver the commencement address at Illyria. I read that the only thing missing from the scene of the crime, the guest-house in which Ro was staying, was his wristwatch. Granted: it was a ridiculously expensive miracle of Italian design; notable for being able to keep time both underwater and on the surface of the moon. Oh, and the murder weapon. That was gone too. It was never found. Wasn't it odd, for what appeared to be so random, such a small theft; that he was stabbed through the heart? The mold ate at the roses. Roman Stone was murdered in Iowa on a hot June night as he sat watching a baseball game on television. He never gave his speech. Ro left his advice ungiven. If he had stood at the dais—what would he have told those kids looking so sincerely to the future?—what secrets would he have divulged about the mysteries of the world? He was cremated: his bones into ashes; and his ashes scattered to sea.

13.

Eloise turned away from him.

She reached for her handbag.

And from it, she pulled out a postcard.

Zigouiller read it aloud.

"—*Have drunk all the wine in the winedark sea.*
Please don't be angry."

"You see?" said Eloise. "She's gone away."

14.

Pru said that she liked Ro.

She said that he had grabbed her.

"Where?" I asked.

"In the kitchen," she said.

"Funny," I said.

She said that she pitied him.

"Is that all?" I said.

"Nothing happened," she said.

We fought then.

I was jealous. I didn't believe her.

She smashed a plate, a glass.

She was angry because I didn't believe her.

15.

In the taxi on the way home, Eloise saw a murder of crows perched upon a rooftop against the darkening winter sky.

An augury of things to come.

This is how the gods will make you mad.

They will make you doubt yourself.

They will make you doubt your own reliability.

As a witness to your life.

Even what had happened only moments ago.

In a hotel room like licorice.

Down a hallway carpeted with roses.

As one came up from the underworld.

Was already a memory.

Eloise had to remind herself, as her taxi speeded along snowy streets; under the moving eye of dark birds watching from window ledges, clustering in doorways, upon rooftops.

One can't outrun the past with—or through—memories.

Making up the ending to fit the beginning.

That's what Louis told her.

That's what Louis said, anyway.

He said that one should live in the eternal-now.

She ran a gloved hand over her lamb coat.

And collected her shopping bag, which contained two books, *Here Comes Everyone,* by Benjamin Salt and *Babylon Must Fall,* by Roman Stone.

The taxi came to a stop.

She paid the driver, thanked him a bit too profusely, and told him to keep the change.

16.

I don't tend to remember conversations quite so accurately as the one Ro and I had that night we walked together to the bar. Something about it has stuck with me. Maybe it was the oddity of finding Roman sitting on the steps with Pru. Or it could have been that he spoke to me with a new and paternal authority; offering me his advice, his admonition, his disapproval, and then, worst of all, his sweet melancholy. I fear that I recall it—as we ambled; the boys running past along the sidewalk, the drooping white mops of hydrangeas in the moonlight, the thick midwestern heat, the houses, the dogs, the gardens, the stars—because I knew that he was right.

That sickening smell of butchered hogs.

Who wouldn't cry out at such a ruthless truth?

He was right.

I wasted my time on words.

My poetry class left off that evening discussing "Leda and the Swan."

I came home to find Ro and Pru on the porch steps.

Do you recall specific days in your life?

Or do they blur into a continuum?

Would you be able to line them up?

To put them in order one after the next?

Or do the images refuse to be orderly?

What was real? And what was not?

We walked.

A sudden blow: the great wings beating still
Above the staggering girl, her thighs caressed

Past houses with windows darkened.
Along those avenues—
Ro chastised me.
What had become of my high ideals?
What about suffering for art?
"Ain't this suffering?" I asked him.
"*Grief without torment,*" he said.
Ro had been reading Dante.
"When are you going to tell your story?" he said.
What was it to him?
Oh yeah, he was my friend. He cared.
I thought that maybe it was something else.
That he was lonely.
Lonely with his terrible knowledge.
Like the serpent who got Eve to take a bite.
What was I waiting for?
Or hiding from?
I wasn't waiting.
Or hiding.
I was holding out.
I wasn't ready for his kind of knowledge.
Ro was ready.
Ro was smart and self-aware.
Educated, inculcated into a world of possibility—
He wasn't bogged down by guilt.
Nor sandbagged by responsibility.
Ro didn't fear anything.
Ro didn't fear any god.
And so he was free to believe in himself.
He was the real god.
Ro and I walked to a bar in Little America.

Though the name of the bar is lost to me.

He spoke of our friendship like a rare object in a museum.

Absurd, tricky, priceless: a Fabergé egg.

Those two boys ran past us kicking a ball.

Over the years I saw Roman do terrible things.

But there was only one thing for which I could not forgive him.

He took something from me.

The broken wall, the burning roof and tower

And Agamemnon dead.

Ro was right.

Pru on the porch.

Pru with a strap having slipped her shoulder.

Roman said I didn't deserve her.

He said that I would destroy her.

Her pale skin, her charcoal-stained fingers.

He said when the time came I wouldn't know what to do.

Pru had money. Heaps of it.

He was right, Ro was.

I never betrayed him.

And this is the greatest proof of my weakness.

17.

Eloise sat at her dressing table.

Along the lakeshore snow fell. They were going to dinner with Dr. Ira Black and his wife, Tiggy, for a belated celebration of the jury's decision. Louis had proven that the girl—the lone survivor of the brutal attacks—was an unreliable witness. That she was suffering from posttraumatic stress and had manufactured a memory to please the authorities and to appease her own unconscious guilt. *Survivor's guilt,* that's what Louis called it.

At the mirror Louis stood behind her.

He straightened his tie.

"Is that a new perfume?" he asked.

She said, no, no, she just hadn't worn it in a while.

"Why not?" he asked.

Her black silk nightdress lay across the bed.

The perfume was a note of rose.

"Will you do this?" she said.

She held her pearls around her neck, the clasp open.

18.

Prudence Goodman was the heiress to the Goody Soda Pop fortune.

She didn't tell me the night that we met. Nor for many nights after. It was her secret. She told me only after our wedding. We were married in a civil ceremony in the Little America courthouse. It was in August 1989—Pru in a pink crinoline dress—

Later—

In the lingering summer evening.

With nothing behind us and nothing before us.

As she lay across the bed.

Naked, nearly blind.

In the darkening hour.

She told me about the soda pop loot.

That's what she called it. Her secret—

She had the rich girl's woe.

Whom could she trust?

She didn't want people to know about the money.

It always came back to the money.

Until that moment—her confession—

She was Pru, the abstraction.

She was my discovery.

She had occurred to me.

In a blur of her own momentum.

A girl in pictures. And then—

She became someone else.

A girl with money.

Prudence, a judgment. A virtue. An admonition—

Her pink hair, a tangle of loops and knots and curls.

Her pink dress on the floor.

An antique stiff contraption of crinoline and bone.

It lay on the floor—on its side, like a fallen heroine.

"You're angry," she said.

On her side in the bed, like a fallen heroine.

"Are you angry?" she asked.

No longer my discovery.

No longer my invention.

"Do you think less of me?" she asked.

"How could I think less of you?" I said.

She laughed, in the darkness.

And she told me her stories.

How her great-grandfather sold bottles of medicinal tonic, lithiated lemon and sassafras soda, two for a nickel. And then a fruit punch that tasted like angel food cake. How her grandfather started Goodman's Bottling Works of St. Louis. How he heaped up the loot. How her father sold the business to a multinational food conglomerate.

And now all this loot was locked in a trust for her.

It would come to her on her thirtieth birthday.

She talked about St. Louis.

"It wasn't so bad," she said. "It's where T. S. Eliot is from, you know?"

Some of it was sugary sweet.

"Do you know what I'm going to do with all that money?" she said. "I'm going to see the world. And when there's nothing left to see, I'm going to find an island and hide out."

"What would you do?" she asked.

I told her that I didn't want her money.

I told her that I didn't want anything from her.

"Why not?" she asked.

She sang that silly catchy jingle:

George Washington may be the father of the country, but Goody is the Pop!

We talked about that fruit punch that tasted like angel food cake.

And the difference between limes and lemons.

And for a while we continued to exist.

On that street called Valhalla.

Pru on her bicycle. Pru walking the primrose path.

Prudence on paper. Pru in looping lines.

Pru upon a sofa. Pru at a window gazing out.

A certain bemused expression on her face.

Pru waiting for water to boil.

Pru peppering plums. Pru reading poetry. Pru with her hair pinned up. Pru defying the future because she had no future to defy. Pru growing pale. Pru with that illness beginning to eat away at her. When did she know that she was done for? Her funny glance; that strange blurry look; she knew. Didn't she? Did the tarot tell her? When did it happen? While I corrected papers. While the swan ravished Leda. And the inhabitants of Limbo and Little America alike felt grief without torment. As Pru painted. Pru washing her brushes. Pru paring potatoes. Pru digging a grave in her little plot of garden for the burial of a dead mouse.

Pru watching a game show on television. Pru with scissors lopping off loops of her hair. Pru smashing plates. *Let anger be general,* she used to say, *I hate an abstract thing.*

Pru becoming more and more unreal in my memory.

"Your name is like an admonition," I told her the night we met.

Riding the streets on our bicycles.

With nothing behind us and nothing ahead of us.

A girl in November—

With a name of admonishing restraint.

Like the streets that she rode on her bicycle in the darkness. As she coasted downhill, as she flew far beyond me. "What does that mean?" she called back to me.

"What does it mean?" she repeated.

She called out in the darkness.

When she came to a wooden bridge over a swollen creek, she stopped.

She held up and waited for me.

She waited on the bridge, looking into the cold moonlit water.

In her plaid coat, her knotted scarf, her black dress.

Pru asked me—"What's the worst thing that you have ever done?"

And then she was off again—

Pru not sticking around for an answer.

19.

Through dinner (at that Spanish place, where they pour chocolate martinis with just a wonderful burning dash of cayenne—) Louis Sarasine talked about bones with Dr. Ira Black, the paleontologist, and his wife Tiggy, the defense attorney (who answered her cell phone at the table three times during the tapas alone) while Eloise (was thinking: what if I took all the treasures in the world—the clocks, plates, cups cracked by the cold—and carried them in a sack out to sea?) rested her face upon her hand and just couldn't decide what she wanted.

They toasted to Louis Sarasine's success in swaying the jury.

"*Survivor's guilt,*" said Ira. "What a strategy."

"Louie, you've got to let me pick your brain," said Tiggy. "About my new case—"

Louie looked at his wristwatch.

"Shall I start billing now?" he said.

They all laughed.

Tiggy had taken on the defense of five high school football players accused of gang-raping a girl, who just so happened to be, Tiggy said, the town whore.

"It goes beyond guilt and innocence, doesn't it?" said Louie Sarasine.

Tiggy said yes. Yes, exactly. It was about belief—

She said, "Is there anything in the world better than a case in which you really believe?"

Was there anything in the world better than a chocolate martini? Eloise thought not. And so she had one or two. The boys had raped the girl. There was DNA evidence. And it was no point in the favor of Mrs. Black's clients that they had videotaped the attack. Still, Tiggy assured Louie and Ira and dear drunk Eloise that these boys were genuinely good, really good kids. And that her clients were not in an indefensible position. There was no question regarding their guilt; but certainly there were things more tangible, said Tiggy, more relevant, than guilt or innocence.

The restaurant was crowded. Amidst the talk, the salsa music, the clatter, the spice, the sweet, the caramel flan and café con leche, by the glow of candles, burning up, burning down—

Eloise was aware of—the scent of rose and pepper.

And smoke and chocolate—

Her face resting upon her hand.

Her hand resting upon her warm cheek—

The pearls roped around her neck.

She was thinking about Zigouiller.

And all the broken things in the world.

Why had he come back?

May whatever breaks

be reconstructed by the sea

with the long labor of its tides.

So many useless things

which nobody broke

but which got broken anyway.

"Don't you agree, El?" Tiggy said.

Yes, yes, Eloise gave a murmur of assent.

And later back at home, Louis said how funny it was that Eloise had agreed with Tiggy that the boys weren't responsible for what they had done. Because he always thought Eloise was the vengeful type. Louis was going to take the dog out. Did she want to come with him? She liked to walk Zola on snowy nights. She said oh that she was going to take a bath before bed. He said, again? didn't you bathe before dinner? Eloise pretended that she didn't hear him. Eloise had already closed the door. She was running the hot water. She had to get that perfume off her skin.

20.

Beatrice called me to the garden this morning.

The tiny bodies of two birds lay in the snow.

And Beatrice stood looking out toward the water.

She is not otherwise squeamish. But she cannot bear to see the bodies of dead animals.

The birds were small and pink and raw, unfeathered. I saw evidence of footprints in the snow. The murders—though I did not say this to Beatrice—looked like the work of my cat. My cat—like *my* island—does not really belong to me. He comes and goes; he sleeps in the sun. When it rains he yowls at the kitchen door, demanding shelter. He is a predator. And he lives as such—stalking mice and rabbits, catching birds; at the shore entranced by minnows; pawing at small darting frogs and snails. He fears only snakes. A beautiful killer, this cat: black with green eyes and a ragged patch of white fur on his flank where a sharp-taloned foe once gave him trouble. I found a shovel and dug a shallow hole for the birds. Beatrice made no pretence toward speech or prayer or profundity. She turned away, and I saw that her gray eyes were dark.

We walked in the light falling snow through the woods to her father's house. It is the best house on the island. Not because it is the largest, though it is, but because of the devotion Dr. Lemon and his daughter pay to its care, its practical warmth and the comfort of the rooms, to the orderly yet chaotic beauty of their garden. I used to find the doctor in the garden on fine summer evenings, asleep beneath the twisted limbs of his beloved crabapple tree in full white flower, with his book fallen to his side, among the birds bathing in the ruined fountain, and the ripening of fruits upon the vine. In a moment, he would wake. His eyes at first showed dazed wonder at the breadth of his kingdom, then bewilderment, then recognition; and finally, sadness. For he went from discovering the world to understanding that it would soon be lost to him. And by way of a game we played of allusions, he would offer me the snippet of a specimen dream. He said: *Behold I dreamed a dream, and, lo, a cake of barley bread tumbled.* I took his arm and we walked into his house. In the elegant dining room, Beatrice set the wineglasses upon the white damask cloth. There were flowers in the summer, and—no matter the season—candles burning, for the doctor enjoyed formality. And as we ate at his table, he talked of apes; or time; or that great cataclysm of desire that had led man to invent the concept of *if*. For both logic and morality; reason and punishment and reward alike proceeded from the very idea of a future. It was only later in the evening that Dr. Lemon asked me if I could identify the source of his quotation. If I could, he showed satisfaction. If I could not he was just as pleased to teach me. *It was Gideon,* he said, and sighed, full of hidden portent, *who saw his enemies vanquished in a dream. And then he vanquished them as such. For what one dreams is always possible.*

Beatrice loves her house. It is a museum of her father's things: in abstract, his lessons; in concrete, his chessboard, his collection of antiquities, his terra-cotta gods and marble goddesses. How many nights did I sit with him, while I confessed, turning over in my hands, a miniature Sphinx? or studying the face of a little ivory Buddha? as the doctor's own face showed no sign of judgment or dispassion. From under a glass dome an antique clock tolled the hour. What could time mean to us? The doctor listened while I told my story. Beatrice brought cake. And her father's medicine. She stood in the doorway. And then she disappeared. She was small and strange. I watched her. I used to see her on the beach collecting shells. When she was a child; she held out her hands to me, laughing. She cares for the doctor in his illness. I too have come to rely on her. She comes to me through the woods with the dogs. I go to her in the evening; I sit at her father's bedside. When he has taken his medicine and fallen to sleep, I drink a glass of port in his library with Beatrice. The doctor's daughter has gray eyes, and I cannot but help myself from touching her arm or her cheek or her mouth or her hair. She does not turn away. The doctor is dying. I feel, in his library, in the pages of his books, his presence.

21.

Eloise had the idea that the course of her life was being penned by some unseen hand.

22.

I buried the two birds by the garden wall.

23.

Eloise walked in her high heels the length of the long hallway upon the plush crushed plum carpet patterned with roses, until she came to the room. She was thinking of licorice. *Everything that one so longs for tastes of licorice.* The door opened. And what did she do?

24.

Snow covers the path through the woods. I came home and lighted the fire. I borrowed a volume of Hawthorne from the doctor's library, but the twice-told tales only darkened my mood. I took down from my shelf a book by Henry James. Pru had no patience for novels. She much preferred to watch television. Or we would go to the movies. She had a terrible habit—she might suddenly burst into laughter during the silence of a dramatic moment. The audience hated her. They didn't seem to understand, did they? how funny she found tragedy. How much she loved the movies.

25.

Zigouiller told Eloise that he was heading back to Paris soon for a role in a World War II epic. He asked her: did she remember his old apartment? and how they had eaten chocolate oranges and smoked Turkish cigarettes? Eloise was naked on the bed. The alarm clock rang. He knocked it to the floor with his open palm. And said damn, he had to get to the theater.

26.

Pru's abstractions—her paintings—are done in her colors: in pink and candy-blue, in orange and lemon. She called them self-portraits. I don't suppose that it matters what you call a thing. A name doesn't change the essential nature of a thing. The later paintings have a creeping darkness downward descending to the edges.

27.

Eloise fastened her black brassiere.

Zigouiller said, "When you were young, you were so beautiful. But I prefer your face as it is now."

28.

Pru—I must go on about this for a moment more—strayed from abstraction in the end. She painted one realist canvas. It was her last. It is a scene, a depiction in green and gray and black, with a sudden almost terrifying whiteness—of the visitation of Leda by the Swan.

It is hanging here in my study against the flowered wallpaper.

I am looking at it now.

CHAPTER 11

Susu imagines that she is the heroine of a novel

IT WAS THE BIRDS that last morning strange green fluttering against the open doors to the balcony calling crying over the chipped and crumbling stone balustrade where soon we would have bread and butter and black plums and oranges where down below in the street on bicycles girls rode along wheels clattering. We drank coffee boiled in a silver pot and poured out steaming with a fine sugary layer of spice and grounds rising to the top and then cream and honey and cakes that we ate with our fingers. The manuscript on the low table—he held his cup. He reached for a spoon. On the balcony the rinds the peels and crumbs and seeds at our feet. He looked at me. He set the spoon on the saucer. He touched my cheek, my hair, the tangled ribbon. He unknotted the knot. It was not a ribbon, was it? It was a rope. It was a string. A looping loop of string. He took it. He picked up the manuscript. The pages were stained with coffee and jam, with butter from his fingers. He took the pages. He took the ribbon. He bound it round the pages. He tied it in a knot. And he said, "The story that I am about to tell you is—"

CHAPTER 12

Eloise mistakes cruelty for a species of kindness

AN HOUR INTO THE BOOK CLUB'S DISCUSSION OF *Here Comes Everyone* by Benjamin Salt, the languorous and beautiful Rachel Rabinovitch, then sprawled across the sofa balancing a wineglass on her stomach, announced that if she heard anyone ("that means you, Greta—") utter the word *postmodern* again she was abso-loot-ly going to puke. At which, Boo Boo Tannenbaum burst out laughing and nearly overturned her plate of fromage, olives, black grapes, figs, and savory canapés; the plate was caught before it crashed down upon Eloise Sarasine's Persian rug by the recently divorced Min Murray, just as the newlywed Greta Conroy refilled her glass with the temperamental ruby Shiraz and asked, "Is there anything better than a good story?"

Greta turned toward the evening's hostess.

"El, you chose the book. You liked the book, didn't you?"

Eloise sat in the lamplight.

The rich chinoiserie of the room threw into relief her dark mood.

She was dressed in black.

She seemed so distant this evening.

So faraway.

She seemed like a bird.

Doesn't she, didn't she, look like a bird?

A raven, no, no, a blackbird—

In a tree, speculating upon the difference between vengeance and wrath.

Her hands were small and delicate.

How could she cling to the branch?

She said that it didn't matter to her who liked the book or who didn't. One finds what one finds in a book. Wasn't that the very point of reading a book?

"Not all books are for all people," said Eloise.

"That's the mystery of it," said Min.

"Oh," said Boo Boo. "I love a good mystery."

Rachel said, "Eloise, tell them about that famous writer—"

"What writer?" said Greta.

"Don't you know?" said Rachel sitting up, smoothing a hand over her dark hair. "El, tell her about that writer who was in love with you, who wrote that book—"

"Really?" said Greta. "That's so romantic."

"He's dead now," said Min. "He was murdered."

Rachel made a gesture; the turn of a knife.

Boo Boo said, "You're awful."

"It's all *so* awful," said Greta.

"It was a long time ago," said Eloise.

"That writer," said Greta. "That dead writer. Did you love him?"

Eloise set her glass upon the table.

She was of two minds, like a tree in which there are two blackbirds.

Her emerald bracelet caught the candlelight.

She said, "I was great with him at that time."

Because she was a liar.

And because she was something of a thief herself.

2.

Does the act of naming an object or idea immediately diminish it; relegate it to the land of named things? Pru's illness—existed before it was named—it grew, unspoken within her. It began as a part of her, and then it took over and consumed her, bite by bite. In that hungry and desirous manner that she might have eaten a plum.

Do you suspect some small speck of demise growing within you?

If it has already begun, how will you stop it?

There is nothing quite like the factual certainty of a plate smashing against a wall. Or a lilac bush bursting into bloom. As the illness ate. I read to her. She tired of words, until she could tolerate only Pound's *Cathay* poems and Eliot's Prufrock. She drank cream soda through a straw. And she would repeat aloud in a sweet morphine dope, the lines that I had just read.

If you are coming down through the narrows of the river Kiang,
Please let me know beforehand,
And I will come out to meet you
      As far as Cho-fu-Sa.

We lived in Little America, Minnesota.

Pound was from Idaho.

And Eliot from Missouri.

Because there was no future, we talked about the past.

We talked about *either* and *or.*

I said that art is called art because it is not nature.

"T. S. Eliot hated girls," she said.

She loved him anyway.

Pru said, "*The silent man in mocha brown*

Sprawls at the window-sill and gapes;

The waiter brings in oranges

Bananas figs and hothouse grapes;"

His rhymes helped her as much as morphine.

Proo from St. Looey.

The hot summers were dry and hopeless.

The winters were unrelieved.

Pru.

With her tangled hair.

With the rise of her hip and the fall of her heel.

What did Eve say to the asp?

This bites!

She spent her days in bed.

She worsened.

And then she spent her days in a hospital bed.

Is one bird more rare or remarkable than another?

Is one person so much more remarkable than another?

And does this quality, this spectacularity that can be found in such small details as a scarf knotted around a white throat or a key fallen from a hand in a darkened hallway—have more to do with the moment or the memory of the moment?

Memory has made me a spectator of my own past.

I watch each scene play out again and again.

I can say that Pru liked cinnamon candies. A soft sort of jelly heart that burned the tongue. And she ate them one after the next at the movies.

That she lived for a while.
And then she did not.

3.

"Oh El, don't torture us. Tell the story already," said Rachel.

4.

Pru died.

5.

Boo Boo nibbled a deviled egg, waiting.

6.

On the burning August day that Prudence Schell died, as I left the hospital, I noticed the billboards were advertising some new television show that she would have liked, but that she would never get a chance to watch.

7.

"I used to imagine that I was the heroine of a novel," Eloise said.

8.

I went on living in the house on Valhalla Street. And then it was autumn, again. Fall fell. And it was beautiful. Each leaf and tree. Each bird and branch. The days were bright. I taught classes. I graded papers. My colleagues offered their prayers, but I wanted none. Faculty wives brought food to my doorstep. My students were dull. The Blue Jays won the World Series. The frost came early. I cut down the roses. And I cleared away the rot of flowers in the garden. Winter followed. With storms and winds and ice. I shoveled snow from the walkway. Neighbors strung up Christmas lights. Children

played in the snow. Girls made snow angels. I had become a widower. My typewriter sat on the kitchen table.

9.
Eloise was dressed in black.

She said that a long time ago—

10.
Show, don't tell, I taught my students.

11.
Eloise had mistaken cruelty for a species of kindness.

12.
Pru had wanted to take her inheritance and see the world. And then
when there was nothing left to see—she would find an island. She
died when she was twenty-eight, before she ever got her long-
awaited soda pop loot. Two years after her death—on what would
have been her thirtieth birthday—the loot came to me. I could no
longer bear the sight of my typewriter with its blacked-out letter-
less keys. I gave up writing. I quit my job. I abandoned Lindbergh
College. And I sought out an island. I found myself this house
among the mourning doves who coo *Perdoo, Perdoo.* For the death
of my wife left me a very rich man.

13.
Eloise told her friends a story. She told them about a room over a
movie theater. About a haunted house. About white flowers in the
darkness. About streets that twisted like an endless argument. About
marzipan, about almonds and cherries and chocolate. And how she
had eaten salted black licorice. And lived for a time by the ocean.

For a moment she faltered. As though on a branch in winter. She didn't know how the story should end. Then she felt her heart flutter upward—and she knew just what to say.

14.

Beatrice is in the kitchen. She is watching *Tomorrow's Edge* on the television as she turns her wooden spoon round and round in the mixing bowl.

15.

Like a hand untying a knotted loop of string. Eloise did not disappoint. She gave her audience what they wanted. Just when they most wanted it. When the women of the book club left Eloise that winter night—each one was happy. And a bit sad as well. For she had heard a love story. With hero and heroine. Separated by fate. Thwarted by chance. Undone by their own undoings. And if it wasn't true? At least it was beautiful. Some say beauty is a form of truth; don't they?

16.

If only I were in love with Beatrice Lemon. Her narrow shoulders; her small breasts; her childishness; her slim legs; her feet in woolen socks on the tile floor. I do not think that I am in love with her. Instead, I feel terror and pity—for the both of us, for the inevitability of us. As though her father wills us as such. Our lack of choice in the matter makes love an impossibility.

If only. If only the past were not the thing that it is.

One day I will forget everything.

Like a drunkard waiting for a shoe to drop.

Like a patient etherized upon a table.

Like a poet on payday.

Like a child at sundown.

I saw Mother give Father his medicine.

I saw Father turn his spoon round in his cup.

I tell Dr. Lemon the same story over and over.

Beatrice was barefoot when first I came to this island.

Now she is eighteen.

She's a good girl, the doctor would say wearily, as Beatrice brought for him a book down from the shelf; he sighed the way that a man sighs over a woman whose life he has lovingly, without intention or malice, ruined. Oh, Beatrice: at dinner with the doctor the three of us used to sit. If I chanced a look, I might catch her lost in the responsibilities that begin in dreams—her face propped on her hands as she stared out the window into the darkness at the dark water.

And still it never occurred to me to fall in love with her.

It never occurred to me that this is what the doctor wanted from me.

He was elegant, in his velvet robe and striped pajamas. He clung to civilization. After dinner the doctor offered me a glass of his cordial—Goldwasser, perhaps. He held the bottle like a small treasure. He did not care for games of chance. He didn't deal cards. He preferred chess. For it relied upon reason rather than chance. I argued that even reason relies upon chance. We sat up late arguing the finer points of impossibility. He was an expert host—offering coffee, tea, sweets and bitters—telling stories.

Later, I was the one who confessed while he sat in silence.

He asked me about my mother, about my father. And about my wife.

He asked about writing, and what it was like to be an artist. He held artists in tremendous regard. *To the life of the mind,* he said, raising his glass of caraway pale aquavit.

We moved our pieces across the board. And thought of the future as a game.

The doctor was already an old man when he came to this island—for solitude—with his books and his collection of rare wines. He married a local girl. Beatrice was the child that he did not expect. His wife died after the difficult labor. And the doctor raised his daughter. He taught her left from right. He taught her right from wrong. On the island all knew her; everyone called Beatrice: the doctor's daughter.

For twelve years, we have shared nothing more, nor less, than a devotion to her father.

He is extraordinary.

His gray eyes see luxury beyond limitation.

So many nights. I sat. And do so still.

I will sit at his bedside and tell him my story.

I can't untangle my years on the island.

I wander the years like Beatrice in the blackberry brambles.

The old doctor fought his illness. He tried to trick his memory into forgetting that it was disappearing. He told us stories. He told about how when he was sixteen he took a train to Chicago. In a jazz club he heard a tragic chanteuse sing her sad songs. When he left the club, outside on the street, he asked a beat cop where he could find a hotel. The cop looked the boy up and down, and he said in brass-button brogue: *Would that be a hotel with hoo-ers or without hoo-ers?*

Whores or no whores.

Beatrice laughed.

The next time that her father told the story, she laughed again. And the next time and the time after that.

He was happy to remember it, but he soon forgot that he had already remembered it. And that he had told it to us. Each time it was a new delight to him.

Beatrice and I learned to forget the story. And to take it as new.

This is how the game is played.

This is how the years pass on an island.

Would you trade a tactical loss for a later advantage?

Beatrice's small feet are scratched and scarred. Bruised berry-blue.

Sometimes in the evening we play chess.

In the moonlight at the glint of her skin—

I feel terrible guilt.

When I do not lament the past too much, I feel the creep of conscience.

When I ponder the future, I do not see myself.

When I imagine tomorrow, I see Beatrice.

When I sleep I dream that I am in a hallway of locked doors.

One day—

A door will open.

And what will I do?

Pru with her hand on her hip.

Beatrice breaking an egg.

Ro on a roll.

Father pacing the floor.

Mother measuring out his medicine.

El and I looking on.

In dope there is hope.

We always said.

In the end the dope ran out. And hope was never quantifiable.

Eloise under the apple tree.

Pru eating a peach.

Pru in the parking lot.

Pru on paper.

Beatrice, bruised.

Dr. Lemon sighing, *Queen takes castle.*

The doctor raising his glass of Goldwasser.

Ro in the snow.

Ro on the ropes.

Ro hitting the bottle.

Ro hitting the road.

Ro hitting the floor.

Ro in the fire.

Ro deep with Dante.

Beatrice is baking a cake.

In a certain light, she is something better than pretty.

What was it that I came here to forget?

Beatrice—

Jars me from such thoughts—

Beatrice stands in the doorway.

"I have the strangest feeling," she says.

"Benjamin Salt is on his way," she says.

"How can I stop him?" she says.

She holds out a letter to me.

And I take her hand.

It was evening.

Beatrice took her cake from the oven.

Beatrice and I had dinner.

There were apples from my own trees and a bottle of Sauternes from her father's cellar.

We ate dark bread.

We spoke of disasters.

We seemed, though I do not know how to explain this: frantically alive.

Like prisoners at a stay of execution—we would not escape. We would never be free, but oh, we longed for one more day, one more hour—without Salt.

We fell upon the food.

Then the wine.

Drunk, we fell upon each other.

And after—in the silence sweetened by a wine that tastes of honey and almonds yet comes only from the rot of blighted grapes—we slept. In my bed, Beatrice lay white, naked, frail—like any other small animal.

When I woke in the night she was gone.

I found her in the kitchen.

She was sitting at the table.

Outside it was snowing.

"Killer," said Beatrice.

Killer, Beatrice calls the cat.

He was lapping milk from a dish.

The cat drank.

He was warm and content.

He brushed against her leg.

He rubbed against her legs.

He leapt upon the table.

He yawned.

And curled there on the cloth.

Beatrice held a knife.

Beatrice looked at me.

"Do we dare?" she asked.

She took the knife.

And she cut two pieces of her beautiful Santa Fe sugar cake.

And she set them each by each upon a plate.

We ate with our fingers.

Perhaps I do, after all, love Beatrice.

One day, when I see an open door, I will run to it.

17.

In the hotel room—

Zigouiller wanted to know about their daughter.

"Where should I begin?" Eloise asked him.

18.

While Beatrice sleeps, I go to my study and find the letter.

There are rules to every game. Even to this memory game.

I tear at the envelope—

To read—

A Frankenstein's monster of a sentence.

What do you know about Roman Stone that no one else knows?

The black cat, his green eyes in the lamplight—

He is sitting at the window.

He is watching me.

Ro had always been a sucker for the ancient world. He fell, he had fallen in love with antiquity. And why not? Athena sprang fully formed from the head of Zeus. In Illyria there were no seasons. And Babylon itself was an infinite game of chance. Work, for Ro, meant sitting in a café drinking ouzo or watching a beautiful girl run naked into the Aegean.

The girl was Susu Schell.

I mean Zigouiller.

Susu Zigouiller.

He went away with her.

Ro's books remain—lined as they are upon my shelves.

Black and white and read all over.

Ro kept at me over the years about my book.

So I never wrote it. So what?

What was it to him?

I don't know if he felt guilt or curiosity.

I don't know if the impact of a meteor crashing to the earth is more or less than the striking of an inked metal key upon a page. I write longhand. And there is barely a sound to signify my fury.

Babylon Must Fall was as impactful on me as an anvil landing upon a bone china teacup.

Ro with eggy fingers tapped out the book on my typewriter.

A book!

Whatta riot!

You should try it.

Ro thought it was hilarious.

It wasn't until years later, when I was back and dug into the Midwest, when my literalism was in full dark flower, that I realized that the joke was on me.

The third rule of storytelling had a name: the fallacy of imitative form. I got it from Ro. I admit this, to some chagrin. But as I am still under the force and exaction of rule one, I must be true. In my defense: Ro learned the theory by happenstance. He said a girl wrote it in lipstick on a bathroom mirror. He thought it was a dirty joke. I am not entirely certain that it isn't. I taught my students about the fallacy of imitative form. They did not understand. I said, "Do not write about a *thing,* in the manner of that *thing.*" They stared at me blankly. I said, "Do not write about ugliness in an ugly way; or about confusion in a confusing tangle. One should be ugly about beauty. And beautiful about vulgarity. One should be disorderly about order. And direct about confusion." They were confused. I was not a good teacher. It was a long time ago. I sit now in lamplighted darkness. As snow falls I have a strange desire; I long to read tragedies.

My father's workshop was in the cellar of our house. When we were children we were not to go down there.

Roman's father read *Babylon Must Fall*. He hated it; and then he read it again. He hated it more; and he read it again. He could not stop reading his son's book. He was looking for clues to his own murder. Really, he was the perfect reader; he was, you see, trapped in the story. He suspected that his wife and son were plotting against him. That they were in love. That his son was a thief. That his wife was a liar. Or maybe it was the other way around. He grew paranoid; a mad king. He began to see words, words, words, all over everything. So the old man divorced the girl—took her to court—and the tabloids ran amok: *Fall of the House of Stone!* Milton Stone was a doddering letch; his wife a gold-digger; his son a lothario. There were photographs in the newspapers, but the courtroom sketch artist rendered the characters in cartoonish beauty. When Mary Clare, waifish in a schoolgirl blue dress, her hair pulled back with a black headband, took the stand, she bore an uncanny resemblance to Alice just as she goes through the looking glass.

Mary Clare said that she did not have an affair with her stepson.

She said that her stepson had never seduced her.

He had never pushed her to the floor, nor torn her dress, nor tied her to a chair with her stockings, nor put his hand over her mouth because her husband was in the next room.

Nor had it happened the other way around.

She never seduced him.

Let alone plotted her husband's murder.

It did not happen.

It had never happened.

Several items of lingerie were entered into evidence.

Ro was called back from California to testify, and he confirmed her story.

He placed his hand on a Bible and swore under oath.

He had simply written a novel.

It was fiction for god's sake.

It was only a book.

It's only a book.

Only a book, Salt!

Not a falcon or a storm or a great song.

Not an eagle or a trumpet.

Not a buttered scone or crumpet.

Not a rock, not a boulder—so how much impact can it have upon a life?

Do not confuse depth with gravity.

Nor heft with heart.

In the grand story of things we all have our utility.

The ant, slug, the cowbird; both balm and bee; the failure and the success. An anvil is weight or counterweight, but you can't drink tea from it; can you?

Who would be Schell when he could be Stone?

Anyone who would rather have nothing than settle for less.

19.

Eloise brought Zigouiller a photograph.

She gave it to him.

He looked.

And his face turned pale.

20.

I took up a widower's life on an island. I had books to content me in winter. In the brief warm season I worked the day through in my garden. If I wanted for the drama of the world, I had newspapers; and I succumbed, I confess, at times to tabloids. I read when Ro got married. He had been writing travel articles for *Esquire*. While examining Southern Gothic—by judging a beauty pageant—he met a young belle called Dibby, a runner-up for Miss Teen Georgia. I know no more of it than any other inky-fingered idolator. I can only say that instead of leaving the girl broken-down or broken-hearted at the door of a rehab clinic; reader, he married her. The girl was an accomplished flaming-baton twirler. Regal Ro and his not-quite beauty-queen baby-doll bride. Thus, his bachelor days behind him, he set about settling down.

Legend says this island is haunted by the ghosts of its first feverish missionaries, who prayed and planted and went mad by the moonlight. What ghost or god or chimera of the grave was it that impelled me to give Roman a wedding gift so light in heft and heavy in symbol?

I boxed up my old Baby Hermes and sent it to him.

I made the acquaintance of Dr. Lemon. We had a standing appointment for dinner and chess, each night. Gray-eyed little Beatrice brought books down from the shelves and bottles up from the cellar; owls nested in the eaves; and so the hours passed pleasantly.

CHAPTER 13

Susu drinks all the wine in the winedark sea

WAIT, WAIT: IT WAS THE BIRDS. In the beginning. August in the grand old Chicago hotel and I crossed the room to him sitting alone in the bar and I came to him in my brown dress and he was spinning coins flipping coins on the table. This is not the beginning. It began the day before. It was only one day before and barely that because it was evening and then it was night at the lecture when in the darkness of the auditorium a cough a rustle of pages a whisper but no more than that, a darkness in which he was the only light and he said, "The story that I am about to tell you is true, though some parts are entirely false," and there was laughter sporadic communal excited everyone waiting to see what to do next and when to laugh or when to be quiet everyone sitting in the darkness looking at him in the light and the high old windows the sky growing darker blue purple winedark summer. He put up his hand and the laughter stopped but he could not stop the darkness creeping in and surrounding us. He said, "Do you want to hear a story? My boys ask for stories at night at bedtime they want to hear of heroes, dragons, and lost kingdoms. They want stories; they need stories to carry with them into the dark world of their dreams. I do not know what tenderness or terror resides awaits waits there for them in that place. I know that as the clock ticks and the hour approaches as the shadows lengthen the boys they will prolong drag out each minute each moment into an eternity until finally both strategy and tactic worn down and suffering the humility of little gods in Superman pajamas tucked into twin beds in the light of a lamp whose distracted globe is shaped like a baseball, they, one, the elder or the younger, will ask, no, no, command: tell us a story. And I do: I tell and I tell and I tell my children a story and I give them what they will need to fight the demons that will rise up from the underworld. It is an underworld of their own creation. It is terrifying for this very reason. And they need weapons. They need poison arrows, swords, daggers, keys, sling-shots and stones to launch, to arm them against monsters. And are stories the same for us? Do stories whether a book a movie a televi-sion drama keep us distract us save us for one more moment one more minute from facing the thing that we fear? Do they distract from some ancient terrible truth? Don't worry, we will not face that ancient truth tonight. Not here. Not now. Tonight here in the dark-ness in this darkness we will turn upend overturn the hourglass. For what is a story? A story is a map to the underworld and how you fol-low that map is, of course, entirely up to you. There is a price for your travels. I won't say that there isn't a price. Remember to keep a coin for the ferryman. He must have his payment. He demands his due. It's warm in here, isn't it? You have listened to me read from a book on a summer night when you could be seducing a stranger or burying a body. So so so I will toss the coin and tell you one last story now, or rather the first story—not from the book, but a story for you because you came out tonight when you might have been commit-ting a crime or taking a wrong turn on a deserted road. A story of monsters and lost kingdoms and children who cannot find their way through the woods. You have been patient." He paused and looked at his wristwatch. "In an hour or so you will be at dinner awaiting the waiter and wondering, when it comes around to it: which part of the story was it exactly that was true? And it may even occur to you that perhaps there was no truth to the story." Laughter, here and there. "You may, as you reach for the salt, utter speak say the word:

liar," laughter, there and here, in the auditorium. "You feel deceived.
I don't blame you. I don't. Because of this deception and because it
is summer and before we move along our separate ways paths into
the night and lose the mystery that binds us together in the darkness
in this darkness before we end, I will I'd like to tell you the story of
how I became a writer." I had arrived late. I was in the back row
watching him in the spotlight. He stopped. His book was open on
the podium. The light from the windows went darker fell was falling.
He stood on the stage. It seemed like forever. But it was not. There
was silence. I waited. I waited. We all waited. He said, "Once many
years ago when I was young I fell in love with a girl. Whether the
girl was beautiful or not should have no bearing on this story. If it
does, the story is at fault from the beginning. And if beauty does not
matter, then the story is not worth telling. Perhaps it is not a story. It
has no substance. It is composed of ghosts. It has no sequence, only
consequence. It has no hero. And the only plot is in a graveyard. It
has a girl who may or may not be or have been beautiful. And a boy
who lost his way in a labyrinth. Though fate would tell us that such
a thing is not possible. A labyrinth is a maze, but a maze is not always
a labyrinth. One wanders aimlessly through a maze, turning, lost and
found, finding one's way; but the path through a labyrinth leads
always to the center. Though each turn may seem like a choice; there
is no real choice. One must move forward toward the worst of it. The
boy was lost. The girl was tragic. This is a form of beauty. This is the
labyrinth. This is the story. Here is your rope. How will you find your
find your way to the monster? to the monster who is at the heart of
every story? I fell for a girl who told me a ghost story. I was young,
did I mention that part? and I, young, foolish, fortunate and favored,
born lucky and prone to games of chance, partial to time and tide, I,
a bit of a liar and something of a thief, I did not want to be a writer;
I became this thing because of her. Because one day or maybe it was

night, along an avenue lined with willows she said to me, she told me, she said, *I have done something terrible.*" He paused, caught in the shadows of his memory or only for dramatic effect; I couldn't tell. "We walked past the willows larch and apple trees." His face was white and damp in the lone light of the stage. "And she told me her story. The story was dark and terrible. *Do you believe me?* she said. We walked. She wore a perfume of roses. Or else the night was dark with flowers that I could not see. We walked. She was quiet. And we walked we passed houses dogs cats gardens we walked on that street for a long time. It seemed like the world would stop. But it did not. It seemed like time might give way. But it didn't. It couldn't. Did I believe her story? How does one answer such a question? How does one—that is: how did I—make a differentiation, let alone a choice between belief and disbelief? There is always a moment of choice; isn't there? a path, a pause between Scylla and Charybdis, between dog and wolf, icing and cake, between sugar and salt, a slip of the tongue between *s* and *z*? What happens when Oedipus meets the king at the crossroads? What happens in that that fated moment when one believes that there is yet the possibility of choice before choice itself is negated by its own existence? She asked me if I believed her. In the darkness. I pulled an apple from the branch, and I handed it to her. It was hard and green. *No,* I said. I said, *No.* She took the apple from me, and she threw it out into the night. And she laughed. She took my hand. She took my hand and she closed it into a fist. She she she raised it to her mouth, and kissed the inside of my wrist. *Do you promise?* She said. *Do you promise never to believe me?* I promised her that. I promised her that I would never tell her story. And I have kept my promise." He wiped his pale damp white brow glowing either feverish or holy in the light. "You, you've been very good to me tonight. I thank you for it. Did you know, have you seen the girls in white aprons carrying trays? did you see them in the hallway? There will be wine and chocolate later. There will be, I saw cake and coffee and cream and sugar. We will stay the ghosts for a time against the darkness. I have been many places and seen so many things good beautiful ugly the desolate the desolation and the unspeakable and yet it is the sight of a cake on a plate that brings me almost to God. I fall to my knees weeping for the beauty of butter-cream. This is civilization. The sound of a spoon turning in a teacup. A key turning a lock. A closed box. We will keep the ghosts away for one more hour one more day or maybe it will be night. I saw my books that I will be signing I am to tell you that they are ah very suitable to read on the beach or in airports my books my newest book very thick in hardcover isn't it? very good to jam under an uneven table leg or to prop open a window or cover your head if you are caught in a rainstorm. You've been kind here in the dark and soon we will have our cake and light the candles and we will talk as though none of this ever happened a vague embarrassment a con-fession a lie a ploy to sell books soon we will have had our wine and coffee and you will say and whisper perhaps he looks odd old ill so much older what's wrong with him? Is it an act? Is it for show? And ladies and germs how was the show? In an hour I will be back in my hotel room and you will be waiting for the waiter to bring your din-ner and talking of today and tomorrow and what will happen next. And perhaps it will come around to you that the story that you heard that the story that I told at the podium was mostly true though parts of it were entirely false and perhaps as you salt the soup it will occur to you that the story was not much of a story and as the waiter sets your plate on the table and you take fork in one hand and knife in the other and you may wonder suddenly and cry out and ask aloud wait wait! how does the story end? For that for this moment in the future, I'll tell you now. This is how the story ends." He broke each word apart slowly, he was tired. He was laboring. "It is not a story. It does not end." He waited. He waited. "If you should in your life be so lucky so so so fortunate as to have a girl tell you a tragic tale and then ask you if you believe her—let me, allow me, please let me give you a word of advice. Lie. A story is only a dream, and I went into my dreams armed with rock, paper, and scissors. I kept a coin for the ferryman. I write and I wrote and I have written book after book. And beneath every story is her story. I became a writer to tell her story. And her story is the one tale I cannot tell. I cannot tell her story. One day I will break my promise. The beginning will begin. The story will end. And it will begin again. Eternity is our punishment. Eternity is our punishment for inventing eternity. It's not so bad, not really. Even a stopped clock is right twice a day. And no story is too long for someone who wants to read it. Or too short for someone who does not. So so so I have eaten salt and sugar. I have been an exile and a wanderer and I have been I am as happy as any wicked king in history. Happy enough to," he laughed here, "grow fat. And wise and ancient as a coiled rope. I know terrible things. I know what she did. And yet, here I am. I continue to exist. It's not so bad, is it? It's not poverty, is it? The glass is yet half full. All signs point to yes. Did I say, did I mention? there is to be cake. And wine. We will talk quietly low pleasantly I'll be signing books they make nice gifts, books do, wrapped up and tied with a knotted knot hiding the terrible things printed on the pages. Oh, I haven't had such a bad life, but I tell you I have done some rotten things," here there was laughter because we all knew of his life, of the actresses, the girls, of Hollywood, of his happiness now, his wife and children. We all knew. We knew all. We longed for more. We laughed. He stopped us. He held up his left hand. "I tell stories," he said. "I lie. I do. I steal. I have stolen, but this is the true part of the story. Believe me—" there was more laughter, now nervous, giddy, one hysterical wail. "Wait, wait," he held up his right hand, "the movies won't save you. The stars won't save you. He who is destined to hang won't drown." And he closed shut the book on the podium before him. The story was finished. It was over. The audience did not realize that it was over. No one moved. There was silence no cough no laugh no scuffled heel or muffled whisper and suddenly all at once applause. The spotlight went dark and the audience went on applauding in darkness. And then the house lights came up and we were dizzy blinded looking for him but he was gone.

CHAPTER 14

Eloise admits to objectification

O N CHRISTMAS EVE, after a dinner (at that Vietnamese place, just down the street, where it's usually impossible to get a table; let alone the nice one in the corner by the aquarium) of salted eel with ginger root (for him) and tamarind pearls (for her) and a shared plate of Buddhist tiger lilies, with smoky tea (*Lapsang Souchong,* she said; though he insisted upon calling it *Russian Caravan*) in japanned cups, Louis and Eloise walked home in silence in the falling snow.

2.

I used to so look forward to my evenings with Dr. Lemon. After the formalities of the meal, with our coffee, we would retire to the library. The doctor and I would sit at the chessboard. He would ask questions. And I would answer. First, I did this out of kindness, because he seemed to enjoy our play at cat and mouse as much, or more, than our game of chess. Later, I began to depend upon my own confession. And I told him everything.

3.

That night Eloise baked a cake.

"Louie, I've done something terrible," she said.

"What is it this time?" he said.

"Don't joke," she said.

"It isn't funny," she said.

Louis poured them out each a glass of a brandy.

"Drink this," he said. "You'll feel better."

The cake sat cooling on the table.

She said that it was a Swedish chocolate cake, with cardamom, elderberry, espresso, and pepper, and that one ate it with oranges.

He asked if she was sure that it was a Swedish cake.

Was she sure?

Because he had had Norwegian cake.

And that was good too.

One ate it with strawberries.

She said that she was so very tired.

"Let's have a fire," she said.

He built a fire in the fireplace.

"Oh," she said. "Turn out the lights—will you?"

They sat in the firelight.

He asked his wife, "Eloise, what have you done?"

4.

We spoke for hours.

The doctor and I.

I told him about Mother.

I talked to him about Father.

There was an apple tree.

The world was accurate.

Or perhaps it was only my memory of the world—

That was accurate.

I told him about Pru.

"These tragedies," sighed the doctor.

"They are like small thefts," he said.

"Fallen coins," he said.

I refilled our glasses.

"These small thefts," he said.

They add up.

We drank.

At a rap upon the door—

Beatrice would open the door.

And bring her father his medicine.

Beatrice would close the door.

The doctor said, "Where were we?"

And I would begin again.

5.

Eloise told her husband everything.

6.

Dr. Lemon listened. I told him—those nights, those years—my story. I told him my story past the time when he could comprehend its meaning. When his illness began to overcome him, he wanted the story to go on. I know this. He wanted me to keep telling him the story.

7.

Louis did not believe Eloise.

8.

The seed of illness took root in the old doctor. The root grew to vine and, oh, it flowered. I began to suspect; to fear; to wonder: were my words an infection? Was the story itself a disease?

9.

Mr. and Mrs. Sarasine spent a quiet Christmas Eve at home.

Among their ovoid Etruscan vases and miniature Eiffel towers.

And a life of mementos and memories.

In their beautiful home.

In their warm well-appointed living room before the fire.

He sat upright in his leather chair.

And she reclined upon the sofa.

She drank.

She finished her brandy.

And he rose and he poured her another.

And she drank.

She held her glass in both hands.

"You don't believe me," she said.

Though the clocks on the mantel refused to tick or tock or chime—

One could not doubt that such a thing as the very concept of time continued to exist.

10.

I told the doctor about my typewriter.

11.

It was Eloise who had the strength to force the moment to its crisis.

12.

My typewriter was a 1960 apple-green Baby Hermes manual. It was once called: *the world's finest portable typewriter.* It was good—fine, even—for the writing of stories.

It was an object and therefore, objective, about the story itself.

I don't suppose that it cared whether Father killed Mother.

Or if it was the other way around.

13.

Louis Sarasine asked his wife if she really wanted to get into this tonight?

He said it was too late, past two.

"Time can't mean anything to us," she said.

He poured another drink.

"You tell stories," he said.

The chocolate cake—the brandy—

The warmth—the fire—

She laughed.

"I tell *stories?*" she said.

He said, "You told me—"

"What did I tell you?" she said.

"You told me how you—"

"Don't," she said.

He said, "The point is—"

She interrupted him, "So now there's a point?"

He continued, "You tell, you've told the story again and again. And every time that you tell me what happened that night—"

"Don't," she said. "Please."

"About your mother," he said.

"Stop it," she said.

"And your father," he said.

"Louie—"

"You change it," he said.

"What?" she said.

He got up.

He took an iron from the stand.

He stood with his back to her.

He shifted the logs in the fire with the iron.

He turned.

It was hard for her to make out his face in darkness.

He said, "The story. You never tell it the same way twice. You remember something new. Or you deny something old. It's always a different version. You dig up bricks and bones, and I begin to build a wall of them—then—without warning—you change the story; and the whole thing, the wall comes crashing down."

"And we have to start again?" she said.

"Yes," he said.

"Even now," she said. "We're starting again."

"Yes," he said.

"From the beginning?" she said.

"If you want," he said.

"If I want—?" she said.

"Do you think that I *want* any of this?" she said.

He said that he didn't know what she wanted.

Eloise said, "I'm telling you."

She said, "I did something terrible and now someone is dead."

"Do you want me to call the police?" he said.

She sighed, and fell back against the sofa.

He prodded the wood, waiting for the flames.

"You've taken your bricks and you've built a maze, a labyrinth," he said. "And we are winding through it."

She rested her head back against the velvet pillows of the sofa.

She covered her eyes with her palms.

"A maze," she said.

"It's only a metaphor," he said.

"No," she said. "It's not. It's *metaphoric*."

With one hand covering her eyes—

She reached over to the table for her glass.

She drank.

Until her glass was empty.

"Eloise," he said.

"Isn't there a monster in the labyrinth?" she asked.

"We'll get to him too," said her husband.

"Yes," said Eloise setting, with some difficulty, her glass upon the table. "He's there. He's waiting, isn't he? It's there waiting for us."

"Our monster," said Eloise.

Eloise closed her eyes.

Louis covered Eloise with a blanket.

Then he poured himself a drink.

And he sat in the darkness before the fire.

14.

Ice scars the windowpanes.

The snowbent boughs of the trees are dark with birds.

Each night I told the doctor my story.

Year after year, as his illness overtook him.

I thought of the story as medicine and disease.

A purge; a punishment; a palliative.

The doctor is confined to his bed. In the evenings I make my way through the woods and I go to his house to see him. I sit at his side. When he wakes.

He whispers: *Tell me.*

He says, *Tell me.*

I do. I do. I tell. I will. I must. I cannot stop telling. As long as the story continues; he lives. He will live. For he wants to know what will happen next.

I have only my story in the whole of the world.

And I cannot not stop telling it.

I remember this: one day—or maybe it was night—
Pru bit into a peach.
Then said that she was dying.
And I laughed.

15.

Louis Sarasine watched Eloise in the firelight.

"In the spring we'll go away for a while," he said.

"Would you like that?" he said.

"Yes," she said.

"I want you to do something for me first," he said.

"What?" she said.

"Write it down," he said.

"The story," he said.

She said, "Everything?"

"Why?" she said.

"Tell what happened," he said.

She said, "Like on television?"

She said, "A confession? Like on a police show?"

"So that you'll remember it," he said.

"I don't want to remember it," she said.

"Eloise," he said. "Tell the story."

"Yes," she said. "You said that. I remember that part."

16.

After forty years in the desert Moses must have hated his god.

17.

After forty laps in the heated Olympic pool, Eloise met Rachel for lunch at that adorable little place where absolutely everything is organic. Rachel pronounced that one could even eat the hemp tablecloths, and when Eloise did not laugh, Rachel said, "Why so glum, chum?"

Eloise said, "That boy; that one whom Louie defended. They found—"

"I know, I know; isn't it awful?" said Rachel. "I saw it on the news this morning."

Said Eloise, "Another girl in the woods."

She rested her face in her hands.

"Louie said that it was bound to happen," she said.

Said Rachel, "I guess he's the expert. God," she said looking at the menu. "I want everything."

The waiter came by.

Rachel asked him about the organic wine.

He recommended a rustic blackberry red.

With a hint of licorice.

Rachel said didn't that sound wonderful?

Eloise did not answer.

The waiter disappeared.

"You're too quiet," said Rachel.

Said Eloise, "I just, I keep thinking about that poor girl."

Rachel said, "Really, El. What can anyone do?"

She reached across the table and took Eloise's hands in her own.

"Is this new?" Rachel asked, admiring Eloise's bracelet.

Eloise turned the bracelet round her slim wrist.

"Did I tell you? He showed me the pictures," said Eloise.

"Those girls," said Eloise.

"Don't think about it," said Rachel.

"I'm worried about Susu," said Eloise.

"She's a good girl," said Rachel.

"People always say that," said Eloise.

"Because it's true," said Rachel.

"—It isn't. I mean, she isn't. She isn't a good girl," said Eloise.

Rachel laughed.

"Maybe not," she said. "But she's *something,* isn't she?"

"Have you heard from her?" said Rachel.

The waiter brought the wine and two glasses.

He poured out the glasses.

El drank.

Rachel drank.

Rachel said, "Look, it's started to snow."

"Do you know what?" said Eloise. "Sometimes I speak entirely in lines stolen from books—or poems. Once I kept it up for three whole days before Louie noticed."

Rachel said that men were such idiots.

And Eloise said yes, she supposed that they were.

18.

I don't suppose that I knew, or maybe I did, that while I was confessing to her father, that while I was telling my story, again and again and over and over in words soaked with plum brandy and every wonderful once in a while, a Cuban cigar with such rich plumes of smoke, as a pawn fell, as a queen triumphed, that Beatrice was listening at the door.

19.

Louie was packing for a trip.

He was going to the annual meeting of the Mnemosyne Society. He had prepared his discussion topic for the gathering: *The Memory Game: What Are the Rules?*

His shirts were folded upon the bed.

He said that she should come with him.

Why didn't she? She could use the sun.

She said that she didn't want to go to California.

He said; he reminded her that it was just for a few days.

He'd be back after New Year's.

He asked her what she wanted him to bring back for her.

"What do you want?" he asked.

She fell back upon the bed.

"Now look what you've done," he said.

"What's that?" she said.

"What have I done?" she said.

"Oh," she said.

She watched as he began to refold—

The shirts—

So neatly, so perfectly—

So that everything fit exactly in his suitcase.

She said that oh Louie she couldn't think of a thing that she wanted.

She said that she didn't want anything.

20.

This is how memory works: pearls that by virtue of string and proximity become a necklace.

21.

Eloise had fought against the things that one fights against in youth, against her own—oh—commodification, against objectification. And then at some point, she had grown tired of fighting it. She was tired of fighting the vague and euphemistic *it*. She had struggled and then stopped struggling. Once it had bothered her to be like a character in a novel. Now she was certain that she lived only on the page.

22.

This past summer on a day in the warmth of June the doctor fell in his garden. He lay among the lilies; there I found him, fallen. I helped him to the house. After a glass of honey liqueur, held with his trembling hands, he recovered some strength.

And we sat in sunlight in the library.

Dr. Lemon asked a favor of me.

He asked me to care for his daughter, after he was gone.

He wanted that Beatrice should be kept safe.

She knew nothing of the world, he said.

Would I do it?

I thought. I pondered.

In sunlight, a bee buzzed.

In the library.

Among the books.

I thought of Beatrice.

The girl.

Running barefoot through the blackberry brambles.

I said, yes.

We celebrated that night, the three of us.

It was Beatrice's eighteenth birthday.

Dr. Lemon said, "It was the ancients who imagined our world; we live by their clock; the mechanism turns, and we dream it is our own doing. History guides us by our vanities. Signs are taken for wonders. We fall to Fate. And Fate herself is a girl with scissors," he paused. He sighed, "—Ah well, we drink to Beatrice." He raised his glass. "In those long-ago times it was good to make an offering to the gods with flowers, salt, and wine; with the smoke of burnt offerings upon a fire."

His daughter's young dreamy face darkened.

"We are no longer ancient," he said.

We laughed, the three of us, though I don't know why or at what.
And we drank Strega and ate plum cake.

23.

Like a character in a novel, like Emma Bovary or Anna Karenina,
like poor Arlova, doomed and defeated, when she tells Rubashov,
You will always be able to do what you want with me: Eloise was
impelled by some unseen ink, across the marble tile, across the
lobby, across the rose carpet, across the page, to meet a fate who was
called in this version of the story of her life, Zigouiller.

24.

I have been reading of the whims of gods and goddesses.

He who seeks to avoid Scylla falls on Charybdis.

Apollo punished Cassandra with the gift of foresight.

She would see the future. She would foretell all.

And no one would believe her.

The wind shakes the trees.

The waves roll.

They say that Zeus came to Leda as a swan.

And with the force of the moment—

In a fluttering of wings.

An empire fell.

Leda gave birth to Helen, whose face launched a thousand ships.

Helen gave birth to Clytemnestra, who murdered the warrior
Agamemnon.

I was speaking of gods, wasn't I?

Of fortune, of death, of wives, of darkness.

The day passed into darkness.

Beatrice came to me in the evening.

At the window she put her palm flat against the glass.

"Let's build a fire," she said.

Is language a prisonhouse?

I am bounded in a nutshell.

Of infinite space.

I live among birds.

I have seen augury and omens.

I have seen Beatrice walking a road at dusk.

And naked in the bath.

With her knees drawn to her breast.

Bare and barely there.

Do you doubt me?

I have heard such cries and questionings.

25.

Eloise and Zigouiller had the entire night before them.

26.

After dinner we watched television.

A crime drama came on.

Beatrice sat beside me.

We were promised by a deep and knowing voice a story ripped from today's headlines.

A disclaimer flashed in white letters upon the black screen saying that any resemblance to real characters or real events was purely accidental.

A hardy-handsome man of indeterminate middle age and obvious fortune sat watching a baseball game on television. He was talking on the telephone. "See you in twenty minutes," he said. There was a knock on the door. He looked at his watch. He rose from his chair. He opened the door. And, he said to his visitor, "Oh, it's you. What are you doing here?"

Two quick gunshots.

In the next scene the room was crowded with police.

One cop explained to another: this was the swanky uptown digs of the famous loudmouth provocateur, Rivers Jackson. Jackson was dead.

There was no sign of a struggle.

A delivery girl had found the victim.

She discovered the body.

Rivers Jackson had ordered dinner: three cheeseburgers, onion rings, and chocolate cake, from a nearby restaurant.

Two tough but tender detectives were on the case: a buxom young woman in ill-fit trousers and her partner, a grizzled old man who chewed on a toothpick.

As he studied the crime scene, the man, his hands in clear plastic gloves, lifted the bun from atop a cheeseburger, turned to his partner, and said, "This stuff will kill ya."

The girl put her hands on her hips.

Her blazer gaped open.

Her breasts strained against her tight blouse.

The body lay pooled in blood on the floor.

The girl said, "And they say that *meat* is murder."

The theme music came up.

And the show went to commercial.

Beatrice and I sat waiting to see what would happen next.

Rivers Jackson: shot while watching a baseball game on TV.

The plot followed the grisly details of his demise.

The author's life was pieced together in flashbacks, while the detectives followed the clues to find out whodunit.

Here was Rivers Jackson telling a dirty joke; eating ice cream; seducing a girl; winning an award; stealing a line; falling down drunk; dazzling an audience; typing; falling down dead.

A gloved hand shot a gun.

Was it the grieving widow? the nanny? the envious friend? the bitter ex-stepmother? I was uncertain about the last suspect—the ambitious young writer. He was only there, I suspected, to lead the viewer down the garden path.

The names were changed.

The places were different.

The knife was replaced with a gun.

Even the final score of the baseball game was different.

Any resemblance to real or fictional events was purely unreal.

Any resemblance to a nutshell was purely spatial.

Beatrice gave a gasp.

She took my hands.

And put them between her thighs.

In the end the murderer was revealed.

The culprit was locked up like language in a prisonhouse.

The case of Rivers Jackson was settled neatly in one nail-biting hour.

While even now: Roman Stone's murderer remains at large.

27.

Eloise opened the curtains.

Outside it was snowing.

In the darkness.

Zigouiller said that he knew the girl in the photograph.

"The girl," he said.

He had seen her before.

Eloise stood by the window.

Where are the eagles and the trumpets?

She wore a black silk slip.

And her hair was undone.

CHAPTER 15

Susu draws a chalk outline around the body

IT WAS NOT A STORY. It had no plot. It had neither sequence nor consequence. It had no characters. There was one shadowy indistinct unnamed girl who might have been any girl. It was not a story, and I heard him tell it in a lecture hall on a hot summer night. No, it was not a story. It was the shape and the space around a story. It had no hero. It had no plot. I listened, and I waited in the audience in the darkness. He stood at the podium. He read from his book, and then he set down the book in midsentence, he stopped, he paused, he poured water from a pitcher into a glass and then drank neither slowly nor quickly but drank in the silence of scuffled shoes and coughs, and he looked out blinking toward the light he shielded his eyes with a hand and thanked and told his audience how good we were and because of this, of this goodness that exists in the silence of auditoriums when a man stands at the podium in the lone light with only his book and his memories, he was going to tell us a story. He was going to tell the story of how he became a writer. Of course, it wasn't a story, not really. There was a story hidden inside of it. It was not a story, but it contained a story. It was not a story. It was a box. It was a bird. It was both tree and forest. It might have been a bough or branch but it was not a story. It had no beginning. It had no end. It was an egg. It was a shell. It was a stone. It was an apple. It was an apricot. It was a house. It was a locked door. It was not a story. I heard him tell it. He talked about desire and deceit. He took the podium and he poured water into his glass and shielded his eyes from the light and told the story that was not really a story and then there was a reception with wine and chocolate and candles. He took my hand. He called me the next day. I went to him at the hotel with roses on the walls, and I drank plum brandy. He wanted me to go away with him. Did I want to go away with him? to the ancient world he said there were snakes and spiders and carnivals and pomegranates and burning kings. He was going away to the ancient world to write his story. I went away with him. We went to the carnival and had our cards and palms read. He talked and I tried to untangle the thread to lead me to the monster. It was not a story. It was a lamp, a vase, a clock, an ax, a cask, a casket. It was a sacked city. A ruined amphora. It was a lilac bush bursting into bloom. He told me the story. It was not a story. It was a spider. It was a swan. It was a snake. It was a king. It was a punishment. It was straw. It was ash. It was fire. It was murder at the hands of children. It was a body. It was not a body. It was the chalk outline around a body. It was not a story. It was every story. And he told me how it would end. Each night he told me more of the story. He started at the end. I walked in late to his lecture. He had already begun. The story was not really a story. It might have been an epic, a myth, a novel, a theory, a theft, a history, a poem, a polemic, a philosophy, rumination, speculation, a confession, a confusion, a lesson, a lamentation. It was a lie. It was the truth. It was a spoon turning in a cup. It was a shovel stuck in the dirt. It was a knife in the heart. I went to meet him at the hotel of roses, in the bar he tossed the coin on the table, and he told me how the story was to end. And the last morning on an ancient island with the birds and oranges the hot dry dusty sun and the singsong girls it was then that he told me how the story was to begin. He peeled an orange. And he asked if I believed him. We stood on the balcony, he scattered bread, and he told me that when it came around to it I would turn against him.

CHAPTER 16

Sheldon digs in the hard frozen ground

O N A HOT SUMMER AFTERNOON in Chicago—not two years ago. Ro came up beside me in the basement gallery of the Art Institute, in one of those reliably lonely rooms containing colonial furniture. Funny how it happened. We just ran into each other. He was in town giving a speech. I was there—on a rare trip away from my island—at the insistence of my niece—for a wedding. Ro and Shelly, we picked up where time had left us. As though we had just seen each other that morning in the dining hall or crossing the courtyard.

Stone & Schell—a little worse for wear—we ambled through the folk art rooms. We passed before a hand-carved coffin; a wooden doll; a miniature winterscape. We paused at a painting of Eve and her grinning serpent. Ro laughed. "Let's get out of here," he said. He wanted to get a drink. He knew a place. And so we left the museum. We found a taxi, and he directed the driver to a Clark Street bistro just about to get too trendy for its own good. On that August afternoon the place was empty. Roman and I walked in and sat down. The lone busboy setting tables for dinner came over and said they weren't serving for a while. Roman said that we just wanted some booze. Could we get some booze?

The busboy brought us gin and ice.

Roman drank. He wiped his brow.

"Sheldon Schell," he said. "The shipwrecked life must agree with you. You haven't changed. You still look like a fucking lunatic."

He told me that he was having an affair with his sons' au pair.

His sons were named Julian and Chester. He called them Jules and Chet. One was a natural athlete. The other wore very thick eyeglasses. He didn't say the au pair's name. Only that she had inspired him to write his latest book.

He always knew how to get to me.

He told me about the girl.

Roman, in an elegant two-button summer suit, drew me into his latest drama. I had no taste for gin, but I drank. The busboy refilled our glasses. I heard a radio playing in the kitchen. Roman's white shirt was rumpled. He wore a necktie, slightly loosened, of light green silk. The line of his oyster-colored jacket suited his broad bulk. His fair hair was clipped short and the recession of his hairline gave his brow a high, sort of holy glow. His affair had inspired him to write a torrid faux tell-all about a suburban scandal.

He knew what his readers wanted. They were *his,* after all. They had moved out of cities; they were denizens of the cul-de-sac, and they didn't want to feel ashamed of it. They didn't want to apologize for their minivans or playdates, for their dashed dreams or catalog shopping. Forty was the new twenty. His readers were responsible fathers and caring mothers. They carted kids to soccer practice; to Sunday school; to animated movies at the Cineplex. They were concerned about rising crime; gangs, drugs; about toxins, terrorism, junk food, and TV shows with content unsuitable for children; about internet predators, obesity, and kiddy porn. They were moral moms and high-minded dads, sure; but once, not too long ago, they had been kids themselves: young and wild and high, fucking strangers in the unisex bathrooms of downtown dance clubs. He knew. Roman knew! He was one of them. He had been one of them. He had seen it for himself. Don't you remember?

Didn't I remember?

He leaned forward. The table shook.

Roman was a frantic drunk. His cheeks burned.

He picked up and drank—that is, he tried to drink—from his empty glass.

"Fuck it," he said.

He looked around. He saw that we were no longer alone.

Waiters moved from table to table. The place was just opening for dinner.

A girl came by and lighted the candles on our table. Ro touched her arm and said something funny. A piano player took on a summertime song.

You're the tops.

You're the Colosseum.

A waiter came by.

We ordered.

Ro wanted wine.

The gin glasses were whisked away.

Roman talked about places that he had been and things he had done.

The waiter brought our food on large white plates. Roman's wife, Dibby, had him off red meat. He was supposed to be watching his cholesterol. He was on a low-sodium macrobiotic diet. He belonged to an athletic club. He worked out. He did yoga and Pilates. In his home, he lamented, his favorite things—cigars, whiskey, cream—were verboten. Roman cut into his rare oeuf au cheval. He salted his pomme frites. That night he really enjoyed himself. He ate. He drank. We sat for a long time. He said that his wife wanted to fire the au pair. Oh well, they would find another girl; wouldn't they? He would find another girl. He buttered his pain de campagne. He talked about Pru. He sighed. It was still a helluva thing, even after all these years, about Pru. He told me that he had once made a pass at her. Did I forgive him?

The platter-like plates; the knives and forks and spoons; the big round-bellied wineglasses: everything set upon the table seemed

suddenly—ridiculously—an oversized prop, a sight gag for our out-
of-date comedy routine.

Roman confessed.

He was not happy.

Or was he just telling me what I wanted to hear?

Just when I most needed to hear it?

"I have one last story in me," he said.

He drank.

"It's the story of a brother and a sister," he said.

"An old story," I said.

"Ancient," he said.

"People want the old stories. Don't they?" I said.

"Who gives a fuck what people want?" he said.

The wine bottle sat between us on the table.

The girl came by and refilled our glasses.

The place was busy now.

And the girl turned away from us.

She moved on to the next table.

He watched her go.

It saddened him, to watch her go.

He lifted his glass.

"All things are a flowing,
Sage Heracleitus says;
But a tawdry cheapness
Shall outlast our days."

He broke off.

He looked down at his plate.

He looked at me.

He set his glass on the white tablecloth.

He picked up, one in each hand, his fork and knife.

And just like that: Ro, the nihilist, was gone.

Gone also, his phantom unhappiness.

He grinned.

And he began to essay forth on the merits of corn-fed Kobe beef.

He and his wife were just back from Japan. He talked about the cartoon crazy fashions of teenagers in Tokyo.

He ordered for dessert gâteau au chocolat.

It grew late and the restaurant filled up.

Soon we left.

Outside as we stood awaiting a taxi, a couple of girls in summer dresses walked by. As they passed us, Roman threw his hands up toward the sky and said with stentorian inflection, "*What a piece of work is man!*" Then, off-balance, he stumbled; he bent over and vomited on the sidewalk. A taxi arrived, and we went back to his hotel. He wanted me to come up for one last drink. "Amontillado?" I said. He laughed. "Have I done you so many injuries, poor Fortunato?" he asked. In his room we drank. And we spoke of the ruined past and great fallen Babylon. Oh that sweet mysterious harlot! He sputtered to a halt in midsentence. He was sitting on the bed. He fell back across the bed. He passed out—in his two-button oyster suit and white shirt, now untucked; with his chocolate-stained necktie of watered silk; his wristwatch indefatigably counting his hours and collecting seconds; his two-tone cap-toe oxfords unlaced; one shoe fell from his foot to the floor—he sprawled on his back like a king in the days of a declining empire.

Somewhere his assassination was being planned.

He gave his speech the next night.

The wedding for which I had come to town was canceled. And I went home, back to my island.

One morning soon after—when I turned on the television—there was stone-sober Roman on a talk show promoting his new book, a based-on-a-true-story account of a suburban scandal. It was picked up by a popular national nonfiction book club. And later developed into a ratings-grabbing miniseries. Roman opened up about his marriage; he talked about how fatherhood had changed his priorities. At the end of the segment, the interviewer, a dowager in a leather skirt, put her hand on Roman's knee. She asked with a skull-tightened smile, "Is there anything better than a true story?"

She said that she couldn't wait to read the book.

I almost felt sorry for him.

I almost forgot—

Roman was my friend and rival and enemy and conspirator.

Roman Stone was a devoted husband and father. He was bright and occasionally brilliant: a best-selling author; an authority; an expert; a household name; a standard-bearer; attention-getter and roundtable-discussion-opinion-giver. He was respected and beloved.

He was murdered.

And he deserved it.

I will say something that is neither deep nor grave. It needs nonetheless to be said. Pru convinced me of the truth that sometimes beauty comes from hate. Pru was big on Pound and Eliot. She forgave them their sins. Because of what they had given to her. For verse and rhymes like candy. She forgave them even their hatred of her. She couldn't stop herself from forgiving them.

I must go back to that summer afternoon in the museum when I ran into Ro.

When we walked by Eve and the snake.

When we ambled artlessly through the gallery.

He was in town to give a speech.

I was there for the wedding of my niece.

Eloise's only child. A spectacular girl called Susu.

Susu was tall and long-limbed. Her eyes were green, her hair black. Just out of college. She had studied *the classics*. She had had no contact with her father, but Susu, to her mother's chagrin, had kept his name. El had married again, to Louis Sarasine, the celebrity defense attorney, whose philosophical, legal, and perhaps immoral specialty was the questioning of the nature of the crime by discrediting the memory of the victim. He called himself a memory expert. Can one be such a thing? Well, memory is a poppy-rich field; for the Sarasines lived the good life.

Eloise and Sarasine planned a black-tie white-cake wedding only to have Susu see, or perhaps imagine, a shadow on her dress. And this the girl took as grave symbolism foretelling (her word) that the marriage was ill-fated. Her fiancé was the son of a prominent family. I never met him. I heard that he was heartbroken.

The evening after Ro and I sat in the restaurant—

Eloise was having the groom's family over for a détente of sorts. There was a commotion about—gifts and guests and caterers. I didn't have a moment alone with El. This was the reason that I had left the solitude of my island: to see her. So between the ringing phone and Sarasine's concerns over whether the iced Absolut would hold out—I made my escape. I was on the street, when Susu—running barefoot—carrying her shoes—caught up with me.

"Where are we going?" she asked.

I told her that I was going to the movies.

She didn't want to go to the movies.

I remember just what she said.

"I don't want to watch other people doing things. I want to do something."

And then I recalled Ro's lecture.

I told her that my old college roommate was giving a lecture.

She was wearing a black dress, for the party. She knelt on the sidewalk and put on her high-heel sandals. She was wearing her large diamond engagement ring.

We caught a taxi.

The lecture was about to start.

The house lights had already dimmed.

We slipped in—and sat in the back row just as Ro was taking the podium.

He was as charming as ever. He was wry and incisive.

He talked of mythology and television.

After the lecture there was a reception.

Susu grabbed my hand.

"Do you really know him?" she asked.

"Who?" I asked.

"*Him,*" she whispered.

She tilted her head. And lifted just slightly one bare shoulder.

And there was Ro standing by a table heaped up with copies of his books.

He had a pen in one hand and a drink in the other.

Susu reached for a chocolate wafer.

"I love these," she said.

And she took a bite.

"Can I—may I meet him?" she asked.

It didn't occur to me—

What a stupid thing it would be—

To introduce Susu Zigouiller, green-eyed ingénue, to Roman Stone, lothario.

I did it. I took her arm. I maneuvered around the girls carrying trays of hors d'oeuvres; through the line of waiting fans clutching copies of Ro's books.

I brought Susu to Roman.

I saw him look at her.

He looked at her.

He took in her black dress, her young face, her diamond ring.

He seemed to take and take and not stop taking.

"This is—" I told him.

She gave him her hand.

Susu leaned close. He spoke into her ear.

The room was hot and the hum of the crowd was rising up into a less-than-literate roar. A woman tapped me on the shoulder and gave a reproving look. I had cut in line.

Aging academics, readers, critics, girls in slacks, their long-suffering boyfriends—

The crowd pushed.

Susu pushed her dark hair from her face—

There were other people waiting to talk to Roman Stone, author.

He had a stack of books to sign.

I should have taken Susu to the movies that evening.

We were about to leave; Ro got up from his table.

And he called out to me—

"Hold up a minute," he said. "I wanted to give this to you—"

And he gave me a book.

Susu took it from me as we walked outside into the night.

"*Here Comes Everyone,*" she said.

She shrugged her bare shoulders and handed the book back to me.

And that—unless you count television—and the grinning ghostly faces in old photographs—is the last time that I saw Roman Stone.

2.

Zigouiller said that whatever he told her now she mustn't hold it against him. Even though she had every right to. She mustn't. Did she understand?

3.

What do I know about Roman Stone that no one else knows?

4.

Zigouiller said, "Just listen."

Eloise closed her eyes.

5.

The story—it was dark and terrifying, as stories told on New Year's Eve in old houses should be—held us captivated around the fire. We had only just arrived that morning. And winter had followed. Snow fell upon the orchard; fell upon the frozen pond and the fields; was falling white upon the woods, which surrounded us. As the bare branches of trees scratched at the windows, we sat together that night, warm and drunk with good fortune. Roman took charge; it was his father's house. Ro stood before the grate, prodding the flames with an iron poker. Wren on the sofa finished off the bottle of Bordeaux. There was a blonde girl sitting beside her. I had taken up refuge near the bookshelves, the better to study the dusty leather-bound volumes. Eloise, wrapped in a blanket, sat upon the hearthstones. There were five of us. I, sitting a bit aside from the others, was lost in the ghost story and jarred strangely awake by its conclusion. It has been only with time; it is only now as I look back that I shudder in a different kind of horror.

The house stood lonely and remote. What possessed Roman's father to keep a house in faraway and desolate South Dakota?

Milton Stone had places like this all over the country; houses on unpaved roads; retreats where should the whim or will take him, should necessity strike; should the market bottom out or his latest wife scandalize him; he could hide out for a while. I had expected a rustic cabin; or a clapboard hunting lodge—and so was pleased to see the rambling Victorian farmhouse. The caretaker had arranged for everything; and upon our arrival we found the kitchen was well-stocked. Wood was stacked by the fireplace. Candles cast shadows from the wall sconces. There were four-poster beds and claw-footed bathtubs. The girls were charmed. Eloise remarked upon the faded floral wallpaper. I went from room to room in suspect—no, vigilant—exploration. Roman plundered the wine cellar where he discovered a store of aged whiskey. At night we sat before the fire. And it is difficult to recall—whose idea had it been to tell ghost stories?

I was nineteen years old.

This was the winter, the exact eve of 1980.

The future was a concept. The past was a theory.

Roman, Eloise, Wren, and I had driven from Iowa to South Dakota in the Range Rover.

We had picked up a skinny teenage girl, hitchhiking.

It was Eloise who made Ro pull over.

When we got to the house, we didn't know what to do with her. She didn't have any place to go. She didn't know anyone. And the house was big and warm. So she stayed with us.

We were spending the winter holiday together.

It was Wren who told the story about the possessed child. And El who pronounced that it gave her the shivers. Roman was restless. He was going to tell us a story. He didn't want to be outdone by Wren. He paced before the fire. He knew the house and the surrounding woods. He had spent time there when he was a child. He hadn't been back in years. Still the old house had not gone completely out of favor; it was loaned for cross-country ski weekends, romantic trysts, and once even occupied by a famous horror novelist in search of solitary inspiration.

And nothing mysterious, let alone amiss, had happened.

"What if I were to tell you the story of two children?" Roman said.

"Is it true?" interrupted Wren.

Eloise said, "The point of a ghost story isn't truth, it's the scare."

"Oh, so now there's a point?" said Wren.

"Don't start," said El. "You'll ruin everything."

Wren said, "It has to be true. You have to believe in something to be afraid of it."

Said El, "Isn't it more awful to be in doubt, to be uncertain?"

Wren said, "Let's hear it, Ro. Let's hear the story."

"Yes, yes," said El. "Tell us your goddamnnedy story."

Eloise could never hold her liquor.

Roman turned to the girl.

"What about you?" he asked.

"What do you think of ghost stories?" he said.

She was young.

She was pretty.

"I like stories," she said.

"Leave her alone," said Eloise.

"Ro," said Wren. "Terrify me."

I was paging through a volume of Poe.

Roman turned his back to us.

I closed the book.

Wren looked at me.

Upstairs—that four-poster bed awaited us.

"Tell the story," I said.

Wren said that she doubted whether Roman knew any ghost stories—

He couldn't really give a girl a good scare could he?

Roman said, "It's the story of a brother and sister."

A log shifted in the fire.

"What's so scary about that?" said Wren.

"It's a true haunting," Roman said.

"How do you know?" said Wren.

"Because one of them told it to me," he said.

"The brother or the sister?" asked Wren.

Ro had his back to us.

"Does it matter?" he said.

"Of course it does," she said. "It matters. It makes a difference; what one person does or another does. Or else how would we know who's guilty and who's innocent?"

Roman threw another log on the fire.

In a halo of sparks.

"*Innocent?*" he said. "That's a big word."

The girl laughed.

She covered her mouth with her hand.

She couldn't stop laughing.

Eloise said she was just now feeling awfully tired.

Too tired for more stories.

Said Wren, "Ro, I want to hear about the haunted children."

Eloise put her hands, palms flat, out toward the fire.

Roman abruptly left the room.

Eloise rose from the warmth of the hearth and said good-night. Then, after a hesitation in the doorway, she followed Ro.

New Year's Day was lazy. There was sun that morning, but it soon disappeared into gray. The girls made pancakes for breakfast. They talked about sledding. Roman said that he remembered a cake that his mother had made when he was little, some sort of Swedish New Year's cake. And Eloise wanted to bake this cake for him. She and Wren were going to drive into town to see if they could find a grocery store. I told her that that was crazy. That nothing would be open. Ro gave them his keys. He said, let them go; let them have an adventure. Eloise decided that we couldn't have a real celebration without Swedish cake. And oranges. She wanted oranges. Oranges on New Year's Day in the snowy desolation of South Dakota. El and Wren asked the girl if she wanted to go with them—but she said that she saw ice skates out on the porch—and was it O.K. if she went down to the pond? Ro was drinking coffee with whiskey and cream. What about you, Shelly? Eloise asked. Up for an adventure? I had a headache. It wasn't a hangover; though the booze didn't help; the change in the weather was bringing on the first sideways throbs of a migraine. I wasn't up for an adventure, no. So Eloise and Wren set out in Ro's car in search of oranges and whatever it was that one needed to make Swedish cake. The girl slipped the ice skates over her shoulder and headed for the pond. Ro tried to get the ancient black-and-white television to pick up a football game, but the screen showed only static. A light snow began to fall. And Ro wanted to collect more firewood. He put on his boots and with an ax he started out that afternoon.

I stayed behind.

And then I was alone in the quiet of the house.

I must have fallen asleep for a while—not long—it couldn't have been more than half an hour. I woke suddenly with a start. It happens this way with headaches; they wake me from sleep, with a sort of ominous sense of disaster. I sat up, sweating, trembling. I was alone. No one had returned to the house. I went to the window. The snow was coming down. I could barely see Ro's tracks, going away from the house. I had a terrible feeling. I put on my coat—

It was already too late when I found them, Ro and the girl in the snow.

She was white and naked. And he was covered in her blood.

6.

Zigouiller sat on the bed.

Eloise stood at the window.

He told her that six months ago he had been on the island where they had gone that time, did she remember?

He said that he ran into someone.

He ran into Roman.

"In the hotel bar," he said.

Eloise drew back the curtain.

"He asked about you," he said.

"It was too hot to do anything but drink."

Eloise waited.

"We drank," said Zigouiller. "Then a girl joined us."

Eloise turned.

"It got late," said Zigouiller.

Roman was drunk.

He got up. He got up from the table.

Roman left the bar.

"The girl stayed," said Zigouiller.

"It was late," said Zigouiller.

"She wanted to look at the stars," he said.

"The girl was beautiful," said Eloise.

"Yes," said Zigouiller.

"She came to my room," he said.

"—But you were thinking about Roman," said Eloise.

"I hated him," he said.

"So you took it out on the girl?" said Eloise.

"Go on," she said.

"How does the story end?" she said.

"After," he said.

"In the morning," he said.

He said, "I saw Roman in the lobby of the hotel. He asked me if I had seen the girl. He said she hadn't come back to his room last night. He said that he loved her."

"Roman asked me," said Zigouiller. "'Where is she?'"

"He set you up," said Eloise.

"You didn't see it coming," she said.

Roman asked Zigouiller, "*Where's the girl?*"

"So you told him?" said Eloise.

"You said that she was in your bed," Eloise said.

"And then he told you who she was," said Eloise.

"Yes," said Zigouiller.

"That she was your daughter," said Eloise.

"Yes," he said.

"Eloise," he said. "El?"

"What have I done?" he said.

7.

I saw Roman. And I saw the girl. She was naked in the snow. She was white. There was blood in the snow. Roman was standing over her. It was snowing. Half of the girl's face was smashed in. I saw the ice skates, far flung from each other. There was blood on Roman; on his hands, his face; on his coat; on his corduroy trousers. His boots left bloody traces—already being covered by the falling snow—as he paced around the girl's body.

"We'll need shovels," he said.

8.

Eloise stood at the window in her black slip.

"Why are you here?" she said.

"Don't you know?" he said.

She stood in the moonlight.

"I thought that you would know," he said.

"You of all people, Eloise," he said.

"I need you to forgive me," he said.

9.

The girl was dead.

10.

"What are you thinking?" Zigouiller said.

11.

Roman told me to go back to the house for shovels.

Roman killed the girl.

I was in the woods.

I came through the woods.

I saw the girl.

And the world was so white.

That you could barely see her against the whiteness of it.

The whiteness of the world.

And the dark limbs of trees.

I heard the wind in the dark boughs.

She was small and white.

Roman was holding a rock.

I saw Roman in the snow.

There was blood on the rock.

In the snow.

On the girl.

There was blood everywhere.

He stood.

He stepped back.

He looked at what he had done.

He staggered for a moment.

His breath hung in the air.

He stood.

He dropped the rock.

Snow was falling.

The snow fell and fell.

He pointed toward the house.

At first I couldn't hear him. Then I heard him. Get the shovels, will you? he told me what to do. And I did it. I went back to the house. I got shovels and kerosene. While Ro waited. Roman was standing at a distance from the girl. He had stripped her naked. Her white legs, bruised. His bare hands were bloody. Roman stood looking at the girl in the snow. We each took a shovel. And we began to dig in the hard frozen ground.

12.

Eloise was thinking about how she met Zigouiller at a movie theater. When she was twenty-one, in Paris. She met Herman Munster. He was an actor. He wanted to be a movie star. She told him that he should change his name to Zigouiller, because the audience would like it. Women would find it romantic. And men always liked a killer. She was right about that. She was right about so many things. She hated to be wrong. They ate double-salted black licorice. And talked about politics and poetry. About time and being. About civilization and its discontents. And truth and beauty. And they laughed and laughed. Then fell silent. In cafés, in bars, in dance clubs, at the movies. He read to her aloud from Kafka: *It happens whether you like or no. And what you like is of infinitesimally little help. More than consolation is: You too have weapons.* The figurative became the literal. Life was like a movie. They spoke of semiotics. Of signs and signifiers. They spoke in lines stolen from books. He lived in an apartment over a movie theater. There was a faded floral paper on the walls. And heavy furniture: a wooden table, chairs, a bed. The twining flowers on the walls. Candlesticks, licorice, paperback novels. There was a brass clock; wasn't it odd? It tolled thirteen. He said he found it in a little shop on holiday. He used to say things like that. *On holiday.* He had learned English from books. Once they went to an ancient island *on holiday.* They swam in the sea, but she was afraid of the snakes and scorpions. She knew too many stories of girls consumed by jealous gods. Or turned into salt for their sins. How he laughed at her then. The holiday ended. They left the winedark water. They left Paris too. They traded the cinema for the movies. And they went to California. So that Zigouiller could be a star. Zig said that fate happens whether you like it or no. She couldn't remember the order of things. She couldn't think of time as a line of events. They had lived in a room over a movie theater. With flowered wallpaper. She was thinking about Turkish cigarettes and marzipan candies in the shape of lemons. They ate chocolate oranges. He ran the film projector. They talked of movies. And the places in the world that there were to see. They would see them all. Wouldn't they? When they were young—everything smelled of smoke and chocolate. And she couldn't get the smoke from her hair. Or the salt from her fingers.

13.

Ro said we had to burn everything. We burned her clothes in the woods. The smoke curled up dark to the sky. Ro started the fire with kerosene. The fire burned fast and hot down to ash.

Our tracks, our footsteps, our footprints were everywhere.

The snow did not stop. It was falling thick and white.

Our tracks were already disappearing.

Each step, each imprint, vanished.

Behind us, as we walked.

We went back to the house.

Ro talked.

He was carrying the ax.

Swinging it as he walked.

My head was killing me.

When we got back to the house the girls were still gone. In the bathroom, I bolted the door. I ran the hot water. I bathed in the ancient tub. The ornate spigots bore the faces of grinning devils. The girl's face rose up before me, pale and hopeless. I closed my eyes. I heard the sound of footsteps on the stairs. A knock at the door; a hand turning the doorknob; Wren saying my name; Ro and Eloise whispering. I got out of the bath. I took my pills. The headache for a while worsened and then began to recede. In bed I fell into an ugly sleep.

14.

Eloise was thinking about how when she was pregnant she had wanted only licorice.

15.

It was dark when I woke.

16.

Eloise was thinking about how once when Susu was small, they were feeding ducks in the park, by a pond. Just then a white trumpeter swan came out of the water with a horrible cry and scattered the ducks away. Eloise lost hold of Susu. Susu ran to the swan. Eloise caught hold of the girl. She grabbed her daughter's hand. Susu wasn't afraid of anything.

17.

I came downstairs to find Ro and Wren and El in the kitchen.

They were drinking.

El's cheeks were flushed.

She was drunk.

"Look at the snow," she said to me.

I looked. I saw.

Snow on the fields and woods and pond.

Snow on the body.

Snow on the grave.

Covering our tracks.

"Snow," said El. "Is general."

Wren said that they hadn't found what they were looking for.

"Oh god, Shel," Eloise said. "We ran out of gas—and we had to walk to this farmhouse—so creepy. Just like in the movies—"

"It was this old lady and her son. And they were so nice to us," said Wren.

"They were," said El. "Guess what they gave us?'

She held her hands behind her back.

"This," she said.

Oranges.

"So we can celebrate," said Eloise.

"Where's the girl?" asked Wren.

Wren asked me what happened to the girl.

"She's gone," said Ro.

Ro opened a bottle of champagne.

Ro poured out a glass.

He poured out one glass after another.

He handed one to Eloise.

And one to me.

We were watching the snow.

And drinking champagne.

And toasting the New Year.

"Where did she go?" said Eloise.

"She said something about Hollywood," Ro said.

"Hollywood?" said Wren.

"Maybe we'll see her in the movies," said Ro.

He laughed.

He thought it was funny.

So he said it again.

The movies.

Wren didn't believe him.

She said that the girl was alone out in the storm.

How far could she go?

The snow falling fast.

It was thick and heavy.

Falling white on the pond.

Falling on the woods.

Ro handed Wren a glass.

Wren drank her champagne.

She set the glass on the table.

"You're drunk," said Ro.

"I'm not," Wren said.

"And a little hysterical," he said.

"I'm not," she said.

"Then maybe I'm drunk," he said.

He drank.

"—And a little hysterical," he said.

"Where's the girl?" Wren said.

"What girl?" said Ro.

"Shut up," I said.

Ro poured himself more champagne.

"Happy New Year," he said.

Eloise was peeling an orange.

"Shut the fuck up," I said.

18.

Zigouiller told Eloise to come away from the window.

She placed her palms flat against the glass.

19.

The hard times, the sour hours; the bloody footsteps of ancient sacrifice, the portents, the omens; the portentous, the ominous. Ro
killed her. Ro killed that girl in the snow. He smashed her skull. It
was his offering to an ancient god of destruction. We took shovels
and lifted the snow. We dug into the hard earth. We dug and the day
darkened. We buried her. We covered her with snow and dirt. The
snow fell and fell. It covered our tracks. It snowed all night. Snow
covered the grave. Year after year, I have awaited a telephone call; a
knock on the door. I have waited for someone to miss that girl. I
thought that one day the body would be found.

This has not yet happened. Will it? She is buried in the woods
beyond that farmhouse. Near the pond, under a willow tree. Ro was
nothing if not poetic. A real artist. Ro knew how to murder and to
create.

In 1981, though the girl's body was not discovered, Roman Stone was. That is, Ro's first book was published. He was hailed as sharp and smart and funny; the sign of the times, the face of the new generation. The *New York Times* sent a reporter out to Illyria to do a story on the latest literary boy genius. Ro was on his way. The face of that girl haunted me. And then after a while, I couldn't remember her face, and I was haunted only by the idea of her.

Ro and I buried the body. And we remained bound together by a gravediggers' hitch. I went out to California with him. It seemed that our general distrust of each other kept us together. After we separated in California he always kept a loosely knotted noose on me. He needed to know where I was. He never feared our secret coming out; it was more of a game to him. A game of odds and chance and memory and probability. Which one of us would break first? Who would tell the story? It was only a matter of time. Stone & Schell, partners in crime. Sometimes I thought that he wanted me to confess, that he was daring me to write a book; other times it seemed that he had forgotten what happened in the woods. He had pushed it from his mind; so much had happened to him since then, so much success, so much happiness. And I too began to wonder if it had ever really happened.

We sat that night before the fire.

There were four of us.

Wren was brooding. Eloise sat at Ro's feet. We drank champagne. Ro began his ghost story. Of course, it wasn't Roman's story.

It was mine.

Do you know what I love about you? said Pru one night long ago in Little America. *You make ugly things seem so beautiful. That's what I call a real writer.*

"Tell the story," said Wren.

We drank champagne.

We ate oranges.

And sat before the fire.

Roman told the story of how I found my mother and father dead.

A true haunting.

His ghost story.

My ghosts.

20.

Eloise was standing at the window.

Her back was to Zigouiller.

She looked out at the city.

She turned from the glass.

She looked at him.

In the darkness.

"I wish I had killed him," he said.

He rose from the bed.

He went to her.

"You called me a whore," she said.

"It was a stupid thing to say," she said.

They sat upon the bed.

They lay down upon the bed.

The drapes were open.

And the lights of the city shined upon the snow.

Eloise on her side.

In her black slip.

With his hand on her hip.

"Do you forgive me?" he asked.

21.

And in all these years; since I became the ghost of my own father; the years since we buried the girl in the snow; the years since my wife died; the years that proved my bad luck by virtue of my lack of virtue, I told my story only to one person.

I told my story to Dr. Lemon.

As we sat before the chessboard.

As we moved our ivory pieces across the black-and-white squares.

He poured me plum brandy.

He was deep and knowing.

I told him about my father and mother.

About my wife.

About my sister. About my book.

About Roman. About the girl.

The doctor could not remember the sins that I nightly confessed to him.

And because the doctor could not remember that what I touched was subject to destruction; he asked me to possess his most beloved object.

22.

Zigouiller asked Eloise if she could forgive him.

23.

The ghost-perfume seeps from the wallpaper. Like roses.

24.

"What are you thinking?" he asked her.

She was thinking of summer and salted licorice and an apple tree and no image that fit in a line with the next image just one thing after the next a ruined vase a cracked kettle a broken clock. She was thinking of Mother and Father. And the house and the tree and the garden and the table in the kitchen an unmade bed a closed door and the light burning burning in the window that you could see when you left your bicycle in the grass so you knew that Mother was reading. Eloise was thinking about Louie how he asked her again and again to tell him what happened. What did you see? he asked her. Do you remember? Did she remember? Father was in the cellar. He was making a box in which to lock all that was bad in the world. Father taught the children to be good. His wrath was a terrible thing. Mother was beautiful. In the garden. With the flowers and the aphids, the snails, the slugs cutting their way through green flesh; boring holes, sucking, destroying the life of flowers. Mother went at night to search for slugs in the garden. She crushed them between her fingers. To save the flowers. Mother's kindness was a terrible thing. At night the moonflowers opened in their twining around the fence; white flowers that hid from the light. See? Mother said. Mother whispered. See? how they open in the darkness? I see, said Eloise. And she did. She had seen. She saw.

She was the one who found the bodies.

"What are you thinking?" said Zigouiller.

She was thinking of the girl.

Of the swan.

Of the ocean.

Of the salt.

"El?" he said.

She was thinking of how her mother taught her to knick the moonflower seed with a knife to break the hard husk so that when buried in the ground the green shoots could push out and up and twine and mingle and knot and secretly at night and in the darkness blossom.

"I forgive you," she said.

25.

There is nothing so much that people will beg for as the truth; and then when given this thing, this *truth,* they will immediately doubt it. Why is kindness repaid with cruelty? The greater mystery is why the bird clings to the branch. Or the mouse plays dead to avoid the cat. When I was a child I used to keep my stories locked in a cedar box. I don't know whether I was protecting my story or the world.

CHAPTER 17

Susu breaks the second rule of storytelling

WE WALKED. The smoke of burning sage and cigarettes. We walked. The white flowers in the darkness. We walked. The dark hours by the light of the lanterns. We drank coffee with honey. At a little shop I bought postcards. We walked. He told me about a box that contained all the misery in the world. It was night. It was not. It was not night. We walked. It was morning. It was a hot dull morning. We stood on the balcony. He broke an orange in two. And he handed half to me. He went back into the room. I opened the box. His manuscript was tied with my ribbon. He untied the ribbon. He undid the knot. His papers fell to the floor. The fallen pages, the papers fluttering. I collected the fallen pages. He sat in shadow. I waited. I waited. I asked him to tell me the story. In the vase the black lilies wilted. In the lobby the statue began to weep. And everyone said that it was a miracle. Then one day or maybe it was night: he was gone. I read about it in the newspaper. It said that he died. And there would be no more of him. I came back here to our room. The night porter's wife asks about him and she brings me coffee with milk and honey but I have no taste for it. I do not tell her that he died. And I am waiting for a ghost.

CHAPTER 18
Sheldon suffers for art

SUSU ZIGOUILLER LOVED AMERICA: the shopping malls, fast food, cheeseburgers and push-up bras, gossip magazines, baseball, poetic justice, and blockbuster movies in which sloganeering heroes jump from jet planes two-fisted with guns blazing. She couldn't help but feel fondness for a certain species of vulgarity, for so much sugar and fat and sex and salt. The highs were high and the lows were low; truth was an artificial construct; beauty was in the eye of the beerholder; and her favorite gods and goddesses had long since ditched Mount Olympus for the Hollywood hills. She understood the sign of her own symbolism. She knew the difference between story and plot. All the history in the world had already happened. And she was in exile on an ancient island.

2.

Dibby Stone, once wife and now widow, in the warmth of a restored post-and-beam New England farmhouse that had been (not once, but) twice featured in *House & Garden* magazine, in a room that despite the absence of the subject had an objective (objectionable?) masculine presence: her late husband's study (he had objected to her calling it a *study,* as he assuredly had never *studied* anything; he was a natural—), touched her fingers to the black keys of his typewriter.

3.

Eloise Sarasine, reading a novel (or rather, not reading—), let the book fall closed.

4.

Elizabeth Weiss held her raku cup in both hands and blew slightly to cool the lime-infused green tisane, and she let the moment linger into a dramatic pause before she answered the question of the girl who sat beside her on the overstuffed sofa. The girl was a graduate student. Her name was Eris. She had bombarded Liz with e-mails, until finally, Liz, both flattered and wary, had agreed to the interview. The girl's hair was bleached white blonde. She was wearing a perfume of green apples, and she was working on her thesis: *Who killed the novel?*

Her theory was murder-suicide.

The girl broke off a bit of her buckwheat scone between her fingers.

And Liz said, "What was the question?"

Eris, caught between bites, set her plate on the cushion, put her hand before her mouth, and held up the other in a gesture, wait, wait—

"How did you meet your husband?" she asked.

5.

Benjamin Salt arrived on Pear Island on the last day of December. His journey began in Brooklyn. He had taken a taxi to the airport.

He had flown from JFK to Detroit, then changed planes and traveled on to Duluth. There he had rented a car. And continued on
toward his destination. He spent the night at a grim motel called the
Stockade; breakfasted the next morning at the Kracked Kettle. Salt
arrived in Damascus, Wisconsin, in a flurry of snow. He smoked a
cigarette and walked along the jetty. Lake Superior was dark. The
water was dark with distant islands. He said aloud in the cold afternoon, *archipelago*. He liked the sound of the word. A posted sign
announced that the ferry was no longer taking passengers across the
lake; but this was no impediment to Salt. He was not to be stymied
by such a small thing as circumstance. He hired a boat to take him
across. And once on the island, he enlisted the aid of a boy from the
inn to take him to the home of Sheldon Schell.

6.
Liz told Eris the story of how she met her husband.

7.
The book that Eloise had not been reading fell to the floor.

8.
"We take the truth and turn it into a lie. This," told Louis Sarasine
to his esteemed friends and colleagues, the members of the
Mnemosyne Society, "is how memory works. We see, we experience: an event, an object, a person—real things that exist in our real
world, made of bone or blood, of stone or steel or paper—and we
say: this is reality. We make an imprint of this reality: a memory; and
recreate and represent, revise and reorder, and change and become,
even with each change and each act of recollection, certain of the
solidity, the factual nature of our art. The drawings on the walls of a
cave, the blood on the doorjamb, the face on the shroud; the sign,

the symbol, the Venus de Milo, the Mona Lisa, the Sistine Chapel: each its own exquisite lie. If these are lies: the recollection of a face, a shape, a shadow; then what do we call truth? In what do we believe? The transcendent thing that signifies beyond significance? This thing called god? The creator, the authority, the artist. What if he is a liar by his very nature? What if he loves ink more than his audience? What are we to believe or to disbelieve? What will we do now? And what of tomorrow and the next day? We fear the truth of our truthlessness. We fear more the idea of an indifferent god than no god at all. We would rather have nothing than settle for less."

9.

Eloise looked around the room: her escritoire; the sofa, the chairs, the woven rugs, embroidered pillows, apples, roses, pens and cream-colored paper, a chess set, a statuette of the virgin, a lamp with a glass dome; the fireplace, a hand-fascinated box, the gilt-edged photo of her daughter.

10.

On the last night of the year, in an ancient city, as she walked to her hotel along a twisting stone street, Susu looked up at the sky to see the stars composing the Northern Cross of Cygnus, over the neon of a McDonald's sign, as though directing her homeward.

11.

Eris looked around Elizabeth Weiss's bohemian home—she saw the framed alpine postcards, the collections on the bookshelves: tin toys, snow globes—

The inkpots and antique typewriters.

She said, "God, that's a sweet story, but tell me—"

"What?" said Liz.

"Is it true?" the girl asked.

12.
Eloise ate an apple.

13.
Susu came to her hotel.

14.
Dibby Stone had inherited the upkeep of her husband's empire, and she was entitled—or obliged—no; obligated—to the excavation of its artifacts. The manuscript of his final novel had been returned to her by the police. Ro had written it longhand on unlined paper. It was found with him, in the room where he died. Tattered, fray-edged: it had traveled the world with him. It was tied and knotted with a length of ribbon. The fact of the book, of its composition of paper and ink, caused Dibby to fear its very persistence; its existence. The murderer—the thief, really—hadn't known, couldn't have understood the value of the manuscript, and instead had taken his watch, that absurd Italian timepiece. Dibby knew all about murder. She liked to read mystery novels. The kind where a body turns up in the garden, and then a sleuth says clever things. This, of course, was not that kind of book. As if kindness had anything to do with it. Dibby dared not untie the knot on the manuscript. It seemed an act of *undoing;* not just of the knot, but of him. As though the knot, more so than the book, were the last of Ro. So she had placed the manuscript on his desk. And there it had stayed: unread. Through the summer and into the fall. Now it was winter. Snow fell, as she stood with her palm flat against the paper, the page—; she wondered: *what is the story about?* and, for no reason more tangible than the force of her desire, Dibby pulled at the string.

15.

It bears noting that when he arrived on the island, Salt was not alone. He had brought with him a beautiful blonde girl. The girl was called Inj.

16.

The knot came undone.

17.

Dibby set the first page on the stand.

18.

A white sheet of paper was rolled into the carriage of the typewriter.

19.

In the hotel lobby: men in rumpled elegant clothing—spies or gamblers or deposed monarchs—sat on worn sofas reading newspapers and smoking Turkish cigarettes. A serene-faced plaster lady in blue with her nose chipped away, but her eyes were forgiving; weren't they? stood near the doorway—patiently—between a potted palm and an elephant umbrella holder.

Susu yawned.

She was tired of bones and candles and the eyes of watchful gods.

20.

A metal key struck a page, inking a letter.

21.

The good will not be rewarded and the bad will go unpunished.

22.

Dibby began typing the handwritten story on the green typewriter with the blacked-out keys.

23.

Dr. Lemon did not deserve the fate that Fate had assigned him. Nor did he warrant the plot imposed upon him by the author of all plots.

24.

Dibby let no pause fall between reading a word and translating it into type. She took the first page from the carriage. And she rolled another sheet into place. She saw the typed words—his words once, her words now—appearing black on the white page. And though she vowed, with a transcriptionist's honesty, to be true to the original—she had to make *some* changes, didn't she? She had a responsibility to fix, to mend and to amend, to correct him, to repair his faults and flaws. His spelling errors, his stream of consciousness ramblings, his words blotted into obscurity with jam or coffee or was it blood? Where was his dictionary? She began to search through his desk. It was as she opened the drawers one by one—that she found in the bottom drawer—a box.

25.

Dr. Lemon was dying.

26.

Mrs. Stone found a tin box. French, a pretty thing—decorated with seaside pictures. Scenes of girls on a beach. Of cakes and oranges and parrots. A little dog ran along the shore. Dibby had never seen the box before. She reached into the drawer. And just then—she heard—

27.

Eloise picked up the fallen book.

28.

Laughter, a crash, a door slammed. It was Olga with the boys. Olga, the new nanny, brought Chester and Julian home from the ice rink. They were in the kitchen, already fighting. Dibby heard them. They sounded so much like Ro. They were hungry. The boys were calling to her.

She looked at the box—

And she drew back her hand.

29.

Even a locked box is right twice a day.

30.

The girl sat beside Salt on the flight from New York to Detroit. She had procured for him an extra pillow and a blanket. When the attendant came down the aisle with the drink cart and gave Salt pineapple instead of orange juice, the girl made a small, but polite fuss. Salt hated flying. The girl said things to calm him. The runway was backed up in Detroit. They had to taxi for a while. Then they lined up in a queue waiting to land. When the flight finally touched down, the girl made sure that they were the first to disembark. They were in jeopardy of missing their connection; the girl grabbed Salt's hand, and she navigated him through the neon-bright airport to make the next plane moments before the doors were locked shut.

The small plane hit turbulence. They kept their seatbelts fastened. Salt went pale. The girl gave him pills from a prescription vial, and he closed his eyes.

The girl, that is, Inger, whom Salt called Inj, was an absolute necessity.

Inj rented the car in Duluth. She drove them on through bleak winter-stricken towns. At the Stockade they slept together in the small bed in the overheated room. And at the Kracked Kettle, he had pancakes; she ordered eggs. While Salt read aloud the crime blotter from the newspaper, Inj looked at the atlas.

Salt did the police in different voices.

Inj plotted their course.

And so they came to Damascus.

They took a boat across to the island.

31.
Snow fell.

32.
Inj paid the ferryman.

33.
The ferryman directed her to the inn. Where—

34.
A black-and-white dog barked at Salt.

35.
The box was a biscuit tin, the kind of thing that a child would use to hide treasures.

36.
Inj was beautiful.

37.

Dibby closed the drawer.

38.

Salt was miraculous.

39.

The black-and-white dog ran delirious circles in the snow.

40.

The boy from the inn put the bags in his truck.

41.

When the bell rang, Eloise was studying the face of a broken clock. She knew who it was at the door. Eloise knew all that there was to know. And this knowledge was no consolation.

42.

It was Zigouiller.

43.

But then you already knew this.

44.

Susu crossed the hotel lobby.

> The pages of a newspaper rustled.
> A match struck.
> Cigarette smoke.
> Lemon wax and rosewater.
> The diamond tiles of the floor.
> A heel scuffed across the floor.

A cough into a rolled fist.

45.

Susu was a remarkable girl.

46.

Where in his small bullish being rested the miracle of Salt? He was not tough or gentle. Neither kind nor merciless. Neither wise nor foolish. He did not tell jokes or say funny things. He was neither loud nor quiet. He was not taciturn or sweet-tempered. If he was not charming; there was an odd irresistible charm to him. If he was not a genius; there was a genius in him. He collected typewriters, puzzles, ink pens, postcards, and keys to doors that he would never unlock. If he had not yet done great things; it seemed that he would, or that he must. And if he had never uttered one brave or prophetic phrase; it seemed that he was just about to do so, at any moment; to say something important. People were waiting for him to do something extraordinary. And they were willing to wait. The universe had granted Salt a gift. He had been given the benefit of the doubt. And because of this, perhaps, *this;* and so much more: Salt had no doubt in his own abilities. Salt believed in himself. He believed in the axiomatic proof of his own genius. He was important. He *was* because he *was*. And he was part of eternity.

47.

Zigouiller took off his overcoat.

48.

While Liz spoke of the moral authority of homo faber in abstract and specific, Eris idly fingered a run in her striped stockings.

49.

Susu on the balcony drank from a bone-white demitasse.

50.

Eloise showed Zigouiller her house, room by room. She showed
him her Mycenaean jars and Egyptian antiquities. Her fat Buddhas
and lean bodhisattvas. Her writing desk and her ravens. A rock from
Gibraltar, a silver knife for cutting paper. Athena, Chronos, a swan,
a weeping virgin, candlesticks. A sofa, a chair, a fireplace. The damask
curtains, the Persian rugs, Russian dolls that opened one to the next
ever smaller, a cedar box, the morocco-bound folios on the shelves,
her books. And he said, "I bet you've read them all."

51.

Zola brought a red ball to Zigouiller.

52.

Susu leaned over the stone balustrade.

53.

Zigouiller rolled the ball across the floor.

54.

Susu looked down in darkness at the street below.

55.

Zola chased after the ball, skidding along the polished wooden
floors.

She brought the ball back to Zigouiller.

He rolled it again.

56.

Is reality rock or paper or scissors?

57.

Each time Zigouiller rolled the ball across the floor to Zola, she brought it back to him.

58.

Eloise and Zigouiller took the stairs one by one.

59.

Louis Sarasine spoke of—

60.

On a nightstand a wristwatch ceased keeping time.

61.

Zigouiller told Eloise that he had played Odysseus in a rock-opera miniseries on German television. And she fell back laughing on the bed.

62.

There was no television in Susu's hotel room.

63.

Eloise's black silk nightdress was draped over a chair.

64.

Salt's dark hair was close cropped; his thick eyeglasses fogged over in the damp. He wore a peacoat, no gloves, no hat; wound about his neck was an impossibly long red knitted scarf. He called his eyeglasses *goggles.* He called his scarf *a muffler.* He called his trip *a journey.* He was on a *quest* for an *artifact.* Like the heroes of old. He was determined to get here; to get to this place. He had traveled such a distance to get to this island. He was not to be stopped by the obstacles that might have thwarted a lesser traveler. His eyes were large and damp and dark. His hands were soft and white. A reporter for the BBC had described Salt's hands as *small furious doves.*

Salt stared up at a black-bellied bird perched on an icy branch.

Inj called to him—*Benny.*

He turned toward her.

And then looked back to the bird.

It had flown.

It was gone.

Oh well, eternity was far away; even from a place called Damascus.

65.

"What are the rules of the memory game?" said Louis.

66.

"People still want the old stories," said Zigouiller.

67.

Sometimes late, out of pity or kindness, the night porter's wife brought coffee to Susu.

68.

Susu had black hair and green eyes. She bore a striking physical resemblance to her mother. They could; they did; they used to place their hands palms flat against each other, and their hands met palm for palm and finger for finger; bone for bone.

69.

Salt and Inj drove on—that is, were driven by the boy who existed, like the ferryman, for only their necessity, for their journey, their story—through the snow to Schell's cottage. Salt looked out the window. Inj watched him. In her hooded parka, her boots, her woolen cap and fleece-lined gloves: she looked, hadn't Salt told her this himself?—like the last girl in the world.

70.

Why didn't Dibby open the box?

71.

Inj was Benjamin Salt's research assistant.

72.

The members of the Mnemosyne Society were dwellers in the field of memory.

73.

Eloise wanted the old stories.

74.

Susu looked very much like her father, too; didn't she?

75.

Salt came to Pear Island to make the acquaintance of a recluse who possessed something that he wanted.

76.

"I call the recollection of images as expressed in a narrative: the memory game. Because," said Louis Sarasine, "like all games it is an enterprise that is both childish and dangerous—"

77.

"Do you believe," Eris asked Liz, "that 'the novel' is dead?"

78.

Inj looked at Benny sitting beside her in the truck. He was wiping his eyeglasses with a white handkerchief. She invested this small utilitarian gesture with mythic symbolism.

79.

Sheldon Schell was in bed suffering with a headache.

80.

Beatrice was in the kitchen watching *Tomorrow's Edge* on the black-and-white television set and turning the spoon round in the mixing bowl, when she heard the knock upon the door.

81.

A French bulldog made her way up a staircase.

82.

Beatrice helped the guests with their bags.

83.

Salt looked around the room. There were flowers on the wallpaper.

Inj sat on the bed. She leaned back against the pillows. Inj said that it was so nice to get out of the city.

84.

Schell turned on his side. He heard bedsprings. He smelled smoke and roses.

And then the scent drifted away.

85.

A red ball rolled step by step down the staircase.

86.

"Why do we admire the way that an actor can memorize his lines? Or revere a painter who can call to mind the shadows of an afternoon long lost to time? Or delight in the exquisite lie of a writer who creates a world within a nutshell of infinite space? And yet," said Louis Sarasine, "when having lunch with a friend who in the course of telling an entertaining story reveals that his story is a deception—we feel affronted. Yes?—Because we were lied to—but when is it, exactly, that we want the lie? Is it only when we set the rules of the game? Does the lie become its own kind of truth? Do we feel anger at having been duped—or experience a secret terrifying pleasure? If the lie can so please us—of what use is the truth? If it affords no real reality or moral high ground, what is its utility? Is it a crime for an actor to address the audience? Or for an artist to admit that he paints his dream of a garden and not the flowers in the vase before him? I say this: truth is the ax wielded by the listener against the teller. It is his only weapon. He demands not: *tell me what you recall;* not *tell the story as you remember it.* He says: *tell me the truth.*"

87.

Zola looked at Zigouiller.

88.

Eloise laughed.

89.

Zigouiller intoned, "I am Odysseus son of Laertes, known before all men for the study of crafty designs, and my fame goes up to the heavens."

90.

Eloise stopped laughing.

91.

Have the grape blossoms opened? Are the pomegranates in bloom?

92.

Eloise's nightdress slipped from the chair to the floor.

93.

Zola gave a mournful sigh and lay her head on the black silk, perfumed.

94.

Schell opened his eyes.

    He did not know where or who he was.

    Then he saw Beatrice's white nightdress.

95.

A white nightdress was draped over a chair.

96.

What did Salt want?

97.

Dibby was typing.

98.

The story was dark and terrifying.

99.

Beatrice caught her reflection in a plate as she set it on the table.

100.

Susu would have rather been called a thief than a liar.

101.

Olga, the nanny, was making cocoa for the boys.

She brought it to a low boil in a pot on the stove, with cream and cinnamon.

102.

Beatrice went into the bedroom, and she whispered to Schell.

103.

Chet and Jules, playing cops and robbers, burst into the study, calling out STOP THIEF! and each boy took one of his mother's hands, lifted the hands, left and right, from the typewriter.

104.

Olga took three mugs from the cupboard and poured out the cocoa into them and set them on the table for Chet and Jules and Dibby.

105.

Salt put his ear to the wall.

106.

"We played games of memory as children. Some games involved repetition—like telephone—the repetition of a phrase that changes for the group as each child reinterprets it. One does not win or lose at this game, only takes part in a chain of meaning. What causes me to move from one word to the next? What causes me to recall in words: a perfume? I can say: it bore the single note of rose; and yet in my experience of this perfume, there were—or are—no words. In the transcription of the sensual into the literal, comes the lie. It is, of course, not the kind of lie that matters. It is the kind of lie upon which we depend for both our dreams and responsibilities." Louis Sarasine paused. "For from that single note of a rose, one suddenly recalls a garden."

107.
Beatrice sat beside Schell on the bed.
    She was tiny and slightly strange.
    With her large gray eyes and dark decisive brows.
    "Has it happened?" he asked.
    "Have they come for me?" he said.
    The curtains were drawn.
    The cat leapt from the window ledge.
    "There's a girl too," said Beatrice.
    "The girl," Beatrice said. "Is beautiful."
    "What girl?" he said.

108.
Eris said to Liz that these days the novel had about as much appeal as a monster from an old movie. One pitied it. One was horrified by it. For a moment even, the thing was adorable. And then one became annoyed that it hadn't crawled off somewhere to die a dignified death. Instead it went around smashing into things and gobbling up girls and stomping on cities like Godzilla.

109.
Inj lay on her side like a fallen heroine.

110.
"No really," said Eris, "What's more silly than a book in which one thing happens and then another thing happens? This," she said, "this

very conversation has already happened. And we can revise it to prove or to disprove any version of reality. Have I told you my thesis? The fixity of the page is a prison of infinite space. In the future," she said to Liz, "the novel will be a polyphonic electric/tronic dialogue between all the readers in the world, and we will have no more of this, this, this monster called the author. We won't be bound by binding or ink. In the future," Eris said, "the future will have already happened. Do you see?"

III.
"She's so beautiful," Beatrice said.

II2.
Liz picked up a plastic dinosaur that Bruno had left on the table.

II3.
"She's like a girl on television," said Beatrice. "She's been places. I can tell. She's done things."

Schell looked at Beatrice in the darkened room.

"Do you want to go places?" he said.

"That's just it," she said.

"What?" he said.

He touched her cheek.

He touched a hand to her hair.

"I don't want anything," she said.

II4.
Elizabeth Weiss felt that a novel should offer—if not moral instruction, then—a roadmap for the reader. It should tell the reader where to go and how to proceed in the world.

115.

At the heart of all things is a knife.

116.

Inj unpinned her hair.

117.

Salt had a secret.

118.

Susu, when she was a little girl, had liked to sit at her mother's dressing table before the mirror; to unstopper the glass bottles and jars; to open the jewelry box; to rope the pearls around her neck; to dab rose on her wrists. Susu had liked to dress in her mother's black silk slip and read aloud from a book of Poe. And when she grew up, she found that what was once a game was the very reality of her existence. Which did not mean that it was no longer fun to play at it. Only that sometimes she felt like the raven and other times like the writing desk.

119.

Bruno Salt, age four, tired of being good for the whole of the long afternoon alone in his room with his trucks and puzzles, tromped into the living room wearing one snow boot (he couldn't find the other) and holding by a tangled leash the long-haired dachshund called Kafka, and announced to his mother that the dog really really really wanted to go outside *now*.

120.

Louis said, "The invention of humanity relies on the device of collective memory. Yet, this collection of shared knowledge, of the very meanings of pain and of pleasure, of yes and no, itself relies on the subset of the individual's memory within the collective. If we locate memory in *difference,* that is, the difference between the real and the unreal; between belief and disbelief; between story and plot; between now and then; or in the skittering ligature-bound variation between *s* and *z:* how will we know where one begins and the other ends? It may be a token of the final illogic of logic, that we must first premise our disbelief on belief. We must pick a point and call it an established truth. Upon which rock will we build our church? We call absence itself presence; and say: it is time to begin. It is time to begin. Here is where we will begin: God is the beginning not because he is known, but because he is unknown. Gentlemen, friends: I will tell you my story. The story of my memory game. It begins, as all stories do and must, with a girl."

121.

Dibby Stone almost forgot—the cocoa was so sweet and warm—
      That Roman was dead.

122.

What had become of the knife that had stabbed him in the heart?

123.

Chester Stone wiggled a loose tooth with his finger.

124.

"Well aren't you something?" Eris asked Bruno.

125.

Said Louis Sarasine, "I'll begin, as I said. With the girl."

126.

Bruno thought that it was a silly question. Between *something* and *nothing,* he would always choose *something.*

127.

Eris was wearing striped stockings.

128.

There were times when Dibby thought that she saw Roman in the darkness. She saw him at his typewriter. And then the shadows shifted. And she knew that he wasn't real. He was a ghost of her memory. Yet, if she could create him—from will or reflex, from habit or desire—who was to say that he wasn't entirely and hadn't always been a monster of her own creation?

129.

Louis Sarasine told to the members of the Mnemosyne Society a story.

130.

The wind banged against the windows—Eloise, naked on her hip, had the awful feeling that somewhere someone was digging her grave.

131.

The story—dark and terrifying, as stories told on New Year's Eve should be—was about a girl who found her mother and father dead.

132.

Susu had a very silly name.

133.

Said Louis, "The girl walked along a dirt road to her house on an October evening. The house was dark. She stood in the garden looking up at the windows. An apple fell from a tree. A bird flew from a branch. She waited. She waited. And then she went in the house. She took the stairs in the darkness. She called out; no one answered. She went from room to room. Calling out. And then she stopped calling.

134.

Eris apologized to Liz, where had the time gone?

135.

Eloise was the one who found the bodies.

136.

Kafka barked.

137.

Eris packed up her laptop computer and collected into an oversized leather bag: her tape recorder, her cell phone, keys, a glove, coins, butterscotch candies, a lipstick, another glove, that she had during the course of the visit spread out across the table to mix with Bruno's clutter of Legos, colored pencils, plastic dinosaurs, and a much-prized grimy white feather. Eris shrugged into her coat. It was blue and furry. Bruno reached out with his damp little hand to touch it.

Liz asked Eris as the girl rose to go, did she have big plans for the night?

138.

Louis said, "What happened next? I confess: I don't know. Her story is unfinished. She won't allow it to end. She tells me the story. I listen.

By day we live in the real world; yes, there is such a place. But at night we wind our way through a labyrinth of her creation."

139.
Eris said that she hated New Year's Eve, and wasn't it stupid? the idea of it; of one year ending and another beginning? It drove her bananas. It really did. She liked to think of the revolution of the planets. Slow, dull, and incomprehensible: like the best novel. It neither began nor ended.

140.
Liz said good-bye to Eris. Bruno took both his mother's hands in his. The girl smiled and pretended that this was adorable. And then Eris said good-bye to the boy and his mother and went off down the street, happy to be free of them, and sad too.

141.
The Mnemosyne Society met once a year, on New Year's Eve. They began long ago with a commitment to the theoretical examination of memory. Oh, but as the years passed, these great men found little and ever-diminishing comfort in theory. They had become, bit by bit: older, whiter, fatter or skinnier, more wanting of story than discourse, more desirous of desire than disproof of the immutable substance of dreams. Memory had long since become remembrance. And so it was that when Louis Sarasine told of the girl who became his wife, who led him nightly through a labyrinth, twining her way in the darkness with a knotted rope of story; binding him with her noose; each man felt looped in the loop himself; bound at the wrist and blindfolded. His bruises were real, or at least real enough; for he had heard a story about truth and beauty.

142.

Zigouiller slept on his stomach, like a hero hiding his fatal flaw.

143.

"I had a recent case," Louis Sarasine said. "No doubt you saw it on the news?—a young man stood accused of rape and murder. Three girls were found, each one packed in a suitcase: one suitcase left by the side of a road; one thrown in a lake; one in a train station. There was circumstantial evidence, but he claimed that he had no memory of the events. He passed polygraph tests. He never broke nor faltered in his denials. He was candid, young, and credible. His sincerity confounded even his most certain accusers. He might have gone free; he might not have gone to trial—but there was another girl, a girl who had survived. She had been found wandering the woods, but she was so traumatized that she couldn't speak for months after, let alone recall specific details, nor could she identify her attacker, until seeing his picture on television. My task was to discredit the girl and engage the sympathy of the jury toward the accused. Which, of course, I did."

144.

Zola, sleeping on the silk nightdress, dreamed that she was a girl and that Zigouiller was in love with her.

145.

Liz and Bruno walked along a snowy street with Kafka.

146.

Eris, who was writing a paper, though no actual paper was involved, on the topic of postfeminist ergodic technoiconography vis-à-vis la morte de la novel as a phallogocentric assault and thusly thrust conversely upsidedownedly: the feet-first kicking breech birth of the eco-polyphonic carnival text, was kinda sorta disappointed that she hadn't gotten to meet Salt.

147.
Salt knew that he had a book within him.
    There was only one problem.

148.
Beatrice pared a potato.

149.
Salt was suffering from writer's block.

150.
Suffering?

151.
Susu closed the door to the balcony.

152.
"The victim could not recall the crime, and the accused could not recall committing the crime," said Louis Sarasine. "Yet a crime had been committed. The case was like a game of telephone; the circuitry of the act had given way to myriad possibilities, not negating reality, but creating subsets to it, inexhaustible what-ifs and why-nots? And it occurred to me; I had a belated revelation, not in the courtroom, but later, on the plane home, delayed by a snowstorm—"

153.
Beatrice set the timer on the oven.

154.
Inj was naked.

155.
Roman was dead.

156.
Dibby had quick small fingers.

157.
Kafka licked the salt from his paws.

158.
"—I understood how my wife had helped me," said Louis. "She told me her story. Each time that she told the story, she changed it. She believed in each version of the story that she told. I understood; I learned from her how it is that the truth is less relevant than a belief in the truth."

159.
Eloise and Zigouiller slept on through the darkening afternoon.

160.
Dibby wanted to know how the story would end.

161.
It was not a story.

162.
Beatrice knocked on the bedroom door; did anyone want to go for a walk in the woods?

163.

Inj buttoned her blue jeans.

164.

Salt had gone dry.

165.

Bruno licked peanut butter from his fingers.

166.

Said Louis Sarasine, "A story is a labyrinth, and all paths lead to the monster. Who is the monster? Is it the storyteller? A good storyteller *must* be a monster. The best stories tell of the worst of human nature. The worst, our broken laws. Our nightmares realized. To write of such things, an author must commit the act himself; if only on the page. And what of us? What of the readers? In the real world, we read our newspapers. We butter our bread. We read of murder, and we are sickened. But in fiction, in the story: we want the dead girl. So—who is the monster? You? Me? Am I guilty? Are you, dear friends, guilty? Because you want to know about a dead girl? Am I guilty for wanting to know what my wife found in the dark house years ago? I want her story. My client told me his memories, that's all. I listened. I defended not him, but his dreams. I defended the story. I defended the right of a dreamer to imagine the worst. I have read the oldest most beautiful stories in the world—tales of rape, destruction, and murder. I have found the beauty in violence. In my mind I have killed so many girls. Yet, I never lifted a hand. I never held a knife in anger, but I did imagine the knife in my hand. Am I guilty? Because what one dreams is always possible? Am I guilty of reading a story?"

167.

Bruno danced to a song on the radio.

168.

Liz at her laptop computer set on the kitchen table, while waiting for the water to boil for macaroni and cheese, was tapping out a particularly relevant passage in her new novel. She was wearing a sweater knitted of organic cruelty-free Peruvian wool. She lived dedicated to the principle of a cruelty-free life. The impossibility of this had not yet occurred to her.

169.

Susu Zigouiller went down to the hotel bar.

170.

In the winter woods walked Inj and Beatrice.

171.

Salt had a story within him, but he had no mechanism—neither ghost nor machine—by which to tell it.

172.

Schell was not sure what was real and what was not.

173.

Louis Sarasine said, "Eloise was not sure what was unreal and what was not. This was the gift—or the grace—that helped me prove, if not the innocence, then the lack of guilt of a monster."

174.

In the kitchen, Salt ate bread and marmalade.

175.

Schell closed the door to his study.

176.

Beatrice told Inj the names of birds.

177.

Said Louis, "I want to know what will happen. Each time she tells me
I want to know. Hearing the story does not diminish my desire. I am
looking for a clue, a twist, a turn, an exit. I am searching for a fallen
candle, a hidden letter, a lost key. I want more. I want to know more."

178.

Salt left a sticky knife on his plate.

179.

Schell picked up his pen.

180.

The black cat went from room to room.

181.

Louis Sarasine went to the window and looked out.

   "There is more to the girl's story," he said. "You see, she had a
brother."

182.

Salt opened the door to the study.

183.

Inj chased the dogs round and round through the pine trees.
   And fell laughing in the snow.

184.

Said Louis Sarasine, "It is the story of a brother and a sister."

185.

Schell put down his pen.

186.

The girls talked about actresses they liked. And how nice it was to be able to talk about actresses they liked without very smart men telling them they should talk about more meaningful things.

187.

The black cat brushed back and forth against the white nightdress, draped over a chair.

188.

"Many years ago, when the brother and sister were small, they lived in an old farmhouse. There was a garden. Beyond the garden: a creek, a path, a wilderness, the woods. The children had a story," said Louis Sarasine. "They kept it in a box. They were writing a story. They wrote it in the woods. There was a key to the box, and the brother liked to lock up the story. Eloise told me that she had lost the key. She said that everything that she told me was true. And I did not believe her."

189.

Salt, seeing his host for the first time, offered his hand. He asked in a manner both sincere and ironic, "May I call you Shel?"

190.

"Eloise did not lie," said Louis. "Does this mean that she told me the truth? She told me about the night she found her father and mother. She told me that there was a chocolate cake on the kitchen table. Or maybe it was an apple pie. She told me that her father's typewriter was green. She told me about a wooden box. Or maybe it was made of tin? She told me about the story that she and her brother were writing, though he always held the pen."

191.

Sheldon Schell took his guest's proffered hand.

Oh, that soft hand was warm and damp.

192.

"I've come to collect on a promise," said Salt.

193.

And didn't Schell feel terror then?

194.

Said Louis, "She opened the box that night. She scattered the pages on the floor. And she set the story on fire. There was no page that did not burn. She told me that she started the fire. She told me that she set the house on fire. And I did not believe her."

195.

Salt said, "I have a sense, an instinct, that guides me like a hand. I speak in abstractions. I should speak only in the concrete. I should be speaking of objects and objectivity. I should be speaking of weight and heft and symbols. Of *the thing* and of the transformation of *the thing*. Does a clock contain the time? Of course not. Does a teakettle contain water? It may. It can. Yet it may not. Or a key, what about a key? If it opens one door, will it open all doors?"

196.
A drink, ouzo—she hadn't ordered it—was set before Susu on the marble of the bar.

197.
The cat slept curled upon the white nightdress in a heap on the floor.

198.
The white nightdress lay in a heap on the floor.

199.
"My friends," said Louis Sarasine, "tell me this: tell me why no version of her story will satisfy me? Tell me why I don't, why I can't believe her."

200.
Salt said, "Do you believe that there is a destiny that shapes our ends? Do you think that there is a connection between time and being? That no matter which course you take, you will end up, you will find yourself at the appointed hour, in the very place where you were going? I do. I do. Let the animals loose of the zoo and some will murder and some will create. Do you see? I've come to you—I am here. For both the ghost and the machine. What is one without the other? Do you think that I'm a fanatic? I must be a fanatic to devote myself so to someone whom I never met. I can barely speak his name. But, I did meet him. A long time ago. It was only that I didn't know that it was him. Let me tell you how it happened."

201.

Salt talked about fate.

202.

The small glass was full.

203.

Fate is a girl with scissors.

204.

Susu did not think about the things that she had done in her short life as being either good or bad. If questioned she might have conceded that the destiny that shapes our ends is like a knot of rope that one grabs hold of when drowning, yet even as one is holding onto it, one's fingers begin to try to untie the knot. She lifted the glass and drank.

205.

Salt said, "I wish that my mother and father had taken more care when they brought me into the world. I should have lived in a ruined abbey. Instead, I grew up in a cul-de-sac. I lived in a circle. The houses were the same one after another. It was a maze of streets, and I lost my way. They called me an idiot. I didn't speak until I was eight. My first word was *planetarium*. Then they called me a genius. I imagined that I was switched at birth with a prince. One day my real father, the king, would come for me. One day I was building a castle of cards when just such a king arrived. This part happens, as dreams do and must, in the present tense. My mother is talking to him. I am under the table. I hear voices. His voice. He lifts the flowered cloth and looks at me. I cover my face. I am covering my eyes. I know that I should not look at him. And then he is gone and there is no more of him. Did it happen? Years later, I am in the library and I take a book from the shelf. I turn it over. I see the picture on the jacket. An old hardcover book with the photograph on the back. And suddenly there I am, under the table looking at his face peering down at me from under the cloth. He is the author. It is he, him."

206.
Beatrice walked ahead of Inj, breaking the path through the woods in the white white snow.

207.
Susu went back to her room with a man she met in the bar.

208.
It was not the first time.

209.
Dibby did not stop typing.

210.
"Roman Stone," said Salt.

211.
Susu was thinking of algorithms and lacunae.

212.
Salt said, "I've said the name. I want to know the truth. I want the story. Will you tell me everything? Tell me about Stone. Tell me how he became a writer. Tell me if he was born to it, or invented his own idiom. Consider me an unruly child ruled by my wants. I want! I will stand on a chair and beat the teakettle with a wooden spoon

announcing: I'll do a dance! I'll sing for my supper! I am like a child demanding a jar from the top shelf; this thing is beyond my reach. Yet I must have it. It is right that I should have it. For I want it so. And if the jar falls upon my head, I'll take my lumps as the price of justice. Justice makes jam all the sweeter."

213.
Inj and Beatrice made their way back through the woods.
    Inj couldn't recall the names of the birds.
    Some were big and beautiful, with such wings.
    Some were small and ugly.
    It began to snow. The snow was heavy.
    Already the sky was dark.
    The dogs ran on ahead.
    The girls walked.
    And the snow fell.

214.
With each page of Roman's manuscript Dibby found a new flaw.

215.
Olga took the laundry from the dryer.

216.
Schell and Salt sat together, as men often do.

217.
On the wall there was a painting of a girl and a god in the woods.

218.
Said Schell, "I'll tell you a story."

219.

Pru used to steal lines. She said: *Let anger be general. I hate an abstract thing.*

220.

Susu had sold off what she could to pay for her wanderings: her diamond engagement ring, a cashmere sweater, a bracelet.

221.

"Many years ago when I was young," said Schell. "I thought about nothing but art, night and day. I had one dream. I wanted to write a novel. And it seemed very obvious to me that before I began to write my novel, I would need to find the perfect story."

222.

Salt pulled his chair closer.

223.

If perhaps a plate or book had suddenly launched flying across the room to land smack against his guest's round face, Schell would have known that it was at the hand of Pru's ghost.

224.

Olga folded a pajama top, leaned down, and set her cheek against the warm flannel.

225.

Schell said, "I began to try to find the perfect story."

226.

"How?" asked Salt.

227.

Said Schell, "I read books. I read book after book, but I did not find the answer. And when I did not find the answer in a book, I went to my father. I asked my father. My father knew all that there was to know—and this knowledge was no consolation."

228.

Susu imagined that she was sailing on a ship to Byzantium.

229.

Schell said, "My father was a casket-maker, and he taught me what he could about the world. He had a workshop in our cellar. When we were children—we weren't allowed there—it was where he devised his plans; it was where he built his monsters. That's what we used to say, my sister and I. A story is a monster, I suppose. A story is an invention. And my father was an inventor. He designed—oh—wooden toys: birds with wind-up wings, soldiers, dancing ballerinas, dollhouses, mazes, jigsaw puzzles, and long-spinning tops. He grew ill, and little by little he gave up everything—except boxes. He worked at boxes. He had a monomania—an idea—he wanted to make a box that would neither open nor close. My mother took care of him. I was aware of my father's misery and my mother's beauty, and that fate had brought them together to live in a house with a twisted apple tree in their garden. I inhabited their little world, and I, as I say, through defense or offense, thought entirely about art." Schell broke off, distracted—

He looked out the window.

The sky had gone dark.

"One night—it was summer. It was late. I was in bed. I couldn't sleep. And I knew that my father was in his workshop—

I crept down the stairs to the kitchen—

I remember—my hand on the door that led down to the cellar.

That door was always locked.

I turned my wrist.

The door opened.

What did I do?

I went down the stairs.

I was so quiet, step by step.

I saw him. My father—

He was sitting at his worktable—

By the light of a lamp.

It was night.

And there was nothing like it.

My father sat at his table.

The table was covered with papers.

The papers were covered with his designs.

He held a pencil.

At first he did not see me.

Then he saw me.

I came closer.

He sat, and I stood.

I stood before him.

I said, 'How do I find the perfect story?'

My father was silent.

I waited.

I waited for him to speak.

He said nothing.

He looked down at his paper.

He began to write.

He wrote for a few moments—

Then he looked up.

He looked at me.

He must have forgotten that I was there.

He set down his pencil.

He picked up a ruler.

He said, 'Be true.'

It was neither a command nor a statement.

It was a measurement.

Just then I heard footsteps.

A ghost?

It was no ghost.

My sister stood.

In her white nightgown.

She had followed me.

She came into the light.

My father looked at us with—

A kind of astonishment.

We looked so much alike, you see.

He marveled at us as at some elaborate invention.

My sister in her white dress.

It caught the lamplight.

For a moment I was angry with her.

I hated her, just then.

I pushed her—and she fell.

My father said nothing.

He gave her his hand, and she took it.

She opened his palm—

In it was a small gold key.

My father turned.

He held a box.

He gave me the box.

He gave my sister the key.

He gave me a box.

A wooden box.

Long gone now—

It was the perfect box for my story."

230.

"And then what happened?" said Salt.

231.

No book flew from a shelf, no plate broke. No picture fell from the wall. No teacup crashed to the floor. No papers fluttered and lost their order. No postcard turned from picture to portent. No branch banged the window glass. No hand moved on the clock. No god ceased his ravishment of a ready virgin. No afternoon gave way to evening. No ghost made herself known.

232.

Said Schell, "One day passed into the next. We had cake. We drank tea. My father killed my mother. Or maybe it was the other way around. I was the one who found them. There was a fire. The house burnt to the ground. My sister and I watched it burn. Then I went to college. And I met Roman Stone. Wasn't that what you asked me? How did I become a writer?"

233.

Salt said, "That *is* a story."

234.

Susu on the bed.

235.

Schell noticed a spot of marmalade on Salt's plaid shirt.

236.

Beatrice did not know what god or grace or ghost impelled Inj to grab her hand. But Inj did. She did. And off they ran running through the falling snow.

237.

With each flaw that she found, Dibby loved the book more.

238.

Salt rapped his fingers restlessly against the windowpane.

239.

Liz would never have believed that readers were not looking for moral instruction; that when they opened a novel, they were not in search of either guidance or escape; but that they were looking always for themselves, along every turn and twist of the stone street and sentence.

240.

The girls ran in the snow.

241.

Susu turned on her hip, unashamed.

242.

Schell was thinking about Beatrice. Her white body.

243.

Let us go early to the vineyards.

Let us see if the vine has flowered.

244.

Salt said, "What about the key?"

245.

Chester was building a fort in the yard when Julian, for no reason more adequate than the force of the moment, pushed his brother's face into the snow.

246.

Louis Sarasine said, "You must know what sort of monster you are, before you know the monster that you will become. Providing, of course, that you believe in monsters."

247.

Dibby saw her boys from the window.

248.

Said Schell, "What key?"

249.

Susu was not beautiful.

250.

Salt got up from his chair.

251.

Olga ran out of the house without her coat and pulled Chester from Julian.

252.

Salt said, "It's too quiet. I'd never be able to work. I love a real hullaballoo. Crash, bang, boom. Say, may I borrow your pen?"

253.
Olga slapped Chester.

254.
Dibby let the curtain fall back against the window.

255.
Susu might have been the model for the statue in the hotel lobby. That is, she was chipped and flawed; yet she inspired in one the utmost faith in the hand of some unseen artist.

256.
Schell gave Salt his pen.

257.
Dibby was typing.

258.
Salt said, "Don't you want to know how my story ends?"

259.
The girls were very nearly to the house.

260.
Said Salt, "Don't you want to know why Stone was in the kitchen with my mother? It wasn't until I saw his picture on the book. That I remembered him. I asked my mother about it. She said that they had dated in college. You went to college with him. Maybe you remember her?"

261.
"There were a lot of girls back then," said Schell.

262.

Salt said, "There are a lot of girls nowWe will run out of everything, won't we? Air, water, land, luck, sugar, salt, gasoline? But we will never run out of girls."

263.

Inj was running.

264.

Salt said, "A typewriter doesn't invent words."

265.

A dark bird sat perched in a cedar tree.

266.

Schell had never quite believed that Salt was real. And now that the young man sat before him with his eyeglasses, with the very ingredient evidence of his existence—the skin, the bones; his luck, his lack; the orange marmalade on his flannel shirt—he seemed less actual than ever.

267.

There were a hundred dark birds in the branches of the cedar trees.

268.

Dr. Lemon had once tried to teach Schell to play random chess, that postmodern variant of the game, in which pieces retain their abilities and function, but may begin from randomly selected places on the board, rather than their standard positions. In a game of tactics; one had to rethink the concept of strategy. Schell had lost very badly. The truth of it was (that is; the way it had actually happened) he had never won at a game of chess against the doctor.

Did this suggest that he was a poor player?

269.

The girls were home.

270.

A door slammed shut.

Inj said, "Benny?"

271.

A picture tilted crookedly against the flowered wallpaper.

272.

In moments of anguish Schell had called out to a god of mercy in whom he had never believed.

273.

Beatrice was in the kitchen.

The black cat pawed the windowpane.

He gave a mournful yowl.

"Oh, you poor terrible thing," said Beatrice.

"Is this what you want?" she said.

And she placed a dish of milk on the floor.

274.

When Salt came in, Inj was sitting on the bed.

275.

Olga took Julian into the bathroom, and she washed the blood from his nose. She asked him, does it hurt? She took him into his room and told the boys that they had to make up, because they were brothers. She told them not to come out until they had made up. After Olga left; Jules said how much he hated her. Chet agreed. Chet asked Jules if he missed the last girl. Jules remembered her. She was pretty. Olga was not pretty, but Olga made cupcakes with melted chocolate in the middle. They were good and sweet and salty. But the last girl had long hair that brushed your cheek when she tucked you into bed and that was good too. The boys were silent then for a while; they played Clue until dinner.

276.
It was Miss Scarlett in the library with the candlestick.

277.
Salt told Inj the story of Schell's coffin.

278.
Salt was thinking about what it would feel like to be stabbed in the heart with a knife.

279.
Louis Sarasine raised his glass.
    And he pronounced, "To monsters."

280.
Inj walked down the hallway.

281.
Black turtleneck sweater, Levi's, woolen socks.
    This is what Inj wore.

282.

It was evening, all afternoon.

283.

Beatrice was thinking about her father. And how he taught her the difference between right and wrong.

284.

Zigouiller touched Eloise's shoulder.

285.

There was. There is a name for girls like Susu.

286.

"Knock, knock—" Inj said.

287.

Eloise wondered if she had made a terrible mistake.

288.

He went to the balcony and stood against the shadows. He asked her if she had heard the story of the statue in the lobby? He asked her did she know that the lady appeared in the doorway one day or maybe it was night many years ago? and that the two men who had brought the statue inside had gone snow white, hair that is, within hours? A girl sick with an ancient fever had touched the lady and was healed. It was true; the girl had grown up and was married to the night clerk. "Do you believe me?" he said. Did she believe him? "I believe you," Susu said.

289.

Susu broke the third rule of storytelling.

290.

Inj closed the door of the study.

Schell rose from his chair.

There was a bottle of vodka on the table.

He poured a drink from the bottle.

He gave the glass to Inj.

He poured himself a drink.

Behind the desk there was a bookshelf.

She turned her back to him.

She looked at the books.

"I bet you've read them all," she said.

She ran her hand, palm-flat against the spines—

Inj picked up her glass.

She sat beside Schell on the sofa.

She drank.

He refilled her glass.

She said, "I bet you know everything that there is to know."

She said, "I don't know about aqueducts, or which king killed which other king or what god did what to *whom*. I don't have every possible poem in the world memorized—"

She reached over and pulled the string on a lamp.

She turned it on, then off.

On then off.

On then off.

"I'm pretty," she said.

"You're beautiful," he said.

"I know," she said.

"I'd rather be important. Or tragic. But I'm not. I'm beautiful," she said.

She said, "Ben is important."

"Is he?" said Schell.

"You probably think that we are very silly."

"I don't," Schell said.

"Of course you do," she said. "Because in some ways we are."

Inj held her glass in both hands.

"I have to tell you something," she said.

He waited.

She turned toward him.

"Benny's gone dry," she said.

"What?" he said.

"He can't write," she said.

"You have to help him," she said.

"Help him?" said Schell.

"Yes," she said.

He asked her, "How would you like me to help him?"

"Don't joke," she said. "I can tell that you're joking."

She drank.

She pushed—in a funny girlish gesture—her hair from her face.

"Is it true?" she said. "That you've lived out here for years—but you haven't written anything? Is that right?"

He said that he supposed that it was right.

"Why?" she asked.

"Why what?" he said.

"Why don't you write?" she said.

"Does it make a difference?" he said.

"Does it matter why?" he said.

"I don't really understand," she said.

"Look at it this way," he said. "Between something and nothing; I choose nothing."

"You're being abstract, aren't you?" she said.

"Do you still like it then? writing, I mean," she said.

"That only matters to children," he said.

"What?" she asked.

He said, "Whether one likes a thing or not."

She paused.

She thought about it.

She seemed to be thinking about it.

She said, "I'm being such an idiot."

She leaned back against the sofa.

She said, "I wish I were thirty-six years old, wearing black satin and pearls."

She drank.

He reached for her glass.

He said, "Perhaps you've had enough."

"No, no," she said. "I've only just begun."

Inj was beautiful in the moonlight.

291.

Isn't Inj beautiful in the moonlight?

292.

Have you had enough?

293.

No, you've only just begun.

294.

"Please tell me what I can do for Benjamin Salt," Schell said.

295.

Inj rested her head back against the sofa.

"It's so quiet here," she said.

"Is it always so quiet?" she said.

"Ben can't stand the quiet. He keeps a radio on all the time," she said.

"What about you?" said Schell.

"What?" she said.

"You," he said.

"Oh," she said.

"You're being deep," she said. "I get it. Metaphysical and all that, right?"

"I am—" she said.

She closed her eyes.

"Whatever he wants me to be," she said.

She opened her eyes.

"Didn't I say that just the right way?" she said.

"May I have a little more to drink?" she asked.

"Didn't I say that just like a girl in a movie?" she said.

He filled her glass.

"Will you help him?" she asked.

"I'll do whatever you want me to do," he said.

She turned toward him on the sofa.

She set down her glass.

"Are you making fun of me?" she said.

He said, no; he wasn't making fun of her.

"Oh," she said. "Then you're being kind?"

He refilled his glass.

"Don't be kind to me," she said.

"Don't pity me," she said.

"I can't stand it," she said. "When men are kind."

She stood—uncertain—and then steadied herself.

"You don't know a thing about me," she said.

It was not an accusation.

It was only a weary statement of fact.

She stood behind him.

Inj touched his shoulder.

She leaned close.

Her hair brushed his cheek.

She whispered—

296.

Louis Sarasine looked out at the ocean. He saw two girls running into the water.

297.

"Don't you see?" Inj said. "You might have dreamed this. I practically don't exist."

298.

Louis said, "One sees a girl—and immediately wants to tell a story."

299.

Susu told him that he had better go. He kissed her on the forehead, and said, "Godnight."

300.

At dinner that night they sat, the foursome, around the wooden table in the kitchen.

The fare was simple: cassoulet, with dark bread and butter. Green plates, chipped cups, mismatched knives and forks; winter squash, blackberry preserves, and a rustic almost brusque bottle of burgundy, still dusty from the cellar.

Beatrice lighted the candles.

Inj watched Salt.

Schell sat at the head of the table.

He filled the wineglasses.

He said a toast to the travelers.

It was New Year's Eve.

They raised their glasses.

To the life of the mind.

Life, well, that was *something* wasn't it?

They ate and drank.

They spoke of such things as places and birds.

They talked of poetry and the Trojan War.

Of which god did what to whom.

And which king killed which king.

Salt, when he had eaten his fill, pushed his plate away—

He said, "Mr. Schell, you know, for the longest time I didn't believe that you were real."

Inj smiled. Like the last girl in the world.

And she rose to help Beatrice clear the table.

Outside the snow fell and fell. It was night. And there was nothing like it. Like night. Like being on an island at night during a snowstorm. Like being in a stone cottage in a kitchen, with a fire burning in the stove and the melting-down sweetness of waxing candles, and a black cat, though a bit ferocious, lurking in the warmth, and a spotted dog sleeping on a woven rug; while girls set cups upon saucers, men talked about the past; while the wind banged against the windows, and waves on the lake rolled up and crashed down. Still, one felt very safe, at the table waiting and awaiting coffee and cake and talking of the past, the past, great fallen Babylon; so it was hard to imagine that the house itself was no more than the fragile shell of an egg.

301.

Over a late supper one year or was it an early breakfast in the next? in a bustling diner amid drunken chatter, they fell upon their food (for her: Adam & Eve on a raft; for him: Burn one, take it through the garden, and pin a rose on it), famished. A jukebox was playing. A girl cried. A glass smashed to the floor. And then the plates were taken from their table by the overburdened waitress who left the man and the lady for a long time to their own devices and then perhaps repenting this inattention brought to them without prompting a banana split so improbable that Eloise felt dizzy with sweetness even as the bowl was placed on the table with two spoons and she couldn't say why the story of her life had taken such an odd turn and she didn't know what the author had next in store for her. She didn't know what was going to happen next as she looked at Zigouiller across the table, and he added cream to his coffee and reached with his spoon into the chocolate and cherries, and he said, "When are you going to leave your husband?"

302.
It is a species of unkindness not to wait for those who are slow. It is a kind of cruelty not to care for those who are weak. There are things worse than anger. The poet says we cannot fall out of the world. We are in it once and for all.

303.
"Let's leave tonight," said Zigouiller.

304.
Susu was happy after he left. And sad too.

305.
Susu was thinking about the starfish, the hermit crab, the whale's backbone.

306.

Eloise was thinking about gold and silver, ivory, apes, and peacocks.

307.

Salt said that he knew that it was late—

What could time mean to them?

Schell looked at Salt across the table.

"Can I have it?" said Salt.

Schell wanted to hate Salt.

He didn't hate him. Nor even did he envy him. He did not envy Salt's youth, his hope, or his ambition. He had only a sense of all the things in the world that were Salt's to lose.

"Don't you have one more question?" Schell asked.

And Salt said, "Is it too late?"

308.

Reality is never paper or scissors.

It is always rock.

It is a boulder.

309.

Salt's glasses caught the candlelight.

So it was hard to see that his dark eyes glittered too.

310.

Inj rested her face in her hands.

311.

Beatrice refilled Inj's glass.

312.
Is the coffee ready yet?

313.
Schell looked at Salt.

314.
Susu looked just like her mother.

315.
The night was cold. The car was hot. Zigouiller was driving. Eloise pushed back the collar of her coat. She placed her cheek against the window. Then felt a slight revulsion and pulled away. She stared out the window. And for a moment, she mistook the shadow of her equipage for blackbirds in the snow.

316.
Schell was thinking about the girl in the snow.

317.
Olga told the boys that they could stay up to watch one year fall to the next, but Chester and Jules fell asleep in their pajamas in front of the television.

318.
Dibby was typing.

319.
Susu was becoming less and less real.

320.
Schell wasn't sure that there had ever been a girl in the snow.

321.

Zigouiller took the key from Eloise's hand, and he unlocked the door.

322.

What happened to that girl in the snow?

323.

Is Eloise going to leave her husband? Is that how her story is to go?

324.

Eris loved disorder.

325.

Susu saw that he had left an envelope on the night table.

326.

Aren't the roasted potatoes wonderful?
    With fennel? Is that right?
    Have you ever had anything so wonderful?
    Is there dessert?
    Beatrice refilled Inj's glass.
    Inj had had too much wine.
    There was talk of fate and destiny.
    Of whether God was a watchmaker.
    Or God liked to watch.
    Inj pushed her hair from her face.
    The time had come.
    To speak of aqueducts and starfish.
    Of cabbages and kings.
    And who did what to whom.

And why?

Waves rose up and crashed down.

Salt said that he was ready—

He asked Schell if he could see it.

327.

It?

328.

Schell rose from his chair.

He left the room.

He came back with the manuscript.

And he set it on the table.

329.

Salt drank.

330.

At home. Amid the chaos. Lipstick, stockings.

Eris reached into her bag.

She opened her closed palm.

331.

Susu looked at the envelope.

332.

Schell wanted to reach out and grab the manuscript back.

It wasn't finished.

333.

"What's this?" said Salt.

334.
A spider crept along the diamond tile.

Susu found her scissors.

335.
Inj turned to Ben.

336.
The envelope was sealed, and written upon in a ghost hand. That's what people say isn't it? A ghost hand?

337.
Susu took the scissors and she cut off her long dark hair.

338.
Of all the gods nailed to the cross, Discord was the most beautiful.

339.
"The story," said Schell. "That you came here for. Here it is."

340.
Salt said, "I didn't come here for a story. I came here for the type-writer."

341.
"The typewriter?" said Schell.

342.
"The typewriter. I collect them," said Salt. "Haven't you read my book?" he asked.

343.

"Of course not," said Schell.

344.

Beatrice burst out laughing.

345.

It began to snow.

346.

Eloise held her wineglass in such a languorous manner that Zigouiller touched her face and said, "In the room the women come and go talking of Joe DiMaggio."

347.

Here Comes Everyone is the story of a young writer named Benjamin Salt who collects the typewriters upon which his favorite novels had been written.

348.

Babylon Must Fall is a love story.

349.

S. Z. Schell preferred tragedy to comedy.

350.

"My typewriter? I don't have a typewriter," said Schell. "I haven't had one for years."

351.

Inj owed everyone an explanation.

352.

Eloise said, "Do you want to hear a story?"

353.

Susu knew that all the poetry in the world would not save her.

354.

Inj said, "The truth is—"

355.

Save her from what?

356.

Eris opened her palm to reveal an ink pen.

357.

Louis Sarasine, his fork in the chocolate cake, said, "The truth is—"

358.

The truth is a knot of green string.

359.

Susu packed her suitcase.

360.

"My client killed those girls," said Louis Sarasine. "He knew it. And I knew it. But the truth was and is irrelevant. The only thing that mattered was how I told his story."

361.

Inj turned to Schell.

She said, "I sent you the letters."

And she turned to Salt.

She said, "Benny, I told you that he wanted to give you the type-writer."

Then she picked up her glass, and she drank.

362.
But why?

363.
"Jesus," Inj said. "You *writers.* You act as though you've never heard of a plot twist."

364.
Eloise said that she knew a story so terrible the telling of it might curse the two of them forever.

"Tell me," said Zigouiller.

365.
The manuscript sat on the table.

It was a symbol, after all.

And one could have used a different word than *manuscript.*

Such as *stone* or *shell* or *bird* or *cat* or *corpse* or *chair* or *peppermint* or *paper.*

Somewhere between *ink* and *ether.*

Between *shoe* and *sock.*

And *tock* and *tick.*

And *scissors* and *rock.*

Between *either* and *or*—

The coffee drip by drop fell into the pot.

The green glass dessert plates were set one atop the next.

And the drifts of snow lay white in the dark woods.

366.

Susu stopped to touch her palm flat to the broken face of the goddess before leaving the hotel.

367.

Inj said, "Benny, his story will help you more than a haunted typewriter."

368.

Salt said, "You want a story?"

369.

Eloise said, "Do you remember the morning that you broke the clock?"

370.

Inj said, "I'm sorry, Benny. I really am."

371.

Zigouiller did not speak, not just yet; because there was no line written for him.

372.

Eloise said, "—When we lived by the ocean? You used to bring me that awful salted licorice."

"I thought that you liked it," Zigouiller said.

"Liked it?" she said. "I hated it. Then I came around to it."

373.

"What do we do now?" said Beatrice.

374.

Zola barked at a shadow.

375.

"Would you like to know how Inj and I met?" said Salt.

376.

"It's a tradition," said Salt. "To tell stories. To tell ghost stories. If you are lucky enough to be snowbound in an old house in the middle of nowhere."

"Where did you hear that?" asked Schell.

"Oh," said Salt, smoking.

He exhaled. "Henry James, I think."

"Ashes," said Inj as she pushed a saucer toward him.

"—To ashes," he said. "Inj and I met at a funeral. Inj in black, crying. Inj with white lilies. Do you know what she said to me? Do you? She came up to me, this girl. Look at her. She said, 'Roman Stone is dead.' It was a stupid thing to say, because I was, because we were at his funeral. Weren't we?" Salt said.

377.

Eloise said that sometimes now she absolutely craved licorice.

378.

Inj said, "Benny, stop."

379.

Benny did not stop.

380.

Zigouiller said, "What clock?"

381.

Eloise said, "My brother killed a girl."

382.

Eloise did not tell Zigouiller the story of the broken clock.

383.

Zigouiller said nothing.

    This was exactly what Eloise wanted him to say.

384.

Salt said to Schell, "Inj wants me to stop. Should I? Would you? Would you stop? No, no you don't even know how to begin."

385.

Inj said, "We met in a graveyard."

386.

Salt looked at Inj.

    "At the heart of all things is a knife," she said.

    "Here comes the end," he said.

    "Here comes everyone," she said.

    "Now you've got the hang of it," said Salt.

    "I do," she said. "Don't I?"

    "You're the cat at a bowl of cream," he said.

    "I love cats," she said.

    "I love cream," she said. "Isn't that stupid?"

    "In the end," he said, "someone is going to be left holding the knife."

"Is this the end?" she said.

Salt looked across the table.

He looked at Beatrice.

"What are you looking at?" he said.

"You're a strange bird," he said.

He turned to Schell.

"She's a strange bird," Salt said.

"Beatrice," said Salt. "Are you ever afraid?"

"Of what?" said Beatrice.

He paused.

He smoked.

"Falling," he said.

"Falling?" said Beatrice.

"You might fall from a branch and break a wing," said Salt.

"Leave her alone," said Inj.

"Beatrice," he went on. "Beatrice—are you superstitious? Do you believe in ghosts? Or poetic justice? If, say, I were cursed," he laughed. "How would I break the spell?"

"You aren't cursed," said Inj. "God, don't say things like that."

"I am cursed." he said. "And stop calling me God."

"Drumroll, please," he said.

Inj pounded the table with a drumroll.

"Sheldon Schell," said Salt with mock reverence.

"Who is S. Z. Schell?" he said.

"What?" said Schell.

"S. Z. Schell," said Salt. "Author. Or not. The has-been who never was. The hermit self-exiled to a life of depriving the rest of us of his greatness. How's that for a story?"

"I don't have the typewriter," Schell said.

"I know about the girl," said Salt.

The manuscript sat upon the table.

No one moved.

Not a spoon, nor finger.

While in the woods the snow fell.

And was falling.

"What girl?" said Schell.

"Have there been? are there," said Salt.

"Benny, don't," said Inj.

"—So many girls that you've lost track?" said Salt.

Salt laughed.

"Let me clarify," he said.

It was quiet.

It was so quiet.

Schell was aware of the falling snow.

And the beating of his telltale heart.

Could everyone hear his heart?

"Your wife," said Salt.

"My wife?" said Schell.

"She died," said Salt.

He paused.

He smoked.

"And she left you a fortune," he said.

"So?" said Inj. "People die all the time."

"Well put," said Salt.

Salt pointed at Schell.

"You're a ghoul," he said.

"He's a ghoul," said Salt.

"What?" said Inj.

"A ghoul. Living off a dead girl."

"Picking her bones clean," said Salt.

"Don't talk about his wife," said Inj.

Salt laughed.

"Look at Inj," he said. "She's going to tell me—to tell us—how to bury the dead. She's been places. She's done things. Just look at her, will you? Look at Inj. How can you not look at her? Whatta face. Where are her ships? Where is her army? She's got a story too. Tell them your story," he said. "Go on. Tell them about Roman and how you inspired him."

"I did so *inspire* him," she said.

"I loved him," said Inj.

"Do you ever think before you speak? Jesus," said Salt.

"Benny," she said.

She put her hand on his arm.

"Don't be angry," she said.

"Benny," she said.

Inj looked at him.

"I'm sorry," she said.

"I'm so sorry," she said.

Salt shrugged.

He smoked.

"So?" he said.

"So Inj lied," he said. "At least she's sorry, right? Inj told me that you promised me the typewriter. I just had to come here to get it. What did she promise you?"

The manuscript lay on the table.

He ashed his cigarette.

And with his white hands like small furious doves—

Rising out of a silk hat—

Salt reached for the manuscript.

Just as he did—

Beatrice grabbed it.

She held it in her arms.

And she ran from the room.

387.

Inj searched the house for Beatrice.

388.

If Susu Zigouiller were, say, a work of art; if Susu were a book: she was not a good book. Not the sort that is easily understood or enjoyed. She was not a best seller or a page turner. No, rather, she was a great novel, a book whose greatness rests entirely in the willing reader's heart. And one cannot say why or how this mysterious greatness is achieved, and yet there it is.

389.

Zigouiller helped Eloise off with her dress.

390.

Louis Sarasine made a compelling case for his own moral objectivity. He defended the innocent and the guilty alike. He was aware of the absurdity of this: the terms *guilt* and *innocence* are antiques—a Grecian urn, a golden bowl, an ossuary box—best placed upon a high shelf.

391.

"I believe," said Louis. "That there are monsters in the world."

392.

What you believe or do not believe is, of course, entirely up to you.

393.

There was a book on Eloise's bedside table.

394.

Schell said to Salt, "Crash, bang, boom."

395.

Zigouiller picked up the book.

396.

"The truth is," said Eloise, "I've never read it. Isn't that stupid of me?"

397.

Eloise had never read *Babylon Must Fall.* She bought copy after copy. Every time that she went into a bookstore she bought a copy. She tried to read it, really she did. She had tried time and again, but she could never go past the first line.

At the heart of all things is a knife.

398.

Salt said to Schell, "We didn't meet in a graveyard. It wasn't a graveyard. It wasn't a funeral. When I heard that Stone had died, had been killed—when I read the details: the knife, the cake—I knew that I had to go to his funeral; but there wasn't a funeral. He was already turned to ash. So I went to the memorial. I don't like that word: *memorial.* She was the nanny, Inj was. An *au pair* they call it. For his boys. I met Inj. In her black dress. I saw his wife. I saw his boys. I saw his life; I—I hated him. I hated him for being real. I hated him for dying. I hated him for being dead. I wanted to be part of the story. I wanted to write myself into his story. I needed his typewriter. I knew that the only way that I could write myself into his world would be to do it on his typewriter. I saw Inj. I met Inj. She got me an ink pen. But, I wanted the typewriter. She told me that you had it; that you would give it to me. She said that she could get it from you. I believed her. I want the typewriter. I need it. I want it. I am part of the story. I always was."

399.

There were many lines, and Eloise had not read them.

400.

"That story about your father—is it true?" said Salt.

"Did he really make coffins?" said Salt.

"Coffins, caskets—" said Schell.

"And he taught you how to do that?" said Salt.

"How to use a hammer," said Schell.

"He killed your mother?" said Salt.

"You must have hated him," said Salt.

"My father?" said Schell.

"No," said Salt. "Roman."

They sat in silence.

As the candles burned.

"Do you know who killed Roman?" said Schell.

Salt removed his eyeglasses.

He set them, bows down, on the table.

He rubbed his eyes.

The candles were burning down.

Salt said, "I think Inj exists only for me. Is that wrong?"

"It isn't right," said Schell.

"No?" said Salt.

He gave a dry laugh.

"But then, what is?" he said.

Schell said nothing.

Schell was thinking about his wife in her hospital bed.

Schell was thinking about the girl's naked body in the snow.

He was thinking about kerosene and turpentine.

About the locust.

And the flood.

And Babylon the great sweet mysterious harlot.

And the difference between sugar and salt.

And the mold upon roses.

Rocks, moss, stonecrop, iron, merds.

A book upon a shelf.

And a name upon a page.

Everything meant nothing.

And *nothing* was the blank page.

There was nothing.

Between one minute and the next.

One letter and the next.

Between breasts.

Between thighs.

The slip of the tongue between *s* and *z*.

"My mother—" Salt said.

In the light of waxing candles.

"Her name is Wren," he said. "Do you remember her? A girl with that name? Did you know her?" Salt asked.

401.

Beatrice ran through the woods.

402.

Eloise said, "You will always be able to do what you want with me."

403.

Schell looked at Salt.

404.

"I didn't kill Roman Stone," said Salt.

  "But I wish that I had," he said.

405.

Eris believed in the novel as the only truly feminine art form.

406.

Zigouiller kissed Eloise and her hair smelled of smoke.

407.

Years later when he was old and prolific and so important that one could barely speak of literature, let alone letters, without uttering his name, Benjamin Salt told an audience of rapt listeners in a packed lecture hall in Oslo the story of how he received—as a gift; a token, an apple of sin; like a box, that he had only to pull the string and untie, unbind—the inspiration for his second novel. He told of his moonlight journey through the woods, through drifts of snow, to take hold of a manuscript that had been stolen from his grasp by a girl—yet he omitted the part about the typewriter. He did not tell that part of the story.

Instead he told his story this way:

"Many years ago when I was young and thought about nothing but art, night and day, I contracted a strange suffocating illness. I went on a journey—a pilgrimage, really—in search of a cure. The cure, in my case, was no unguent or herb, no pill or injection; no, the remedy was a story. I traveled a distance to find the man who could tell me this story. You see, I was suffering from writer's block. How was I to live without words on the page? I lived in a terror of emptiness. I did not know yet the lesson to be learned from lack. As I say, I was young and took symbols where I could find them. So what could I do? I did what dreamers do. I did what is done in the movies: I headed out on the road with a beautiful girl. Well, that didn't work out," he paused, as the audience laughed. "We were young," he went on, "and love was an inevitability. The man for whom I searched had promised to give me the manuscript of his memoir—he was peculiar, a recluse. I won't speak his name, as he so valued his privacy. He would only allow me to read this memoir on the condition that I came to visit him on his island. He was lonely there, lonely with his terrible knowledge. We arrived on New Year's Eve just before a storm, and found ourselves—the four of us—snowbound. This recluse had a girl—no more than a child—living with him. It was rumored that the island was haunted, that the inhabitants were possessed. These were rumors, of course—" he seemed to lose his way in the telling of his story. There was silence; it lasted almost too long. No one moved. No one coughed. Or whispered. And then in the dark and hush of the auditorium, Salt spoke, "On the night before I was to leave—he gave me his manuscript and promised that with the reading of its pages would come a cure to my affliction. How could this be? I held out my hands to receive my medicine, my antidote—the perfect story—when just then that girl, that strange possessed child, stole the manuscript, gathered it in her arms, and made off with it into the woods—into the snow. What could I do but go after her? I followed her by the moonlight. She led me through the darkness. I called out to her. She ran on ahead of me. She lost me. She eluded me in the trees. She fluttered up as a bird. I chased her shadow. She disappeared. —I fell; I lost my footing on an icy incline—I slipped and fell down, down—and when I landed, as I lay on my back in the snow, in the cold, staring up at those starry twins, Castor and Pollux, and the vast blue of the black sky; I knew then, not fear, nor anger—but a story—word by word—complete, whole—a world of words. I knew every word and the space between every letter. I knew; I knew what had happened. And what was yet to happen. I opened my eyes to the heavens—and there before me was a house. Do you believe that there is such a thing as the house of fiction, ladies and gentlemen? I do. I saw it that night. I saw the house of fiction rise up out of the wilderness and all her lights were blazing."

He said the woods were haunted.

He lost his way.

He fell in the snow.

He lay in the snow staring up at the black sky.

And then he saw the doctor's house rise up before him.

And he saw light in Beatrice's windows.

He went to it.

408.

Beatrice was kind to Salt. He would have to spend the night. He couldn't go back through the woods. She showed him her father's house. Salt looked in astonishment at the ruins of a botched civilization: the books and paintings; the marble statuettes and figurines. They drank plum brandy. And when it came around to it, Salt asked her for the manuscript.

409.

Eloise was thinking about what Roman had done to her.

410.

"I should have gone with Benny," said Inj.

In the kitchen, she stood at the window.

The room was warm. The fire was bright in the stove.

"There's a path through the woods," Schell said.

"He'll get lost," she said.

"He'll lose his way," she said.

She placed a hand against the glass.

The clock ticked.

Snow fell.

Inj turned from the window.

On the table was the Santa Fe cake.

Schell took up the knife and he cut two big slices.

He set them each upon a plate.

She sat.

"Have you ever had Santa Fe cake?" he asked.

She said no, she hadn't.

She picked up a fork.

"Do you miss him?" she said.

"I hadn't seen him in years," Schell said.

"He wasn't the kind of person that you can forget," she said. "Was he?"

Schell said no, he supposed that Ro was pretty hard to forget.

And God knows that he had tried.

"Oh," said the girl. "You're joking again."

She set down her fork.

She broke a bit of cake with her fingers.

"I hate jokes," she said.

"I saw Ro hit a girl once," said Schell.

"Did you?" said Inj.

"Yes," he said.

She said, "What happened to her?"

"What happened to the girl?" she said.

He said that it was a long time ago.

"Look," he said. "It's stopped snowing."

It really had stopped snowing.

And everything in the world was perfectly still.

"Does it bother you to talk about Roman? I like talking about him," she said. "I like saying his name. You told me that *like* is a word for children. And I felt so stupid," she said.

"I'm sorry," he said.

"Are you? For what?" she said.

"You don't have to apologize to me," she said. "It only makes it worse. I'm not the sort of girl who needs apologies."

She ate.

"Do you want to hear my story?" she said.

She laughed.

"The truth is that I don't have a story to tell you," she said. "There is nothing mysterious about me. I didn't have a lousy childhood. Nothing tragic has ever happened to me."

She ate with her fingers.

"This is so good," she said.

"Do you want to know about me and Ro?" she said.

She rose and brought the coffeepot to the table.

She liked coffee with her cake.

She didn't like cake without coffee.

She liked the bitter and the sweet together.

She filled his cup.

And then her own cup.

She added cream.

She turned her spoon round in her cup.

"He threw me over for another girl," she said.

"I didn't hold it against him," she said. "How could I?"

She went on, "Ro died. And I met Benny."

"What about the typewriter?" he said.

"Benny wanted it," she said.

"I don't have it," he said.

"I know," she said.

"Why did you write to me?" he said.

She turned her spoon in her coffee cup.

"I'm sobering up," she said.

There was a bottle of brandy in the cabinet.

He got the bottle.

He poured some into her cup.

She drank.

"Ro used to talk about you," she said.

"And your sister," she said.

"Why do you read books?" she asked.

"Some people," she said. "Read books to learn things, or to escape."

"I'm so envious of other girl's tragedies," she said. "I guess that's why I read books: to imagine that I'm that tragic girl around whom the whole wide world revolves."

"I was a little envious," she said.

"Don't be," he said.

He said, "I hadn't seen him in years."

"Not of you," she said.

She pushed her hair from her face.

With a palm against her forehead.

"Of your sister," she said.

She drank.

"I sent you the letters," she said.

"I'm sorry," she said.

She smiled.

Sad, wan—

"I'm not really sorry," she said.

She looked down into the cup.

She looked up.

"He was waiting," she said.

"Waiting?" said Schell.

"For you," she said.

"He said he couldn't write his book until you wrote yours."

"He was waiting for you, and—you; you were waiting to tell the perfect story," she said.

"Do you know what I think?" she said.

"I think every story is the perfect story," she said.

"Isn't that stupid of me?" she said.

"You loved him," he said.

"You make it sound ugly," she said.

"You make it sound like an accusation," she said.

"I suppose it was ugly," she said.

She drank the last of her cup.

"Did you write your story?" she said.

"I did," he said.

"Why?" she said.

"It's my story," he said.

"Who else would tell it?" he said.

"Now who's being stupid?" she said.

"So you did it for Ro," he said.

"Yes," she said.

"I think, I thought—it's what he would have wanted," she said.

"And you always did what he wanted," Schell said.

"I did," she said. "Didn't you?"

411.

"Beatrice," said Salt.

He set his glass on the table.

Her face was strange in the lamplight.

She leaned back against the sofa.

The tapestry flowers, the brown, the forest green.

He touched her cheek.

He touched her dark hair back from her face.

"Don't you know who I am?" he said.

He took her hands in his own hands.

He put his hands over hers and held them together.

Beatrice did not pull away.

He raised her hands to his lips.

And kissed her fingers one by one.

"I know just who you are," said Beatrice.

Salt looked at her with his dark damp serious eyes.

"Who's that?" he said.

"You're the monster in the maze," she said.

"I hate you so much," she said.

"Then why don't you stop me?" he asked.

"I can't," she said.

Salt pulled the chain on the lamp.

He knocked a glass swan from the table.

It fell to the floor.

And shattered.

412.

The black-and-white dog sleeping by the warmth of the fire awoke.

413.

Olga carried Chester on her hip, and she led Julian by the hand, from the television to the bedroom.

414.

Dibby, in the study where no one did, heard Olga putting the boys to bed.

415.

Susu, waiting in line to have her passport stamped, looked at her wristwatch.

416.

Eloise was thinking about what she had done to Roman.

417.

Elizabeth Weiss was watching a crime drama on television.

418.

A hand—though deft, though quick—could not have stopped the fall of the china swan to the floor, where it shattered; its long neck snapped.

Oh well, it was an ugly thing anyway.

Salt let go.

Beatrice cried out.

419.

One can neither win nor lose on the topic of aesthetics. Whether the swan was ugly or not had little to do with the fact that it was broken, in glass pieces on the floor. One could have collected the pieces and perhaps with patience and glue reassembled the cygnet to its former majesty. One could have done and still might do so many things.

One likes a thing or does not like a thing. Even if *like* itself is the province and provenance of children, one still *likes* a thing or does not *like* a thing.

The swan was white, with an orange beak, with claws, and it stood on its legs rising upward, its wide white wings unfolded. It was a regal stance, this posture; a threatening position, but it betrayed the flaw of the maker's design. For when an errant hand in pursuit of the chain on the lamp brushed against the statue that had stood upon the edge of the table for years and years as though waiting for that hand; when that elbow knocked the swan from the table to the wooden floor, first the legs broke, then the neck snapped; the beak chipped, the wings fractured; the dark eyes stared up into the darkness.

One shouldn't confuse one's own ugliness with the ugliness of the world.

420.

In Sheldon Schell's study, the dim light of a desk lamp cast a shadow against the flowered wallpaper, upon a painting done in green and brown and white of a girl being raped in the woods.

421.

Bruno Salt awoke in his bed.

422.

Dibby typed from one year into the next.

And then suddenly it happened.

423.

What?

424.

The customs agent looked at the pages of the girl's passport. He looked at the girl. He asked her to remove her sunglasses. She did. He asked what she had done on her travels. She said she had seen the world. She asked with a small amount of irritation, if there was a problem? He said, no. He said there was no problem. Susu said, good, because she was going home.

425.

A hand fumbled, an errant elbow knocked; the fingers of a fist uncurled.

426.

Dibby came to the end of the manuscript.

427.

There is a theory. It says: The closest definition of art that one can come to is beauty plus pity. One is sad when beauty dies. And beauty always dies. The manner dies with the matter. And the world of subjectivity dies with the individual.

428.

The book was unfinished.

429.

The typewriter was green. It was not heavy. It was light. It was portable. The Baby Hermes was a modern miracle of Swiss ingenuity. It had still after all these years its original clamshell metal case. It was bought new in 1960 by a very pregnant Mrs. Eloise Schell. As she had always wanted to write a novel.

430.

If Julian or Chet Stone had awoken and crept along the hallway toward the door, ajar; he might have seen Mother in the room they called Father's; seen Mother knotting and unknotting a green ribbon; Mother opening a desk drawer; Mother holding a tin box in her small hands.

431.

There was something else in the bottom of Eris's bag.

She had taken from his house a memento more meaningful than Salt's pen.

432.

Olga was in the kitchen baking cinnamon bread. Won't it be nice to have warm with butter in the morning?

433.

Louis Sarasine, thoroughly convinced of the validity of his own position, was trying to persuade his fellow members of the Mnemosyne Society that memory was a game.

They were inclined to believe that she was a goddess.

434.

The ruined fountain in the doctor's garden was constructed of stone and had been fed by a now-barren cistern. Once it held a water so cold that the original settlers had claimed that it healed their woes. That it was a poison to dark spirits. That men who bathed in it spoke the truth. That birds who drank from it would never die, and flowers that grew around it were a honey for bees and a balm for heartbroken girls; it was said that the perfume of the garden led one into a sleep whose dreams foretold the future.

435.

Eloise watched the snow falling.

436.

It was snowing. And it was going to snow.

437.

Eloise Sarasine in a black nightdress sat at the executioner's table among relics, indulgences, and treasures: winter apples, a silver knife, a cedar box, a fountain pen. She rested her face in her hand. In the other hand she held a red ball.

438.

Eris had stolen Bruno's little plastic dinosaur.

439.

The cistern had gone dry.

    This is only a metaphor.

    Or at least it is metaphoric.

440.

Inj wanted to finish the brandy.

    She took the bottle into the bedroom.

    Schell followed her.

    She sat on the bed.

    She drank.

    The room was warm.

    With the woodstove in the corner.

    A heap of kindling, a bundle of newspapers.

    The door to the stove was open.

    The fire was the only light.

    Schell added wood to the fire.

    She was so close to him.

    Her hand on his arm.

    There was a burning sweetness to her skin.

    She said, "Roman told me that you lie."

    She shrugged her shoulders.

    "I don't mind liars," she said.

    She said, "He told me that you married a girl with a lot of money. And when she died it came to you."

    "It's true," he said.

    "Troo troo troo," she said.

    She laughed.

She stopped laughing.

"He said that you killed her," she said.

"Who?" he said.

"Your wife," she said.

"Why would I do that?" he said.

"Because you couldn't stop yourself," she said.

"Because you are tragic," she said.

"Your life is a Greek tragedy," she said.

"You are Sisyphus," she said.

"Pushing a rock up a hill," she said. "As punishment."

"Is that what you do?" she said.

"That's not so bad," she said.

"Hey," she said, "at least you have a rock. And a hill to push it up."

"That's something, right?" she said.

"Some people don't even have that," she said.

"Nothing terrible will ever happen to me, will it?" she said.

"No one will ever murder me," she said.

She seemed disappointed.

A log shifted in the stove.

"Did Ro tell you," said Schell.

He drank from the bottle.

"—How he stole my story?"

She laughed.

"No one can really steal a story," she said.

"No?" he said.

"Because every story is—" she said.

"Like a snowflake?" he said.

"You're making fun again," she said.

She closed her eyes.

"Oh well," she said.

"Tell me," she said.

"Have you kept the key all these years?" she said.

"What key?" he said.

"To the box," she said.

She turned toward the stove.

"What a nice fire," she said.

"What a nice fiery fire," she said.

"Is this the story?" she said.

"Are you telling your story right now?" she said.

"Is it happening now?" she said.

"Am I in it?" she said.

"Am I prettier in the story than in real life?" she said.

"Is it an old story?" she said.

He was thinking about the black cat.

He was thinking about birds.

"People like them," she said. "The old stories."

"Don't they?" she said.

"I do," she said.

"This is what I would do in the story," she said.

She kissed him.

She was beautiful.

Or maybe she wasn't.

It was only that so many other things were ugly.

The fire burned in the stove.

The room was warm.

The fire was fiery.

She overfilled the glasses.

She was naked on the bed.

She said, "Do you think that the novel is dead?"

And she laughed.

By the light of candles.

441.

Eloise rolled the ball across the floor.

    Zola chased after it.

442.

Eloise followed Zola.

    Or Zola followed Eloise.

    Each time that Eloise rolled the ball.

    Zola brought it back to her.

    Eloise went from room to room, rolling the ball.

    Round and round, past her clocks—

    Her vases—

    The weave and weft of tapestry—

    The floral, the plum, the shadow, the umber.

    Her tables and chairs and lamps—

    Her paintings and photographs.

    Her cedar box.

    Her desk, an escritoire.

    The statuettes, the gods and goddesses.

    The unsmashed idols.

    The unread books—

    The ball rolled.

    Her pearl-handled letter knife.

    She picked it up from the desk.

    It was a gift from her daughter.

    Sent from far away.

    Eloise held the knife in her hand.

    There was a reassuring solidity to it.

    It was small and feminine and fit nicely in her hand.

    What a terrible thing for that boy to stab those girls in the woods. One girl had lived. She had crawled along the road—

Louie had disproved the girl's testimony at the trial.

He had made her doubt herself.

Made her doubt more than her memory.

Made her doubt her own broken bones.

Her own blood.

How could Louie do such a thing?

That boy had been found *not guilty.*

There was another word for it.

The ball bounced.

The girl was not a reliable witness.

Guilt was not tangible.

Innocence was not relevant.

Girls were not reliable.

They showed those girls over and over on television.

From home movies. From videotape—

In school plays, ballet recitals, in pageants and prom dresses.

Bloody faces and broken bones.

One face after the next.

One girl after the next.

Eloise took the knife.

She took the stairs, one by one.

Zola chased the ball.

Eloise held the banister.

And went up the staircase.

One step after the next.

She stood in the doorway of her bedroom.

Zigouiller lay sleeping.

He wasn't real.

Or maybe he was.

Then the shadows shifted.

And he was real.

Or at least real enough.

He was Zigouiller, as she had named him.

She stood watching him sleep.

443.

All at once, without regard to sequence or consequence:

A glass swan fell to the floor and shattered.

A sleeping dog woke.

A remarkable thing happened to Beatrice.

Salt had a sentence in his head.

Dr. Lemon dreamed a dream, and, lo, a cake of barley bread tumbled down.

Beatrice collected the broken pieces of the swan.

The last light in the doctor's house was extinguished.

A bird flew from a branch.

Snow lay white in the woods.

Snow fell upon the ruined fountain.

Inj lay naked on her hip.

She lighted a candle.

Inj asked Schell, did he? had he really killed his wife?

How did he do it?

Did he plot? Or was it done in anger?

Schell laughed.

The roses on the wallpaper trembled.

The black cat leapt upon a table.

The waves crashed upon rock.

Eloise stood in the doorway looking at Zigouiller asleep in her husband's bed.

Eloise was thinking about the burning roof and tower.

And Agamemnon dead.

Bruno cried out in the night. He woke from a dream in which he was being chased by a flock of geese. He called for his mother. And when she came to him, he asked her for a story.

While reading to her son from his favorite book—the one about an impossibly curious little bear who gets his head stuck in a honey pot—Elizabeth Weiss paused upon the page.

Bruno tugged at his mother's sleeve.

She began reading where she had left off.

The bear cracked the pot. And ate the honey.

When the last page of the book had been read—

Bruno turned back to the first page.

And Liz began again.

Olga, in the kitchen, covered a pan with a dishcloth.

Dibby sat on the floor in her husband's study with her legs curled beneath her. In the desk drawer, she found the tin box.

She turned the box over in her hands.

Chester, no, it was Julian, no, it was Chet, nearly opened his eyes. A thought, an idea, a desire, almost woke him. He wanted scrambled eggs for breakfast.

Dibby lifted the lid.

And then she stopped, as though waiting to be stopped.

No one stopped her.

Just like in the movies.

She was small.

She was dressed in black.

Dough began to rise.

Dibby opened the box.

It was empty.

Except for.

One photograph, blurry.

A picture of Roman and a dark-haired girl on a beach.

Dibby didn't recognize the girl.

Dibby sat on the floor.

Looking at the photograph.

The girl was not beautiful.

Dibby reached into the desk drawer.

Her hand found—without looking—

Her fingers rested upon the scissors.

Dibby took the scissors.

She cut the photograph into two.

And she cut each piece into two.

Until there were many tiny pieces.

There was no Roman. There was no girl.

Dibby threw the pieces into the fireplace.

She rose from the floor.

She stood at her husband's desk; the monumental mahogany desk—and then she sat in his Herculean chair.

She took a blank sheet of paper.

She rolled the paper into the carriage of the typewriter.

Dibby set her fingers to the keys.

For a moment she faltered.

Like a branch after the bird has flown.

And then her heart fluttered upward.

And she knew just what to say.

She knew how to finish Roman's story.

The bear found the honey.

And a train chugged up a hill.

Bruno fell asleep.

Elizabeth kept reading.

A spider spun silk in a bathtub.

Eris held the dinosaur in her hand.

Inj was naked.

Like a girl painted on a Grecian urn.

Inj kissed Schell.

Snow was falling.

Everything fell.

The snow.

The blankets from the bed.

The bottle from the table.

The bottle spilled.

Knocking over the candle.

The flame caught the path of brandy.

And followed it—

The fire crept along a strand of green twine.

The green twine bound a stack of newspapers beside the woodstove.

The newspapers caught fire.

The fire spread to the wallpaper.

It burned the flowers.

It climbed along the curtains.

The fire spread to the kitchen, where it ate cake.

To the study.

It read every book.

It read each letter.

It crawled. It crept.

It roamed.

It ran.

It wasn't afraid of anything.

The fire ran along the walls.

And took hold of a painting.

First the swan.

Then the girl.

Then the dark woods burned.

Susu Zigouiller before the mirror in an airport bathroom studied her face.

On a mantel over a fireplace a broken clock began to tick. And kept up time for eighteen minutes before suddenly, and perhaps even reluctantly, giving up the ghost.

Eloise stood beside the bed, holding the knife.

Louis was arguing the rules of the game.

Susu was boarding an airplane.

A red ball rolled.

The knife fell.

Eloise let the knife fall from her hand to the floor.

So no one knew.

No one suspected.

Except a French bulldog.

That time could stop and start.

Of its own mechanism.

Of its own desire.

Of its own free will.

Such miracles will happen now and again.

CHAPTER 19

Eloise lets the dark flower blossom

ROMAN TOLD HER ABOUT THE WOODS. It was the night when he and that girl, the actress, what was her name? Harlow—had that fight and she fell into the champagne fountain in her white dress and the picture of her ran in the tabloids. He pushed the girl into the fountain. The photographers kept snapping flash after flash,

and Ro was laughing. The girl lost it. They had to drag her away
into an ambulance. Ro was talking about the actress, how stupid she
was. How stupid actors were. He said, he asked her, "Why'd you
have to go and marry an actor?" They drove home through the dark
night. He said—

"Eloise."

He had a story.

Maybe it would be the beginning of his new book.

Did she want to hear it?

"The story starts in an old farmhouse," he said. "They went out
into the woods, three of them, that day. Two boys and a girl."

"It was snowing," he said. "One on each side of her, they
walked, and the girl between them. She was carrying ice skates.
They walked toward the frozen pond. And when they returned in
darkness, there were only two of them."

She said, "Shut up please please please, will you?"

He said, "Something terrible happened in the woods."

He said, "The girl was dead."

She said, "Stop it."

He said, "No one ever found out about the girl. And so the boys
never talked about it or her again. They never talked about the girl
or the woods."

Did she like the story so far?

At first he had been sickened by it.

Then horrified.

Then guilty.

And then the story had taken hold of him.

He thought about it.

He imagined it.

He tried to understand it.

"Envy," he said.

"What?" she said.

"The girl," he said.

"What about her?" she said.

"The gods must have envied her," he said.

She wanted him to stop talking, but he didn't stop.

Or wouldn't.

He talked of gods and girls.

He was talking.

The car stopped.

They were home.

Home?

The house by the water.

It was a hot night.

He took her arm.

In the dark.

It was quiet.

They walked to the house.

He said something about the sky, about the stars, about the constellations.

Wasn't the sky beautiful?

Wasn't Discord the most beautiful of the gods?

Or was she a goddess?

He said Fate was a girl with scissors.

They sat in the kitchen. And wasn't the light the sky the world beautiful then? They drank. She drank. He kept filling the glasses. He smoked. He said that he hadn't written a word of the story. He liked to know how a story was to end before he began writing it on paper. He said that he didn't know how it ended. Her dress was black. The green typewriter was on the table. He said, "If you were writing it, how would it end?" He picked up the clock. He said that he was going to write a book about what happened in the woods.

He was winding the metal clock. She told him that Zig would be back soon. "*Fatherland,*" she said. "What?" he said. She said, "Zig's movie, they're shooting it at night." He said, "Who the hell would want to be in a movie?" He said, "Wouldn't you rather be a character in a book?" Then he would always know where to find her. He said that he would like her to be a girl in a novel. He said that he would always know just where she was in the world.

He said, "Do you believe me?"

The clock was on the table.

He took her arm.

He took everything.

Was it late or too late?

It was too late.

Metaphorically speaking anyway.

Zigouiller was standing in the doorway.

Watching them.

He was angry.

He took the clock and threw it smashed it up against the wall. It stopped. He smashed the clock against the wall. He called her a whore.

It was.

It really was.

A stupid thing to say.

Wasn't it?

Ro hit Zig.

Zig hit Ro.

Or maybe it was the other way around.

Things were broken.

Cups, the clock, a plate.

Time stopped.

Literally, figuratively.

What did it matter?

What did it signify?

Things get broken every day.

As though smashed by some invisible hand.

Glass, bottles, bones.

What happened to that black dress?

Zig smashed the clock.

Ro picked up a broken plate.

He laughed.

Ro said that he was hungry.

He asked Zig, are you hungry?

Ro poured himself a drink, and one for Zig.

They drank.

She took the eggs from the refrigerator.

She broke them in a bowl.

Zig did not look at her.

He found a screwdriver.

He had the pieces of the broken clock on the table.

He was putting the clock back together.

Shelly came in, then.

The day was hot and ugly.

The clock was broken.

Shel asked her.

Did she want to go to the hospital to see the actress?

He wanted to get flowers.

Would she go with him to get flowers?

The girl liked yellow daisies.

Zig and Ro were eating eggs.

She didn't really want to get flowers for the girl.

But she went with Shel to that flower market.

Where you can buy flowers one by one.

He got the girl yellow daisies.

They had coffee.

They had cake.

They were like children.

They could eat cake.

And who would stop them?

Shel looked at the flowers.

Were they wilting in the heat?

He said El.

He said Sodom was sensational.

And Gomorrah was great.

California was a gold rush bust.

He said, "We can't fall out of the world."

He said, "We are in it once and for all."

He ate his cake.

Chocolate, on a green plate.

Shel drank his coffee.

She drank too.

With cream and sugar.

It had cream and sugar.

But it tasted of smoke and ashes.

The daisies were tied with green twine.

"I like the yellow flowers," she said.

He said, "But you like dark ones best."

He went to the hospital to give the flowers to the girl.

She didn't go with him.

Because the flowers were yellow.

And she liked the dark ones best.

Zig used to bring her licorice. In a little paper box with violets. He had a camera. He liked to take pictures in black and white.
What happened to that clock? and the photographs? Those pictures

that he took on the beach? Those blurry snapshots. He called her a whore.

And that was the end of it.

She had thought that that was the end of it.

If there is such a thing as an ending.

Is there such a thing as an ending?

Because here she was.

In her kitchen. And it wasn't—

And it isn't over yet.

All these years later.

When she met Zig he was reading a book of poetry. He was sitting outside a cinema smoking a cigarette and reading poetry. He handed the book to her. He asked her to read the line.

She said, "In the room the women come and go talking of Joe DiMaggio."

He worked the projector.

She went to the movies.

They ate chocolate and smoked cigarettes.

They talked about the future like there was one.

Which is why he gave her the clock.

So that she could tell the time.

They went to Hollywood.

He broke the clock.

What time is it?

Late? early?

What would she do?

Play a game of chess? or stay up all night?

She could eat chocolate cake.

Or drink coffee with cream and sugar.

She could burn the house down.

Or burn down the house.

No one would stop her.

Zigouiller was in the movies.

And she was married to Louie.

Look at her house.

It's so beautiful.

Isn't it?

Look at her dog.

Zola chasing her ball.

She was so beautiful.

Louie wanted her story.

He said that the story is a ruined castle.

He would rebuild the ruins.

Brick by brick.

Memory by memory.

That was his metaphor.

Is it a metaphor?

Louie said that perhaps they would go away in the spring.

Louie never had a tragedy.

Nothing bad had ever happened to him. So—

He wanted her stories.

Louie wanted a story—

Louie asked her to write the story.

She couldn't think of the word.

For what Roman did to her.

She couldn't think of the word—

For what she did to him.

For what she wanted.

Of the word for licorice.

The black licorice, that at first she hated, but then she came around to it.

To love a thing, you must hate it first.

You must come around to the worst of it.

Underneath the salt, she found the sweetness.

She loved the salt.

She never lied.

She told the truth.

Even though she did not believe in such a monster.

It was Louie who wanted more.

Louie didn't want the story to end.

He wanted one more twist, a turn.

So she changed it.

She told it to him again.

It was the story of a brother and a sister.

They lived by a salt creek.

There was a garden with an apple tree, with plums and roses and lilies.

In the woods among the rotting rotten things, the flowers, the mud and the birds, the leaves, the branches, the moss, and vine and violet; they wrote a story.

They locked the story in a cedar box.

She read books. She dreamed.

She wanted. And then she went to Illyria, and she met Roman Stone.

She told Ro the story.

The night they met.

Told him in a doorway.

Dark fluttering wings—

She was the one who found them.

Mother was on the bed.

Father was beside her.

She lighted a candle. She took the candle and went room by room. Lighting small fires as she went. The house was on fire.

Everything was burning but she walked through it, and nothing could or would stop her. There was a cake on the kitchen table. She cut a piece of cake, and she ate with her fingers. While the house burned. The door to the cellar was open. She took the steps one by one, down. Down down—she went down to the cellar. Father's design was unscrolled. She read and read until she could read no more. She read until she knew all that there was to know. She touched the black keys of his typewriter. There was a sheet of paper rolled in the carriage. There was chocolate on her fingers. She could taste smoke and chocolate.

Maybe it didn't happen like that.

But that's how she remembered it. Louie had heard the story a thousand and one times. Each time it was not quite the same. She remembered. Or she forgot. Once she was certain of every object in each room. Like the clock on the table. And the nightdress on a chair. Like a book. And a shoe. Like the cups. One had fallen to the floor. Louie told her—

Louie said that the evidence is crucial to an understanding of the event.

Once she told him of a typewritten note.

She didn't remember that now.

She didn't remember that it said: *At the heart of all things is a knife.*

How could she remember a thing like that?

She remembered the cold night sweetening the hard apples.

And that Father had left the door to the cellar unlocked.

Mother had baked a cake.

Roses grew by the salt creek.

Even the flowers tasted of salt.

The cake was on the table.

There was a knife beside it.

She told Sheldon what she saw.

She saw their bodies.

And so she knew what it meant.

To come to the end of things.

She ate chocolate cake.

She burned the house down.

She took the typewriter.

Shel wrote stories on paper.

And the house burned to ashes.

She told Roman.

She told him that she had burned down the house.

She told him the story.

One night in Illyria. Along those shady lanes. Ro kissed her in the darkness and she didn't know why.

He said that he had always envied orphans.

She pitied him then.

She mistook cruelty for kindness.

And envy for sweetness.

She told Ro everything.

No one had ever envied her.

Or kissed her in a doorway.

He listened while she told her story.

She told Ro.

That was a long time ago.

What about now?

And what about *now*?

Ro died.

Had they come to the end of things?

She did not believe—

That they had come to the end of things.

Even now.

There was.

There is no ending.

One night in California.

Ro told her about the girl in the woods.

"Shelly killed her," he said.

"Shelly killed the girl," he said.

She told him to be quiet.

She was quiet.

Then she said—

"Promise me something."

He smoked in silence for a while.

"What do you want me to do?" he asked.

She said, "Wait."

"Wait?" he said.

He thought about it.

She could tell that he was thinking about it.

He filled his glass.

He filled hers too.

He said, "Your brother killed that girl."

She said, "And you want his story."

He said, "El, I didn't kill the girl."

"Just wait," she said.

"For what?" he said.

"For him," she said.

He said, "Jesus."

"Please," she said.

"Let him tell the story," she said.

"Wait for him to tell it," she said.

"Jesus," he said.

"Do you think that he's going to confess? He won't confess,"
said Ro.

"I saw what he did to that girl," he said.

"Please shut up please," she said.

"Zig will be back soon," she said.

He said, "How does the story end?"

She said, "I'm not the writer."

He said, "How would you end it?"

She said, "The girl doesn't die."

He said, "What happens to her?"

She said, "She sails away to Byzantium."

She laughed.

It wasn't funny.

But that didn't matter.

She laughed.

She said, "She lives by the sea. And has a dog."

He said, "That's how it will end."

The clock ticked.

They didn't speak.

It seemed like forever.

He smoked.

He ashed his cigarette.

Then he said—

"Rock, paper, scissors me for it," he said.

"What?" she said.

He said, "Rock, paper, scissors me for the story."

He set down his glass.

"Really?" she said.

He put his hand over hers.

And rolled it into a fist.

He took his hand away.

"One, two, three," they said.

"Go—" they said.

And hit the table: one, two, three times.

He opened his fist.

She opened her hand.

She was scissors.

And he smashed her with his rock.

She lost.

"Jesus," he said.

"You always choose paper," he said.

He refilled his glass.

He drank.

He said, "Shel killed that girl."

"He's my brother," she said.

"I have to take care of him," she said.

"He killed that girl," he said.

"Stop," she said.

"Stop saying it."

He drank.

"I'll wait," he said.

"But you won," she said.

He said, "I'll look out for him."

"I'll wait," he said.

"It won't make things any better," he said.

"I know," she said.

"Every time that you look at him," he said.

"You'll see what he did to that girl," he said.

"I know," she said.

"You'll hate him," he said.

"I won't," she said.

"You should," he said.

"I know," she said.

"I'll wait," he said.

He said that he would wait.

And he would look out for Shelly.

He would wait to write his story.

She started to get up from the table.

He put his hand on her arm.

"Tell me," he said.

"Do you believe me?" he said.

And didn't she feel terror then?

She knew all that there was to know.

And this knowledge was no consolation.

He held her arm.

She struggled.

She stopped struggling.

He let go.

She stood.

He said, "I promise."

He said, "I promise to take care of your brother."

The sky was light.

The stars were gone.

"I'll keep his secret," he said.

"I'll look out for him," he said.

"Just say that you believe me," he said.

He pushed back his chair.

Ro stood.

The sun on the water.

He said, "Do you believe me?"

Ro in sunlight.

He looked. He looked—

Ancient.

Did she believe him?

He waited.

He waited.

She said, "Yes."

He kissed her.

He kissed her then.

It was too late.

It was early.

The sun was coming up.

Isn't that stupid?

The sun coming up.

Like Apollo riding his chariot across the sky.

The waves were crashing against the shore.

Like Poseidon in his kingdom.

And the sea girls singing each to each.

Isn't that stupid?

He tore her dress.

Her dress was torn.

He did not know.

And she did not see.

The shadow in the doorway.

Like Odysseus to Penelope.

The sky was red like pomegranate seeds.

Like the eyes of old weeping Zeus.

Like the Sirens singing sailors to the rocks.

The door opened.

Zigouiller stood in the doorway.

He had brought her licorice.

He called her a whore.

He broke the clock.

She broke the eggs.

Roman and Zigouiller ate.

Because they were hungry.

Isn't that stupid?

Zig collected the pieces of the clock.

There was no hope for them after that.

Was there?

It seemed that there wasn't.

But here she was.

In another year.

Another winter.

It's so cold.

Should she start a fire?

She could have cake.

Or stay up all night.

Or sleep.

And dream of great fallen Babylon.

She had a brother.

She did not hate him.

She loved him.

Jesus, what a thing to say.

It's funny how things go.

She saw the actress. The girl—

She saw Harlow on television the other day.

She was on a soap opera.

She played a widow accused of murder.

Funny.

Roman kept his promise.

He never told the story.

He died and a little bit of the story died with him.

But not all of it.

Roman Stone is dead.

Fate is a girl with scissors.

She's so beautiful.

Zig asked her to choose.

How could she choose?

When she was a character in someone else's novel?

Louie told her to write the story.

How could she write a story?

When someone else was already writing it?

It was the story of a sister and a brother.

How could she write; how could she destroy a story?—when she was, when she had always been—a reader.

She found the bodies.

She started the fire.

She burned down the house.

But she did not burn the story.

She took the cedar box.

She hid the box in the woods.

She did not open the box.

She had not opened the box.

Not in all these years.

She could not open it.

The story was locked inside.

She didn't have the key.

She had the box.

She gave her brother the key.

When they were children. In the woods.

He put out his hand for the key.

And she gave it to him.

So that he could lock the box.

Locked inside the box—

There was.

There is.

Their story.

The first story.

It was the story of a brother and sister.

A girl and boy who kill their parents.

It was only a story.

It was a dream in the woods.

They dreamed in the woods.

What one dreams is always possible.

She hid the box beyond the salt creek.

She gave her brother the typewriter.

So that he could tell his own story.

She set the house on fire. She stood watching the house burn. She waited for Shelly. She told him that she was burning down the house because the story had come true. He took an apple from the tree. He cut it in two halves. And he gave her half. He said, "El, it's just us now."

And then he said, "We'll start again."

Once years later.

It was day or maybe it was night.

She saw Roman.

She heard him call her name in a hotel lobby.

It was snowing.

She held her daughter by the hand.

She did not let go.

She did not turn.

If she had turned—

She would have turned to salt.

And god knows she loved salt.

And sweet.

Each word is a symbol.

Each word replaces a thing.

A clock.

A bird.

An apple.

A girl.

A minute.

An hour.

A day.

Or maybe a night.

A story is a memory game.

This is the memory game.

Choose one moment.

Choose one word over another.

Choose rock or paper or scissors.

She didn't want words.

She didn't want memories.

She didn't want licorice.

She wanted chocolate cake.

On a green plate.

Maybe she would stay up all night.

Zig was sleeping.

Ro was dead.

Sheldon was living on an island.

Louie wanted a story.

She rolled the red ball across the floor.

Zola chased it.

She threw it.

Zola caught it.

She took the ball from the dog.

She threw it; it bounced.

It knocked a vase from the table.

The Etruscan vase fell to the floor.

And broke.

On the Persian rug.

She laughed.

She might stay up all night.

She might stay up one thousand and one nights.

After all, who would stop her?

Eloise she was named after her mother

Eloise she named her daughter.

She sat on the velvet sofa.

And picked up her book.

It was open to the first page.

She began again.

CHAPTER 20

Sheldon explicates the egg

W E ATE BAKER'S BREAD THICK WITH MARMALADE, honey, and butter. There were garden roots, al forno: red potatoes, yams, carrots, quince, and peppered turnips. The black cat stood at the windowsill. The morning sun did not impress him, as though he knew something about destruction that the rest of us did not, or could not, or pretended not to know.

We talked of dreams.

Salt said, "Last night I dreamed I was at King Arthur's grave. And the great old ghost in a coat of armor pointed his sword and held up his shield, and he said to me, "Benjamin Salt! Benjamin Salt? You have a very stupid name. Are you ever called anything else?"

Inj laughed. In sunlight.

The day was promising, wasn't it?

Whatta day!

And then I remembered the fire.

It had burned everything to ash.

"I woke up," said Salt. "And I knew just how my story should go."

Beatrice peeled a hard-boiled egg.

Ben and Inj and I set out for the jetty after breakfast. Inj swung her arms as she walked. Ben talked. He spoke of pine trees; ash and candle; of paper and ink, pepper and plum liquor. I let him go on ahead of me, and his voice was lost against the cries of the birds.

I had a terrible desire—

A nearly sickening want—

To confess to her.

In the woods.

To tell my story to a girl.

Who never had a tragedy to call her own.

One could love or hate a girl for this.

For being so easy. For not being difficult.

For being a girl, just at the moment when one wanted a girl most.

She turned and looked back at me.

There was nothing tragic about her.

Nothing terrible had ever happened to her.

Nothing terrible would ever happen to her.

Salt had made his way far beyond us.

Into the woods.

Deeper, darker.

She took my hand.

Salt went on—through the thick trees—into the sunlight.

He was so taken with the day.

Can you imagine?

A day so bright—

That you couldn't see the past.

Only the future.

Only the path before you.

A day so promising.

That you couldn't see the shadows of the pines.

I held her hand in mine.

And then I let go.

She opened her hand.

Palm up in the glittering sunlight.

Her cheeks were flushed.

She said.

She told me—

From beyond us Salt called out.

"Inj," he called.

"Here's the boat," he said.

Inj pulled away from me.

Inj closed her hand.

And kissed her rolled fist.

"Benny," she called.

She ran to him.

The lake was dark blue.

The ferryman waited.

Inj waved to me from the boat.

The boat moved slowly, cutting through the cold dark water.

Benny was staring straight up at the sun.

A cloud came across the sun.

It began to snow.

I took the path through the woods.

To the doctor's house.

Thinking about Inj and her questions.

And why I answered them.

I could describe her face.

But I won't.

I want to remember Inj.

The idea of a girl.

The memory of a girl.

Inj at the window.

Pru on her bicycle.

Wren waiting to hear Ro's ghost story.

Eloise in the woods, running.

A girl in the snow.

I want. I want.

I want the doctor to wake so that I can tell him my story.

I want to begin again.

I want to repair the ruined fountain.

How will I rebuild the ruined fountain?

Perhaps in summer.

It is winter.

Who is S. Z. Schell?

The author of his own silence.

Here in the doctor's library—amid—

Such magnificent marble, these statuettes, these books—

This proof of a great civilization.

I will begin.

The glass swan is broken.

It must have fallen from the table.

It was one of the doctor's curiosities.

The pieces are on the table.

A snapped neck, a broken wing, a terrible accusing eye.

I'll start again.

My house burned.

I saw the fire.

It wasn't my house.

It was only a shell.

I lived there for a while.

Before scuttling on.

The house had never been mine.

Should I care for ashes?

Inj and I and the fearsome black cat took refuge in the doctor's house.

Beatrice held the ragged cat.

"Oh you," she said.

"You monster," she said.

She kissed his ear.

The ragged cat.

Who lived by murder.

Who prowled the garden looking for birds and mice.

Beatrice held the cat.

I said to her that everything was gone.

"It's gone," I said.

Beatrice said, "Good."

This morning I found my manuscript on the table in the library.

I'll start again.

I'll tell what happened. I'll tell—

The story of how I killed my wife.

Pru had a garden. She grew ill, and the garden thrived. The disease spread. There was no stopping it. It was wild and tangled. It was a dark flower. Pru died, and her garden flowered through the fall: the asters, the Russian sage, and catmint, the black grapes in damp sunlight.

Pru in her hospital bed.

She said. She said to me.

Tell me a story.

And so I did.

I told her a story.

Of a girl in the woods.

Pru against the white pillow.

The fine bones of her face.

Her pale mouth.

A girl with a name of admonishing restraint.

A girl who once asked me—

What is the worst thing that you have ever done?

The story was the answer.

She closed her eyes.

That night she died.

She died in August.

The roses bloomed in October.

This is how I killed my wife.

With a story.

It is the kind of murder that comes from kindness.

A Halloween frost killed the last of the flowers.

I kept the typewriter on the kitchen table.

I killed her, I suppose.

Is there a better word for it?

Snow is falling on the ruined fountain.

I'll start again.

Dr. Lemon is dying.

The doctor has taken a turn for the worse.

I anticipate the end.

It is snowing.

And it is going to snow.

Beatrice has a terror in her eyes.

I am writing in the library.

I can do only what I know.

And continue on with my story.

As though telling it to her father.

Who listened with such sweet sagacity.

Language is the cracked kettle on which we beat out tunes for bears to dance to, while all the while we long to move the stars to pity.

That's Flaubert.

I used to want to move the stars. When I was young and wanted to be a storyteller, but I had no stories. When I longed for experience.

I wanted a story.

I have lied. Once or twice.

In the telling of a story.

I did not find the bodies.

It was Eloise.

This is what happened.

I came home.

In the dark of an autumn evening.

Doesn't it get dark so early in October?

I was riding my bicycle.

Listening to my transistor radio.

The Dodgers were playing the Yankees.

It was darkening.

Then it was dark.

There was a brightness up ahead.

I saw the fire.

Eloise called out to me.

She was under the apple tree.

Watching the house burn.

The typewriter beside her.

Later the story of the fire was on the news.

A murder-suicide.

Though there was no real evidence to suggest who killed whom.

Or whether one killed the other.

Only that both were dead.

And the house had burned down.

Eloise told me that there was a note.

Eloise had found a note.

Left in the typewriter.

We were quiet.

While the cold ripened the apples.

While the house burned.

We were seventeen. I am running so many autumn evenings together. We are children running down the street in the darkness. Shel and El, what the hell. Father used to say: he who avoids Scylla runs on Charybdis.

Did Father kill Mother?

In one version of the story it was Mother who killed Father.

Like the ancients, she followed after; to care for him in the next world.

And then it was just us.

El & Shel.

We had no one else in the world.

No one else in the world.

Eloise.

Her hair smelled of smoke.

And her fingers of chocolate.

The house by the salt creek burned down.

And then we went to Illyria. We got on a bus and headed to Virgil's Grove. I met Roman. And Roman met El. We let him seduce us, respectively. We were drawn in, collectively. We could not resist him. It did not occur to me until later that he also fell; he could not resist us.

Our tragedy.

It was like smoke and chocolate.

I'll begin again.

I will start again.

So there I was—eighteen, and just off the bus.

So there I was—young.

There I was with the image in my head—with an image that could not be replaced by the view out of the window or the burning red burnished landscape of autumn in Iowa or the glass bottles of orange soda or the hardbitten yellow apples—of my mother dead.

And how she lay across the bed like a fallen heroine.

With her dark hair upon the pillow.

And her palms turned upward.

My father was beside her.

The story overtook me.

I'll start over.

So there I was—eighteen and just off the bus.

There we were in Illyria. It was night. And there was nothing like it. We sat outside. We drank orange soda. Me and Ro. There was nowhere to go.

The next day.

It must have been.

Or the day after.

Ro and I were sitting together in the cafeteria.

Eloise sat down with us. She set her tray on the table.

Ro looked at her.

I saw him look at her.

Until she blushed and turned away.

This was the brash bravado that made Ro a hit.

Here comes Ro.

Everyone wanted to be his friend.

Ro was wearing a pink Izod shirt—you know, with the collar turned up and the little alligator?

I hated him from the first.

Maybe Fortunato hadn't done me quite a thousand injuries.

Maybe the shirt wasn't pink.

Does that part matter?

I'll start again.

El and I went to Iowa.

We were eighteen and had no one in the world but each other.

What one dreams is always possible.

I had the image in my head of Mother and Father.

Though I never saw them like that.

Eloise saw.

And she would not let me look.

Though she saved me from reality.

She could not save me from my own dreams.

She set the fire.

That burned the house.

That burned my story.

She saved the typewriter.

So that I could start again.

I'll start again.

One day in Illyria, where there were no seasons.

One day in Virgil's Grove, where the shades came to rise.

One day Ro's mother arrived, like some marble-white goddess.

Carried upon a palanquin.

And Ro, prince that he was—

Showed me dirty pictures of the queen.

The pages were frayed.

He wasn't afraid.

Of anything.

He showed me the pictures.

The evidence of her beauty.

Dirty pictures.

He had heaps of them.

That's not poverty, he said.

One day—

One day or maybe it was night.

At night along those quiet streets.

In our apartment on Bard Street.

When Ro, oh Ro, you know—

He was going on and on about what he had done to whom.

About what he had learned.

About what he knew.

What he wanted.

About the taste of it.

And I could no longer bear to listen, to hear—

About his experience.

About the world.

I said to him.

"Here's a story."

I told him a story.

Mother killed Father, I said.

"I found them," I said.

"I was the one who found the bodies," I said.

I told Ro a story.

I told him how I found the bodies.

How I walked down the hallway.

How I stood in the doorway.

I told him my story.

He was quiet.

He listened.

He drank.

He kept refilling his glass.

And when I was finished.

He said.

"That is a story."

I looked at him.

And didn't I feel terror then?

At what I had done.

What had I done?

I lied.

And the lie became a story.

The story became a truth.

I lied.

It was Eloise's story.

Eloise under the apple tree.

I told Roman my story.

And he stole my story from me.

He took it.

As an elemental thing.

A thing, a theft, that would make all else possible.

The spark that leads to a conflagration.

I'll start again.

An event, a scene; it only lasts a moment.

The memory of the event is inexhaustible.

It is not bound by time or space or reason.

The doctor's house is a maze.

It is full of beautiful things.

I cannot find the secret to their possession.

Beatrice is baking a cake.

If her father dies in the night, she will belong to me.

What will I do? With such a thing as Beatrice Lemon?

Who is small and fragile.
Who has dark hair. And gray eyes.
Who might fall from the branch and break a wing.
Who has freckles across her bare shoulders.
Who knows nothing about the world.
And everything about the wilderness.
Like the smell of snow.
And the taste of blackberries.
Who feels despair at the bodies of dead birds.
Whose skin is like snow and blackberries.
When first I came to her island—
Beatrice was a girl.
I saw her by the water's edge.
She was a child.
She called out to me from the beach.
Your name is Schell, isn't it?
She opened her hands.
And held a clamshell, halved.
How will I learn?
How to get to the end of things?
Beatrice turns the spoon round in the bowl.
She knows things that I cannot know.
She knows her way through these rooms.
Each door with its own possibility.
What one dreams is always possible.
I am winding through the maze.
I am bound by my own infinity.
If I keep telling my story—
The doctor will live.
Awaiting always the ending.
The ending that never arrives.

I begin.

I've begun.

I began.

I saw Roman and the girl.

I looked at Ro.

I looked at the girl.

Ro said, "Jesus."

The girl's hair, tangled and matted with blood.

That was one day in South Dakota.

When I was young.

And could justify anything.

Even why I thought—

She looked beautiful.

A girl in the snow.

I'll start again.

The farmhouse.

The snow.

The winter.

January 1980.

The girl buried in the woods.

And that night the four of us sat around the fire.

Wren said, "Tell the story already, Ro."

Ro said that a terrible fate might befall the teller of such a tale.

We sat waiting.

We drank champagne.

And felt a certain terror.

Even with the crackle of wood in the fire.

At each sudden spark or flame.

Ro began.

To tell his story.

"This is the story of a brother and a sister."

It was Ro's ghost story.

And as he spoke—

Wren sat rapt.

Eloise kept drinking champagne.

Ro told the story.

Ro set the scene.

The autumn evening.

A tire swing creaking in the wind.

The rustle of dry leaves.

The apples ripening on the trees.

The girl ate an apple.

The boy left his bicycle by the gate.

He went to the house.

There was a light in an upper window.

The door opened.

He called out.

No one answered.

He took the steps—

Slowly.

He was on the second floor.

Slowly.

He was walking the dark hallway—

He had his hand on the doorknob.

He opened the door to the bedroom.

The girl was under the tree. Waiting for him.

She felt a chill all along her skin.

As she ate the apple.

She heard nothing.

Only the leaves.

And the wind in the branches.

She dropped her apple to the ground.

And she ran to the house.

She ran.

She ran up the steps.

She took the steps two at a time.

She stumbled in the darkness.

She came to the bedroom.

The door was open.

She went in.

She went into the bedroom.

And there she saw—

The moon.

The bed.

Father.

Mother.

And the boy standing over them—

With a bloody knife in his hand—

Ro stopped.

Just like that.

Wren was wide-eyed.

Wren said, "Go on."

Go on.

Wren was leaning against me.

There was salt and warmth to her skin.

"Tell me how it ends. Please," said Wren.

Eloise looked up.

Eloise looked at me.

She looked just like me.

And I looked at her.

I looked just like her.

Eloise turned away.

Wren was so close.

Her breath was warm.

"Don't stop," she said.

She wanted to know what the boy had done.

She wanted to know about the knife and the moonlight.

Wren was waiting for the story to end.

It was nothing without the ending.

And there was nothing like an ending.

Wren's lips parted.

Her mouth opened.

Wren said, "Oh."

"Ro," she said.

"Oh," she said.

And here I saw.

I could feel.

And see.

What a story could do.

Ro stopped.

Ro wouldn't take her to the end.

Of the story.

Wren fell back. Against the sofa.

In a soft cry.

He turned toward the fire.

Ro wouldn't end the story.

For a moment I thought that he was being kind.

Then I remembered the girl in the woods.

Wren had her hand on my arm.

I could feel the flutter of her heart.

I knew that the world was his.

To do with as he wanted.

And my story—

Was no longer mine.

It was his.

And he could change it.

As he willed.

And as he wanted.

It was his.

Wren said, "Shel your hands are so cold."

She put my hands between her thighs.

We sat before the fire.

And Ro told my story.

He went where he wanted.

And no one could stop him.

From going where he wanted.

Even if there was nowhere to go.

In Roman's version of the story:

I was the one who killed my father.

And my mother.

I'll start again.

That summer night in Chicago—

After dinner; Ro and I saw two girls on the street. And we caught a taxi. Ro wiped his brow. He grinned. He looked out the window as the city went by in lighted darkness.

"I never thanked you. Did I?" he asked.

"For what?" I said.

"The typewriter," he said.

We got to his hotel.

And walked a hallway carpeted with roses.

He unlocked his room.

He sat upon the bed.

In his oyster jacket.

And his white shirt untucked.

There was a bottle of scotch on the table.

He opened it.

He poured us each a glass.

I took my glass.

I stood at the window.

The curtains were open.

I looked out.

I drank.

I asked him the question.

I asked him.

"Do you remember that girl in the woods?"

He drank.

He loosened his tie.

"What girl?" he said.

"What woods?" he said.

We drank.

The room was cool.

The coolness of the room made the hot night more miserable.

"Hey," he said. "Do you know what my mother said about you?"

I waited.

"*Yond Cassius has a lean and hungry look,*" he said.

He laughed.

He leaned back against the pillows.

"I always stay here when I'm in town," he said.

He said, "Once—this was years ago—I was in the bar. It was snowing. I thought that I saw your sister in the lobby with," he said. He drank. "The girl, the little girl."

"Susu," I said.

"Is that what they call her?" he said.

He raised his glass.

"To Susu," he said.

"She's going to be married," I said.

"I'm here for her wedding," I said.

"Let's drink to the bride," he said.

He drank.

"I'm getting sentimental," he said.

"You were always sentimental," I said.

"Was I?" he said.

"I loved her," he said.

"Who?" I said.

He set his glass against his forehead.

"Do you want ice?" he said.

"I could have them send some up," he said.

I didn't want ice.

"My sister——" I began.

"Your sister?" he said.

"We don't have to do this now," he said. "Do we?"

"This isn't about her," he said.

"It's about the story," he said.

"What story?" I said.

"If you want to do this now," he said, against the pillows of the bed, "I'll order up some chocolate cake."

He reached for the phone.

Spilled his drink.

Distracted, set the phone down.

Held the glass in both hands.

His face was damp and pale.

He laughed.

"I saw her," he said. "Your sister. With the girl. In this hotel. This very hotel. I come back here. Because maybe I will see her again."

"Sheldon Schell," he said.

"Where's my cake?" he said.

"There is no cake," I said.

He said, "You were always so literal."

"Your sister," he said.

"Her hair smelled like smoke," he said.

"Her fingers tasted like chocolate," he said.

He laughed.

He fumbled for his cigarettes.

The pack was empty.

He looked inside the empty pack.

"Where the hell is that cake?" he said.

He crumpled the cigarette pack.

And threw it to the floor.

He said, "Shelly, you know—if it weren't for you. If it weren't for you and your sister and your typewriter, I never would have become a writer."

"So thank you," he said.

"—For being a liar," he said.

I did not speak.

He looked at me.

"Jesus," he said. "Don't be so downhearted."

"At least you have a sister," he said.

He filled his glass.

He drank.

"All the poetry in the world won't save us," he said.

"From what?" I said.

"Jesus," he said.

"From what we did," he said.

"What did we do?" I said.

"You really are something," he said.

"I always said that you were something," he said.

He said, "Put it in your book. I'll be the first to read it."

I looked out the window.

I said, "There is no book."

"What?" he said.

"There is no book," I said.

"Jesus," he said.

"All these years," he said.

"The story," he said.

"It wasn't a story," I said.

"It was about a girl," he said.

"What was it?" he said.

"You tell me what it was," he said. "If it weren't—wasn't a story."

There was a book on the table.

Left open—spine-side up—pages spread.

The face of a serious young man with eyeglasses stared at me from the jacket.

I closed the book.

"Is it good?" I said.

He laughed.

"It's a mystery," he said.

He raised his glass.

I raised my glass.

"*Be true,*" I said.

He drank.

He coughed.

He laughed.

He clapped his hands.

"*Be true,*" he said.

"It was a helluva rule for a liar," he said.

The glass rolled on its side.

He picked up the fallen glass.

Looked down into it.

He looked at me.

"I'm dying," he said.

"It's my heart," he said.

"Don't kill off your protagonist," I said.

He laughed.

He might not have said *heart*.

He might have said *ticker*.

I might not have said *protagonist*.

I might have said *main character*.

He was weary.

He was drunk.

He was. He might have been dying.

But then aren't we all?

I said, "Never talk about truth in a truthful way."

He raised himself on his elbow—

And then fell back.

"There is no story," I said.

"No girl, no book?" he said.

"No story?" he said.

"What the hell," he said.

"No girl?" he said.

"No book?" he said.

He rested his head on the pillow.

He slipped off one shoe.

It fell to the floor.

He cradled his glass on his belly.

The glass slipped.

His eyes closed.

I noticed.

Just then.

The faint scent of licorice.

Like the story says.

And the hills were like white elephants.

The glass fell from his hand.

And rolled across the carpet.

I left the room.

I closed the door.

The next night I went to his lecture with Susu.

It was two days before her wedding.

And she found a dark spot on her white dress.

She took this as a portent.

I took her to see him.

He talked about television.

He told the old stories.

And he gave me Salt's book.

He took Susu by the arm and whispered—

I couldn't hear what he said.

Caught up in the clamor of Ro's readers.

She bent her face against his.

Her dark hair.

Her silly name.

She pushed her dark hair from her face.

Susu and I walked out into the night.

I looked at the book.

I asked her if she wanted it.

She said, "Oh god no."

And laughed.

She opened the book.

"What did he say to you?" I asked her.

She tilted her head.

The summer night.

She said, "In the room the women come and go talking of Joe DiMaggio."

"I don't know what it means," she said.

"Do you?" she asked.

"Whatta riot," she said.

"Whatta mystery," she laughed.

And she took my arm.

She didn't want the book.

She was so tired of serious young men.

It is night. Beatrice and I had a quiet dinner. Of mushrooms, artichoke hearts, dried love apples, bread, pomegranate jam, and almond butter.

She rose and collected our plates.

"Why don't you go to Father's library?" she said.

"I'll bring you coffee," she said.

"And you can finish the story," she said.

"I'll bring you cake," she said.

Beatrice said, "Don't tell me how the story ends."

It is not a story.

It was never a story.

And I did not write it.

I did not write a book.

I did not begin.

Not until I knew that Roman was dead.

Not until Salt asked.

And then I began this story.

I thought Salt wanted a story. He wanted my typewriter. He wanted a machine and instead he got a ghost.

I wanted to believe in Salt.

I wanted to see for myself—

If Ben Salt could save us.

Because all the poetry in the world won't.

Salt has been here and gone.

He came to my archipelago.

He was here. He was real.

Or at least: real enough.

If he is a monster.

Then he is my monster.

Beatrice in the kitchen has fallen asleep at the table.

I find her.

With her head cradled upon her folded arms.

She wakes.

Her gray eyes open.

Like Pallas Athena.

Who was born of her father's wisdom.

Her dark hair is tousled, and her face is soft. She gives me her sleepy girlish ramble of words alluding to her dreams and eluding what monster chased her through them.

And I see only her father.

There is a saying that the hand of God is in every story.

It is just as likely that at night the great black cape of Mephistopheles shrouds the sky.

And that the descent to hell is the same from every place.

I will start here.

I will keep my vigil.

I will keep telling my story.

It is not a story.

It is a confession.

It is not a confession.

It is a thing.

Like a flower.

Or a bird.

Like a knife.

Like an ax.

Like snow.

Like a table.

Like a chair.

Or the girl tied to it.

Like a grave.

Or the girl buried in it.

I'll start again.

I met Prudence Goodman.

Who was good.

As her names implies.

Who painted abstracts in pink and blue.

And just when I thought—

That I could escape the past.

Pru took ill.

Or the illness took her.

It would not relent.

It bashed her. It beat her.

It knocked her down.

It had its way.

With her.

While I watched.

And could do nothing.

Pru grew ill.

(*Oh Shel*, Pru would say here. *Shut up already. Get to the good part. Tell them how you gave me the boot and then got all the loot. Tell them that part*, she would say.)

Pru began her last painting in dark green and brown.

Pru was dying.

Pru was painting a picture.

Of a girl in the woods.

Who fought and struggled.

And then stopped fighting and struggling.

And gave in.

The picture on the canvas began to take shape.

Each day as the canvas darkened.

As there was more of it—

There was less and less of her.

Pru never finished the painting.

The blackbirds lined up on the fence.

And the garden grew wild.

With no one to tend to it.

I did not pity her.

Because whether it was Mother who killed Father.

Or Father who killed Mother.

Is entirely irrelevant.

I was—I am—I cannot escape being their child.

When the time came—

I gave Pru the medicine.

The story.

She died.

I went on living—

With the image of her waiting on that bridge for me on her bicycle the night that we met: in her scarf and coat; waiting by the dark water.

Waiting for me to answer her question.

And when she asks me.

When she asks again.

What is the worst thing that you have ever done?

I will know what to say.

It is not a story.

And I will keep telling it.

One night in Little America.

Where boys rolled the universe into a ball and kicked it along those dark shady lanes.

One night in Little America.

Pru slipped a strap from her shoulder and kissed me by the scratching hands of lilacs.

One night.

Or maybe it was day.

In the full sun of summer.

Pru told me that she was dying.

And I did not believe her.

"Let anger be general," she said.

I hate an abstract thing.

One night in Iowa.

Roman Stone died.

While watching a baseball game.

Roman Stone is dead.

But then you already know this.

It is not too late, I think.

Nor is it too early.

It is time to tell the story.

If it was. If it were.

A story.

I would tell it like this.

Pru died. She left me her soda pop loot.

I am a very rich man.

Here in my prisonhouse.

On an island of fathers.

A refuge of birds.

Here on my island.

I did not write a book.

I wanted the perfect story.

I stocked my cellar.

I watched Beatrice.

I watched as she ran through the woods.

I saw her from the distance.

And she grew.

And she came to me.

I never wrote my story, no.

I told it again and again. Perfecting it—

To Dr. Lemon.

Infecting him with the sickness of words.

I told him how Pru died, in summer.

And all the knowledge in the world couldn't help her.

I told him.

That I did not pity her. I said that—

My father wanted to build a box.

A box that would neither open nor close.

And would contain memories. I said—

My father had the crazies, and my mother did not pity him.

My sister and I were twins, the same and not the same—

As same as any he & she can be—

We had to be very quiet.

So we invented a game.

A game to pass the hours.

We wrote stories.

Each of us taking one sentence.

Like a twist, and then a turn, down a hallway.

Through a maze.

Leading to some undeniable conclusion.

We built a story.

We wrote together.

Our book.

Waiting for an ending that never came.

I wrote my initials on the page.

I locked the story in the box.

There was one key.

It was my sister's, and I took it from her.

Then it was my key.

I kept it.

I had the box. I had the key.

I had the story. And then—

One day, or—no, wait—

It was night—

Mother and Father died.

And Eloise found the bodies.

She told me what happened, her story. We sat—

Under the apple tree—

And she told me.

I was angry. I was envious.

It was her story.

I wanted her story.

We called our story a game.

To pass the hours in silence.

Can a story be a game?

Salt is gone.

He took with him his girl.

His head full of words.

And my favorite ink pen.

Oh well, let him have it.

I have others.

He took Inj.

Let him have her.

I have others.

I have a sister.

Here comes the tragedy.

Here come the ghosts.

Here come the girls.

Here comes everyone.

I have tragedy.

Let Salt have the words.

I have more.

Let him have the story.

It is not a story.

It is only the space around a story.

It is the grave.

It is not the body.

Snow is falling.

I'll take up the shovel.

I'll begin again.

Sugar-drunk on orange soda and Everclear, on the first night in Virgil's Grove, Eloise in the men's bathroom in my dormitory wrote on the mirror in red lipstick: BABYLON MUST FALL!

She always knew just what to say.

And Ro loved her for it.

Love?

Isn't that stupid?

Roman loved Eloise.

He did. And that was the problem.

With kings, with gods—

Love is destruction.

Call it what you will.

The wrecking ball.

An upped jig.

A cooked goose.

The wrack and the screw.

Crash, bang, boom.

A real hullaballoo.

Destruction.

A love story.

The perfect story.

The story is a sickness.

The story is a flower.

The story is the monster.

Don't tell stories.

They spread.

They infect.

They conquer.

They ruin.

Don't tell stories unless you keep a coin for the ferryman.

He exists only for the sake of your journey.

He demands his due.

One day Salt will understand this.

And that will be a terrible day.

Or maybe it will be night.

Who knows what a monster can create.

Once it rises from the table.

And is born into belief.

Salt loved Ro.

Salt believed in Ro.

Ro fed on belief.

Awaiting his own destruction.

The ghosts demand retribution.

Beatrice told me that she could not stop Salt. She could not stop him from reading the story. Salt read my manuscript. In her father's library.

In this room.

He did not read this page.

For it had yet to be written.

He will steal the story; this much is certain—

And the story that he steals from me will be a lie.

It will spring forth like water from a rock.

It will be a story of love and destruction.

A masterpiece.

It will be the story of the life and death of Roman Stone.

He ran ahead through the woods.

I can go on without him now.

I have seen Salt. I have seen his hands.

Like furious little doves.

One night on the Isle of the Father.

Salt lay upon the operating table.

A lump of wax and ash.

A creature composed of stories.

I shaped his face.

I cut his jib.

Hoisted his petard.

I glued his fingers to his hands.

I gave him the words.

And he said them.

Then he broke free—

He rose from the table.

He cried out in a howl.

—for all the things that he wanted.

Like any other monster.

Or a child.

Tell me a story!

I could not give him the machine—

I await the ghosts.

The count is 0 and 2.

And what will I do?

This one goes out to the cheap seats.

Here is—the document.

It is not a story.

When I was young I longed to move the stars to pity.

Now I find the greater heartbreak in a dancing bear.

I cannot stop myself.

From telling it again.

And trying to get it right.

When the telephone rings.

When there is a knock on the door.

I think: Are they coming for me?

Have they found her yet?

Have they found the girl we buried in the woods?

One day they will come for me.

And what will I do?

Oh, I know.

I'll start again.

Each night the doctor forgot the story that I had told him the night before. He forgot that I told him about Father and Mother. He forgot what I told him about Eloise. He forgot that I told him about Pru. He forgot that I told him about the woods.

This was the nature of Dr. Lemon's disease.

He forgot.

And I confessed again.

I remembered.

This was the nature of my punishment.

I could not forget.

I drank plum brandy.

Down to the bottom of the glass.

I told the doctor how I watched his daughter in the black-berry brambles.

How I waited for her.

How small and strange and beautiful she was.

How I watched her.

Year by year.

As the literal became the figurative.

And she collected by the shore her shells and stones.

I told the doctor.

That Eloise found Father and Mother.

In their bed in the moonlight.

I told the doctor—

That my wife destroyed me.

For I came to understand that I did not love her.

I loved her sickness.

That I had known it was there, growing in her.

Even when she did not yet know.

I sensed it gnawing at her.

Destroying her.

I told the doctor.

That Ro and the girl and I started out into the woods together.

In the snow.

The three of us walking in the woods.

We came to the pond.

She tied her skates and went onto the ice.

She was skating in circles on the frozen pond.

Ro and I sat drinking whiskey from his flask.

He called to her.

She skated the loop of an eight.

And back again.

She came back.

She sat with us.

Ro had a silver flask.

He gave her booze.

She drank.

She drank more.

She was taking off the skates.

Untying them, white skates.

Ro talked to her as though she were a child.

He started to tell a story.

It was the story of Pandora.

Who opens a box and unleashes all the woe in the world.

And hope too.

Her cheeks were flushed.

Her mouth drooped slightly.

We were sitting on a fallen tree near the edge of the frozen pond.

She sat between us.

"Is it an old story?" she said.

Her eyes were blue.

"Tell me another," she said.

He kissed her.

"Tell me another story," she said.

He held her face in his hands.

"I'm cold," she said.

He put his arms around her.

He asked her what she wanted to be.

He asked what she wanted to do.

And where did she want to go?

She said, "I want to go to Hollywood."

He kissed her.

She didn't stop him.

Her mouth was damp.

She rested her head on his shoulder.

She turned just slightly—

She looked at me.

"What are you doing?" she said.

"Watching us?" she said.

There was nothing childish about her then.

"Go away," she said.

"Make him go away," she said to Ro.

I looked at Ro.

He thought it was funny.

He reached into his coat for his cigarettes.

The girl took off her woolen cap.

She ran a hand through her hair.

Ro was lighting a cigarette.

He cupped his hand around the match.

He handed the cigarette to her.

She took off one glove.

She smoked.

One glove fallen in the snow.

The knot of her scarf, her white neck.
The smoke, the white sky.
I stood.
I began to walk away.
I walked.
Into the woods, in the pines.
When I came upon an old fire pit.
Among rotten branches.
With heavy rocks and blackened stones.
I picked up a rock.
It was dark and ancient.
I turned.
And I looked back.
It was snowing.
I couldn't see them.
I began to walk back.
Until I could see them in the distance.
Then I stopped.
I could see Ro and the girl.
And I watched them.
I walked back to the pond from the woods.
I was quiet.
I came closer.
I was behind them.
Ro and the girl.
Her coat undone, his hand under her sweater.
I was standing behind the girl.
I could see her breath.
And her cigarette in the snow.
I took the rock.
I hit her.

I hit her with the rock.
She fell away from Ro.
She fell to the ground.
She lay still.
Her eyes were open.
And she called out.
She was bleeding.
She grabbed my hand.
The sky was white.
The world was white.
Her face.
Her mouth.
She was trying to say something.
She took my hand.
She was going to beg—
Wasn't she?
For kindness?
Or pity?
I would have given her kindness.
If only she would ask.
She opened her mouth.
And bit my hand.
She bit through the skin.
I had no pity for her then.
I raised the rock.
I hit her again.
Ro had fallen back in the snow.
He was on his knees beside the girl.
The girl was crying.
The girl was weeping.
"Jesus," said Ro.

She wept.

I hit her again.

She struggled.

"Jesus," he said.

I dropped the rock in the snow.

He picked it up.

He took the rock.

And he hit her.

She stopped struggling.

She was covered in blood.

Her eyes were open.

She did not move.

She was not weeping.

I undressed the girl.

She was naked in the snow.

Ro stood. He staggered.

He fell back down to his knees.

He lay a hand on her stomach.

His bloody handprint on her bare white stomach.

I said that we had to burn everything.

"Jesus," he said.

I told Dr. Lemon what I did.

That I hit that girl.

And she lay bleeding.

As she lay bleeding in the snow.

Ro took the rock.

He smashed her head.

He killed her.

The snow fell.

I undressed the girl.

I looked at her white body in the snow.

The doctor's eyes were gray.

With knowledge.

And he forgot.

He forgot.

He did not remember that I told him how—

We dug a grave and buried the girl in the woods.

And that night we sat around the fire, the four of us.

Roman told my story.

I told the doctor.

That I did not know who killed Roman Stone.

But I wished that I had done it myself.

I told the doctor that Roman stole my story.

First he told it aloud.

Then he wrote it on paper.

His fingers to the black keys of my father's typewriter.

I spoke.

Till there was nothing left to say but this.

Roman took my story.

His theft—his crime—was worse to me than murder.

Worse than killing the girl in the woods.

And burying her body.

And burning her clothes.

He stole my story.

The story of my childhood.

The story of the fire.

My story was a lie.

He stole my lie.

It was mine.

That's what I said.

The doctor listened.

I began again.

I had my rock.
And my hill.
Each day Sisyphus pushes a rock up a hill.
Only to have it roll back down to the ground.
And he has to start again.
And yet one must consider Sisyphus happy.
Like Inj says—
At least he has a hill.
At least he has a rock.
Some people don't even have that.
Some people live their whole lives.
Without a tragedy to call their own.
Some brothers don't even have a sister.
The days grow hot, O Babylon!
Hey Shelly, Pru would say if she read this.
Don't be so glum, chum.
That's what Pru would say.
I forgive you, she would say.
If she read this.
Which she cannot.
Because I killed her.

I open the door to Dr. Lemon's room.
 He is small and frail against the pillows of his bed.
 The curtains are open. If he opens his eyes, he will see—
 When darkness goes to black.
 Descending around the edges of the day.
 How even in winter the garden awaits him.
 I sit beside him.
 His eyes open.

Does he see?

The beauty of his kingdom?

Dr. Lemon is dying.

And with him will go his knowledge.

And every story that he has ever heard.

Though his trees will burst into bloom.

And that summer sweetness will come again.

He knows this.

His will be done.

He commands.

He whispers.

He asks.

Tell.

In the farmhouse, as the snow fell and fell, and the girl lay buried in the ground, and the ice was thick on the pond, we sat that night around the fire, the four of us. Roman told the story of the brother and sister who were haunted by a murder. We drank. I staggered to bed with Wren. Later when I woke she was gone. I lighted a candle. I walked the hallway. I heard voices, a girl. I thought that it was the girl. I thought: she is not dead. We buried her alive, and she has come back. She is back from the woods, a ghost. I went downstairs, my hand trembling as I held the candle. The wax burning my skin. There was a blaze in the fireplace. It lit, it lighted, it illuminated in shadows and shapes the room. I saw Ro and the girl—I watched them—I watched her—I did not turn away—her ghost skin; her ghost body in the firelight; the wood shifted in the fire; a flame leapt; the light caught her. I saw her face.

I saw the girl.

It was not a ghost.

She turned; I saw.
It was Wren.
Eloise was in the kitchen.
She was baking a cake.

I'll start again.
Father taught me how to type.
The metal key hit the paper.
Inking each letter.
Father taught me the truth.
Father knew the truth.
The world is a monster.
Eloise and I wrote a story.
I suppose there are worse things.
Than killing your parents.
In a story.
I planned how I would kill them.
In a story.
I set pen to paper.
Eloise ate an apple.
And then they died.
So perhaps a story is not a story.
It is the ghost of desire.
I told the story to Ro.
I'll start. I will. Again.
This is how the first house burned.
Eloise set the bed on fire.
She took our story.
Handwritten pages.
She scattered pages.

And she lighted a candle.

And she set the bed on fire.

She was named after Mother.

And I was named after Father.

She was under the apple tree, waiting.

With the typewriter.

It was fall.

And I fell.

We stood by the salt creek.

We watched the house burn.

The story should end here.

It does not end here.

One thing happened.

Then another.

We went to college.

We met Roman Stone.

Ro wanted a tragedy to call his own.

Paper covers rock.

And rock smashes scissors.

I know that the story did not end.

The story does not end.

Because it is not a story.

And scissors cuts paper.

I'll begin.

Not with the rock, but the idea of the rock.

Not with the girl.

But the idea of the girl.

Eloise under the apple tree.

Susu in the dark auditorium.

Wren with Ro.

Pru with a paintbrush.

Leda with her swan.

Beatrice among the blackberries.

Inj in the woods.

When Inj stood in the woods.

When Salt went on ahead.

Through the pines.

Blackbirds in the branches of the cedar trees.

I said, "Don't you have one more question for me?"

I opened her hand.

I gave her my key.

Her palm caught the sun.

And the key glittered.

I said to her, "Now you have a tragedy—"

She said, "You know who he is, don't you?"

"Who?" I said.

"Salt," she said.

The wind was in the trees.

I almost couldn't hear—

"He is," she said. "He's—"

"Roman's son," she said.

"Roman is his father," she said.

The jetty was up ahead.

She kissed her hand.

She ran.

She ran to him.

If you don't believe a story can kill you—

You haven't heard the right story.

In the myth: Zeus takes the form of a swan and rapes Leda. She gives birth to an egg, from which cracks Helen. Prince Paris chooses

Helen as the most beautiful woman in the world; he gives her the golden Hesperidian apple—a gift that causes such envy amongst the goddesses that it brings about the Trojan War. Or does it? Were events set into motion with the cracking of an egg? Or the fluttering of wings? There is a version of the story in which it is not Helen who breaks from the egg, but her twin brothers, Castor and Pollux. In some tellings, there is no egg. There is always a swan, and a girl, and rape.

This is the place to start.

Start with the girl, the god, the rape.

Prometheus steals fire.

Pandora lifts the lid.

Eve eats the apple.

Lot's wife looks back.

Moses is not allowed to enter the Promised Land after forty years in the desert.

He comes down from his mountain, and he smashes the commandments. In every version of the story there is a broken law.

Time is a winter evening.

Time is a white sheet of paper.

Snow White eats the poison apple. When the woodsman, who has come from the wicked queen, finds the girl fallen in the forest; she is so beautiful that he can't bring himself to kill her with his hatchet. He kills a deer; and with his knife cuts out the heart, puts it in a box, locks it with a key, and he brings it to the queen.

Egg.

Apple.

Swan.

Shell.

Rock.

Stone.

Water.

Law.

Hatchet.

Knife.

Heart.

Hope.

Oh, and the girl.

I mustn't forget the girl.

In every version of the story there is a girl.

Time is no measure of meaning.

Snow is falling.

This afternoon—just when I thought the story was ending—

A strange thing happened.

And everything began to begin again.

I heard a knock on the front door.

I thought that perhaps they had come for me.

I waited. I waited.

Beatrice came into the library.

"There's a girl here," she said.

There was a girl in the kitchen.

A girl—

Susu Zigouiller in her coat.

Susu sat at the kitchen table.

Her dark hair damp with snow.

"God," she said. "It's taken me forever to get here."

"How did you find the place?" I asked her.

"Whatta question," she said.

Susu looked around the kitchen.

"This is a nice house," she said.

"Whose is it?" she said.

"My father's," said Beatrice.

"Oh," said Susu. "May I have some cream?"

"I got to the island. And I started walking," Susu said. "I saw the lights, your lights, and I followed them."

"Through the woods?" said Beatrice.

"I love the woods," said Susu.

Beatrice gave Susu the cream.

Susu poured it into her cup.

We sat at the table.

"How did you get here?" I asked.

I asked, "How did you get across the lake in this weather?"

Susu held the coffee cup in both hands.

She said, "I gave a coin to the ferryman."

Happiness is a monstrosity!

   Punished are those who seek it.

I am winding my way through the labyrinth. I am chased by fate. I avoid one monster to fall on another. Has Beatrice shored up enough against the ruins to keep us safe here? Will the wine hold out? Will there be sugar and salt enough to see us till the end of time and beyond? Will I devour like the locust? Will I obliterate like the flood? Will the dove find the fresh green breast of the new world? How many times can the hourglass be upended? I will run out of soap and flour and milk. I will run out of truth and beauty. I will run out of things to run out of. I will run out of the desire of wanting. I will run out of the fear of objects. I will run out of tragedy. I will speed to my fate. So slowly. So slowly. That I will miss it as it happens. Though it is happening now. I am speeding to my fate. I will run out of girls.

I will never run out of girls.

Dr. Lemon entrusted me with his greatest treasure.

Not a painting. Nor a vase.

Not a signed first edition of a leather-bound tome.

He asked me to take care of his daughter.

When he was dead and gone.

No one is ever dead and gone.

I said, yes.

I will devour, like the locust.

Like the flood.

Like the flame that turns to holocaust.

Everything before me.

I said yes.

As a symbolic gesture.

Before I realized that there is no such thing.

Not an eagle or a trumpet.

Not a buttered scone or crumpet.

Later, in the evening. Susu closed the door to the doctor's library behind her, and she said to me, "I came here to tell you what really happened."

Susu told me what happened.

"Roman found me," she said. "The day after you introduced us. Do you remember? At that lecture? The reading? We were late. We walked in late, remember? He called me. I went to him at his hotel. It was so—so sophisticated. You don't know how a girl longs for that."

She said, "To be sophisticated. To be grown up."

I was silent.

In the library.

I waited.

"We got along so well," she said.

"Do you want me to tell you how it was," she said. "Between us?"

"Do you want me to be vulgar?" she said.

She stood at the window.

"I can be vulgar if that's what you'd like," she said.

I said nothing.

She went on.

"I went away with him," she said. "We ate oranges. We swam in the sea. He called me his fate. Is that stupid? I know it's stupid," she said.

She laughed.

"We saw ruins," she said.

"He wrote his book," she said.

"Did you read it?" I asked.

She said, "What good can a book do for me? I went to the beach. We were happy. He said that we were happy, anyway. I never really think about things like that."

"That's when it happened," she said.

"What?" I said.

"I met him one night—in the hotel bar. He wasn't alone. He was with a man. An old friend whom he hadn't seen in forever. They drank. I drank too. Then it was late. I didn't, I don't know where the waiter had gone. The friend went to find the waiter. And Ro, he turned to me. Ro asked me to—" she said.

She waited.

"He told me what he wanted me to do."

"You don't have to tell me this," I said.

She had her back to me.

She turned.

"May I have a drink?" said Susu.

I poured her a glass of vodka.

"I did what he asked me to do," she said.

"I always did what he asked me to do," she said.

She drank.

"I spent the night with his friend," she said. "When I went back to our room in the morning—Ro was gone."

"He left you there?" I said.

"He left a plane ticket for me. That was it. I don't know," she said. "I went home. I went to the movies every day. I saw everything at the Cineplex. One day, or maybe it was night, I saw this picture— this movie about the Trojan War. Have you seen it?"

"No," I said.

"The man," she said. "Ro's friend. From the bar. He was in the movie."

Susu said that she watched the movie. With a terrible ominous feeling. She waited for the credits. And then she saw the name of the actor who played Priam.

"The king," I said.

She said. "The king."

"Who was it?" I asked.

"Zigouiller," she said.

"Zig," I said.

"Jesus," I said.

"In the hotel—" she said. "Where we stayed. There was a statue in the lobby. Ro called her Our Lady of Situations. There was a story that she could heal the sick and all that. It made the place pop- ular with tourists—they came to see the lady. To take a picture with the lady. It bothered Ro that the place was becoming popular with tourists. He said, he said—'the world may change, but not me.' That's what he said. So he always tried to knock her over," she laughed. "When he walked by. Gave her an elbow—a shove. He couldn't help himself. Some people said the hotel had been built around the lady. But the night porter's wife told me that the owner of the place won the statue in a card game."

She laughed.

"I knew that Ro was going to Iowa," she said. "He had told me about it. How he was going to give a graduation speech. At his old school. So I went to Illyria. I went to him. He was staying in a guesthouse. The door wasn't locked. I walked in. He wasn't even surprised. He asked me was I hungry? He had just ordered dinner. 'I'm so happy that you came,' he said. 'You always know what I want. Just when I want it,' he said. I—I told him about the movie, that I saw, that I had seen the movie. That I knew who his friend was. He laughed. He said, 'So you saw Zig?' He said, 'Poor old Zig.' He said that he had never liked Zigouiller. He said that actors were stupid parrots; weren't they? I asked him why did he trick me? I asked him why did he do that to me? He seemed, oh—sad. 'To you?' he said. 'What does it have to do with you?' he said. It was a joke on Zig. That's what he said. He said, 'Zigouiller has nothing to do with us.'"

"And then I knew," Susu said.

"Or maybe I had always known," she said.

"Knew what?" I said.

She looked at me.

Her smooth forehead. Her moon-round face.

Her green eyes. Her dark hair.

"I knew that Roman was my father," she said.

I was looking at Susu.

"You don't mean?" I said.

"You mean—?" I said.

"Don't be vulgar," she said.

"He said that we could go away together. Someplace where things like that didn't matter. I wanted to go with him. I really did," she said.

"I asked him, 'What about my mother?'"

"'Your mother?' he said."

"Do you know what he said then?"

"He called her a whore."

Susu laughed.

"*Whore* is such a funny old-fashioned word," she said.

"'Your mother,' he said, 'lost a bet, and here you are.'"

"'Do you believe me?' he said."

"Did I believe him?

The television was on. He was watching a baseball game.

He said that it was just us now.

And didn't we have an understanding?

Didn't we get along so well?

He came toward me.

There was a pearl-handled letter opener on the table.

Wasn't that just like him?

To leave such a dangerous thing lying around?

A sharp silver knife.

A beautiful thing.

He came toward me.

He didn't stop.

He saw me looking at the knife.

He said that he had gotten it for me as a gift.

Because it was so beautiful.

Because I was beautiful.

And because I always liked letters so much.

That I should have a silver letter opener.

He handed it to me.

Its handle toward my hand.

I took the knife from him.

I pushed it in.

As hard as I could.

I stabbed him.

He fell back.

I took the knife.

He wanted me to have it.

It was such a beautiful thing.

Oh, and this. His watch.

Because mine had stopped.

He didn't need his anymore.

What could time mean to him?

Do you think it's ugly?

I'll sell it when I run out of cash.

I took the watch and the knife.

Then I left.

I got on a plane that night.

I haven't been back since.

And now here I am," she said.

Susu sat by the window—

Just as Ro had all those years ago.

"I look like him, don't I?" she said.

I couldn't look at her.

"My mother spent my whole life trying to protect me from him,"
she said. "Maybe she should have tried to protect him from me."

"Does she know?" I asked.

"I came to you," Susu said.

She came toward me.

In her hand was an envelope.

She handed it to me.

She put it in my hand.

Then she turned away.

She asked for a drink.

I filled her glass.

She drank.

On the envelope was written: *S. Z.*

I opened it.

Inside there was a folded sheet of paper.

I read it.

There was one sentence.

Handwritten, inked—

How does the story end?

Susu stared out at the water.

The birds flew dark-winged—

Snow was falling.

Night fell and was fallen.

I tried to give her the paper.

It fell from my hand.

It fluttered.

To the floor.

She picked it up.

She crumpled it in her hand.

And she threw the paper in the fire.

She watched it burn.

She laughed.

She held out her glass.

She wanted more.

"I'm a monster," she said.

I handed the glass back to her.

She tapped her fingers on the windowpane.

"He knew," she said.

"He knew all along. And he thought that it would be a good story," she said.

"Is it?" she said.

And she stood.

She drank.

She set down her glass.

She sat.

She sat across from me.

I looked at her.

She became her father.

A storyteller in love with a story.

"I killed him," she said.

"Why?" I asked her.

She paused.

She stared into her empty glass.

"Because that was how the story had to go," she said.

She laughed.

Susu leaned back in the chair.

She rested her cheek against the velvet cushion.

Her features softened.

She was her mother.

She was Eloise Schell with that look on her face—just before she would call out, *Hey Shelly—no hands—*and plunge downhill on her bicycle.

When Father taught us right from wrong.

When Mother's kindness was a beautiful thing.

"Aren't you afraid?" I said.

"Of what?" she said.

"Getting caught," I said.

"Caught?" she said.

"I don't worry about getting caught, no," she said.

"I only had one father," she said.

She held her glass out to me.

I refilled it.

She drank.

"I loved him," she said.

"Love?" I said.

"Am I being too vulgar?" she said.

The snow fell and fell.

"What will you do now?" I said.

"Now?" she said.

"What would you do?" I asked.

"If you had a lot of money?" I said.

She set her glass on the table.

"I'd go away," she said.

"I want to give you," I said. "Everything."

"Your wife's money?" she said.

"It's mine," I said.

"I don't want your money," she said.

"Why not?" I said.

"It seems like a punishment," she said.

"It is," I said.

"Rock, paper, scissors me for it," I said.

"A game?" she said.

She was quiet.

She did not speak.

She placed both her hands flat, palms down on the table.

Then she made a fist.

We counted out.

One, two, three.

She chose scissors.

"Did I win?" she said.

There was a rap at the door.

Beatrice stood in the doorway.

She asked did we want coffee?

Did we want chocolate cake?

Susu said that chocolate cake sounded good.

She rose.

She stood—

And then she saw the broken swan.

A snapped neck; a wing; a black glittering eye.

Susu found the broken statue.

She held the broken glass in her hands.

And she began to piece the swan back together again.

Whores or no whores? That is the question.

That night the story ended.

Dr. Lemon passed from this life into the next.

In the manner of a saint.

I would not believe it if I had not seen it.

I saw it for myself.

I was with him as he lay upon the bed.

Under a white blanket.

At his head was a candle.

There were candles about the room.

Beatrice had lighted them.

A cold wind passed through the room.

And the candles flickered.

I felt all the pain of knowledge pass from me.

And there was an attar of roses.

Beatrice reached forward and closed her father's eyes.

She did as he had asked of her.

She always did what he asked of her.

She placed a new penny upon each closed eye.

As payment to the ferryman.

My hair has gone to silver.

Like Moses before the burning bush.

Or any other witness to a miracle.

CHAPTER 21

Susu puts the broken swan back together

WE SAT AT THE TABLE IN THE BARROOM of that grand old Chicago hotel out of the sun and the heat, and he drank whiskey, and he ordered for me plum brandy. He said, "I am going to tell you a story." He said, "Let me tell you how it ends first. This is how it ends: you are going to kill someone." I laughed. He laughed. And the waiter came by with another round. "Who?" I said. He drank. He tossed the coin on the table. "Me," he said. I watched the coin. "What?" I said. "You?" I said. I had never been drunk before in the afternoon. I said, "I couldn't kill anyone." He said, he joked, "Not even me? I'll tell you how. I'll teach you." He said, "It won't be so difficult." He laughed. "Believe me: in the end you will want to do it. You'll look forward to it. You will understand why it has to happen," he said. I said, "You sound like someone in a movie." He said, "Do you like movies?" He covered the coin with his hand. He asked me then, did I want to know how the story was going to begin? I said, "If you are trying to get me to sleep with you, I'll do that anyway, so you don't have to be mysterious or talk about murder or." He spun the coin, no; it was my ring. He spun the gold ring on the white cloth. He said, "Don't be vulgar." He said, "You're so beautiful, it doesn't suit you, being vulgar." He opened his palm and my ring disappeared. It was gone. I wasn't afraid. I saw him. I saw him look at me. I saw that he was in love with someone else. He was in love with a story. It was not a story. It was a ghost story. I went away with him. The clocks stopped and the bells rang off-time and the night porter's wife brought bread and raspberry jam in a chipped bowl. It was sweet. It was good, and we ate and ate we ate walnuts, pistachios, dates, figs, bread, and cheese we ate sunwarmed grapes and drank wine and glasses of liquor spirits ghosts of anise of wormwood of black plum and licorice and cherry we ate olives, eggs, and honey cake and we drank coffee and he wrote while I went wandering ruins. I swam in the sea. The sea did not scare me. The stars did not scare me. On the beach among the rocks there were snakes but the snakes did not scare me. He who is destined to hang will not drown. Each morning I asked him a question. He would not, would never answer. I asked him how the story was to begin. Each morning I asked him my question. And then one morning he answered. I knew that this was the last morning. I do not believe that the story is over. I do not believe that it is a story. This did not stop him from telling it. He told me he taught me he led me by the arm down twisting streets by the light of lanterns through a carnival where girls sold flowers and we ate salt and we ate sweet. It is not a story. It was not a story. It was an ax. It was a fire. It was a flood. But it was not a story. It was a carnival. And we walked. A boy ran in front of us, snapped our picture with an instant camera, and then, waving the photo, held out his hand. We paused against the water to watch the picture go from shadow into us we stood and then we became us and we walked on in the flickering green lights and the ting ting tang closer closer as we passed by a boy a child a brother banging a drum while a dog jumped hop hop hop up and down and the flower girls laughed and a sister danced and he threw handfuls of coins so many they scattered the coins rolled the girls laughed and he threw coins into the basket and watched the girl dancing for her brother's drum her skirt her stockings her little shoes and he took my hand in his. He is gone now and there will be no more of him. No more missed trains or days between stations. Or bread and butter and pots of jam. No more chocolate stars coins tossed or cards fallen. No more carnivals. No more omens or fortune-tellers or oracles or prognostications. No more soliloquies cigarettes or stolen lines. No more of him. I did what he asked of me. I did what he wanted. He asked me to kill him. He told me that this was how the story had to go. The author asked me to do it. He wanted me to end his story. He told me to. He dared me to. Because I was young and I wasn't afraid of anything was I? Because I was his. I belonged to him. Because it was his story and this was how it had to go. I saw the burning king. I saw the king burning. I remember I remember. We were lost in a carnival a day all of flowers a night of falling darkness and we walked twisting streets he took my arm away along the water strung with lights. I was walking with him winding our way along a seawall stone steps children lighting our way with candles twined with burning knots of sage and we went down like we were making a descent down down down to his underworld. He said, "One day you will turn against me." The sky was dark. The sea was dark. The night was burning. I said, "I won't." He said, "Then maybe it will be night." A girl ran past us. He watched. There were effigies of straw strung up from posts and the night was lit by stars and small fires and colored lights strung in loops. The girl cried out in the darkness. A bell tolled, an hour passed, tea went cold in a cup, a bird flew from a branch, a spider crawled along a faucet, a hand pulled the chain on a lamp. We did not move. We stood on the stone steps. He held my face in his hands. It seemed like forever. A boy bounced a ball against a stone wall. Torches were lit. He said, "You would do anything that

I asked, wouldn't you? You aren't afraid, are you?" He took my hand as the narrow walk gave way to a wide esplanade where children took up the burning torches and lighted the bodies on fire and girls sold flowers and we followed the stone street its turns along past girls holding wreaths of white with petals scattering past little boys throwing balls past the lemon and licorice sellers past the burning king and the children singing singing in paper crowns. I said, "Tell me the story." There were ships with dark sails on the water. We walked. We passed a fortune-teller a strongman a tiny lady. He said, "There are rules to telling a story." The bodies were burning in smoke and straw and flame. I waited. I waited. It seemed like forever and it might have been. A girl handed me a knot of flowers tied with a green string. He took the flowers from my hands. He untied the string. He dropped the flowers, the white flowers, to the ground, the petals scattered. He took the string and he tied back my hair. He held my face in his hands. And he said, "The rules apply to everyone else in the world, not to you." And we walked. We passed we walked we passed men holding torches. Past women selling sweets. He bought figs and sugared dates there were pomegranate jellies and caramels and bright taffies salted and wrapped in waxen twists that we unwrapped as he talked of deceit as we passed the bearded lady and the fatman and the two-headed snake and he talked about desire as we saw the fire-eater the tightrope walkers the jugglers of knives as he talked of disease oh he talked like the ting tang ting of the tin drum coming from up ahead of us the hot night by the light of lanterns and strung with colored lights as he ate hot toasted sesame crisps from a little paper funnel poured them out into my hand burning my fingers as we walked and I said tell me about the sea about the stars tell me everything tell me teach me tell me about the future tell me about the monsters tell me about the ghosts, tell me. And he told and he told as we passed the mind readers the spoon benders the mermaid lady with her mournful calling refrain a card fallen is a card played tell me about the hearts and the diamonds tell me tell teach me every word and say every word but never say her name never say her name he never said her name until the last morning no tell me about the burning king as we walk through the world. We walked through the world. Past girls carrying white graveyard flowers with drooping tragic faces losing petals along the path and lilies they held lilies out to us as we passed. He only said my name once. It was a hot dull morning. We had coffee and oranges on the balcony. He stood at the crumbling stone peeling an orange. He looked down at the street below. He said, "I saw you years ago." I came to the balustrade and stood next to him, holding my demitasse. The coffee was bitter black boiled through with cardamom and sweetened with honey. "It was snowing," he said. "I called after you. I called Eloise, El—" He looked at me in the sun, and I pitied him. He put a hand to my face, and I knew that he wasn't really talking to me, that he was talking to her, to my mother. He said, "You wore a coat with a fur collar." He said, "You looked like a ghost." And then he broke the orange into two, and he handed half to me. He said, "I'm sorry." He said, "I'm sorry about the world. I'm sorry that this is all that is left for you, just bones and rotten broken things." He looked down at the street. This was the last morning of coffee and oranges and green birds on the balcony looking for bread, because he fed them his crusts and crumbs: a croissant, a jam brioche, a napoleon, sesame wafers, seed-cake, sugar crackers, crisps, biscuits for the awaiting birds. It was morning, and he talked, as he watched the girls on their bicycles, as we stood on the balcony. He was tired. He was weary. He had aged a thousand years in a night. A bird flew low, fluttered. I said, I asked him, "How does the story begin?" He picked up from his plate a heel of bread, buttered. He broke the hard floury crust to bits and scattered it for the birds. He licked the butter from his fingers. He turned. He went from the sun of the balcony back into the room all shadow. He went to the table. He sat. His back was to me. He did not answer. Each morning I asked him this: the same question. And he would never answer. Each morning I opened the box in which he kept his pens and he would choose one. I opened the box. I collected my things for the seaside: my postcards, licorice, a mystery novel that sentence by sentence unraveled so that I could not remember the sentence that came before the one that I had just read even as it passed before my eyes. He sat at the table. I was at the door. I looked back. A shadow fell across his arm as he chose a pen. I had a terrible feeling. I felt. I thought. I felt too young. I thought that I might never see him again. I hoped that I would never see him again. I was going to leave and then, because I was young, and I thought that I would never see him again, because the green birds and bread and oranges prophesied, promised omens, and that the foreign sky was too old, too hot, too ancient for me; I went back to him. I waited. I waited. He set down his pen. I did not know how to begin. And he said, "Start with the girl, the god, the rape." There was sun from the balcony, but he sat in shadow. He untied the knotted ribbon that tied his manuscript. A sheet of paper fell to the floor. I saw my name written on it. And didn't I feel terror then? He took my hands, one in each of his hands. He turned them over, palms up and open, and he kissed first one, then the other, the inside of my wrist. Then he closed my hands into fists. And he let go. It was not early. It was not late, but it was time to go. I left our room. I ran. I began to run. I ran through the lobby, past the men on velvet sofas, past our lady of situations, and out to the street, even though the morning was gone to afternoon, hot and dusty. I ran. I was happy to be free of him and sad too. My fingers tasted of ink and oranges, and the birds collected their butter and bread and twigs and bones and took them to dark dark places. I ran all the way in sunlight down to the water.

CHAPTER 22

Sheldon rebuilds the ruined fountain

IT IS JULY. I have written as accurate and true a recollection of events as can be expected of a liar.

My manuscript, untitled—with the pages inked and demarcated by my initials—is finished. I want no one to read it. As the words gave me far more pleasure—and pain—to write than could be felt by any reader. I keep the story in a box. The box fits my manuscript exactly. Or is it the other way around? Will you believe me when I say that I myself built this wondrous box? It is cedar, with hand-fascinated corners. It is a puzzle of a thing. It is so smooth, and the grain so rich, that the box seems neither to open nor close. Is it a box? It is perhaps a shell. Or shall I call it a symbol? Fate finds forms for all things. And man makes his own metaphors. The little world of the story is a strange place. I sometimes wonder if these characters were real or only the monsters of my solitude. Who but a monster would be so lonely for a story? As for me: I have no more stories to tell. I live in the doctor's house. I am repairing the house. I have begun with the garden. I have a shovel, a hatchet, and a spade. See? The ruined fountain runs with water from the ancient cistern. The roses climb and tumble. The vines tangle. The first grapes are ripening. They are hard and sweet. The flowers are in bloom. The birds have returned. The water, the dogs, the gods, the ghosts, the trees— are the same and not the same. In the fall there will be apples. My cat brings me mice. Beatrice is expecting a child. She hopes for a girl. She hopes for a girl with black hair and green eyes. At night I hear strange cries from the woods. Beatrice says our life is perfect. Beatrice says that we are happy. Perhaps she is not altogether wrong.

After dinner at that little place where in the summer one sits outside on the terrace under the stars to stare up at Orion the hunter and Cassiopeia and the Dippers Big and Small, so that one barely looks at the flowers and the candles; and a girl goes from table to table asking to read your fortune in her cards; and the waiters discreetly pour your glass but leave the bottle——, he had fruits of the sea (with mollusk, oyster, prawn, and crab) and she the pomegranate soufflé; and then a movie (that war epic; a big hit at the box office) during which in the darkness when he put his hand under her blouse she nearly burst out laughing; and then back to the hotel for dessert (Schokoladeneis—already melting but no less sweet or bitter or delicious—) and Turkish coffee in cups painted with the faces of saints; it was late or maybe it was early. There was time for all things. There was time yet for some talk of you and me, and Eloise asked him to tell her a story. He said, "A story?" He said, "You are making this far too difficult. It's easy. It's very easy. It has been a story all along. It has been nothing but a story. El, it's just the kind of story that you like: the good are rewarded and the bad will be punished. That's what you like, isn't it? Don't I know you?" he said. "Don't I know what you like?" Louie touched her cheek. She kissed the palm of his hand. She said, "Let the black flower blossom as it may."

In a place to which you will never go; in a city to which you have never been; in a house on a side street where the shadows are the only relief; up the steps—a door is open, and a cat sleeping in the doorway out of the heat; there is a girl in the kitchen. She is singing along to a song on the radio, but you don't know the song. She is boiling milk on the stove. She pours the milk into a bowl, and puts the bowl on a tray, and fills a small pitcher with cream, and there is a dish of sugar cubes and almonds, a jar of honey, and a spoon; and bread and butter on a plate; she carries the tray up the narrow staircase to a room on the second story. He is at the window. She speaks low; you don't know what she says. It isn't a language that you know. She sets the tray on the table. And while he watches, she places—the bowl, the plate, the pitcher, the sugar and almonds, and arranges them on the faded cloth. She waits for him to say something, but he says nothing. You will never see her face, so it doesn't matter what she looks like; only that she is young and strange; she is wearing a flowered dress; and he likes to look at her. He sits at the table—before him: the bread and honey; a knife; a spoon; volumes of poetry by dusty old authors whom you once vowed to read, but have not as yet gotten around to it; caramels, a key; there are coins, scissors, and a box. He opens the box. The room overlooks a garden. The girl has gone into the garden. After a time, he hears the girl in the garden talking to a little boy. The boy throws a ball against the garden wall. Then the evening is quiet. It seems almost wrong—it does not seem entirely right—to break the silence with words; and he sets his pen to a sheet of paper. Roman Stone is writing a book. It is a story about a brother and a sister. He writes by hand. He writes from memory. He makes it up as he goes along. He writes for a long time. It is dark. It is night. Later: the girl comes back to him. She smells like flowers and licorice; like smoke and chocolate and oranges. In the darkness—she turns her back to him. She takes off her dress. She is naked on the bed. He imagines, perhaps: the world.

Susu in a black string bikini stares up at the sun on a white sand beach. She begins to write an address on a postcard she found in that little curio shop; do you know the place?—where the bright green parrot called Balzac sits in the window reciting dirty limericks and at closing time mournfully coos: *Perdoo, Perdoo*—

Upon the postcard is a picture of the talking parrot.

He is something of a local celebrity.

The day is hot. A dog runs along the shore. The dog runs loops and circles. Susu laughs. She leaves her postcard in the sand. And she runs after her dog. Susu runs to the sea. The water is so warm one could stay in it all day. She doesn't even mind the salt.

Colophon

Let the Dark Flower Blossom was designed at Coffee House Press,
in the historic Grain Belt Brewery's Bottling House
near downtown Minneapolis.
Fonts include Bembo and Copperplate Gothic.

COFFEE HOUSE PRESS

The mission of Coffee House Press is to publish exciting, vital, and enduring authors of our time; to delight and inspire readers; to contribute to the cultural life of our community; and to enrich our literary heritage. By building on the best traditions of publishing and the book arts, we produce books that celebrate imagination, innovation in the craft of writing, and the many authentic voices of the American experience.

Good books are brewing at coffeehousepress.org

Funder Acknowledgment

COFFEE HOUSE PRESS is an independent, nonprofit literary publisher. Our books are made possible through the generous support of grants and gifts from many foundations, corporate giving programs, state and federal support, and through donations from individuals who believe in the transformational power of literature. Coffee House Press receives major operating support from Amazon, the Bush Foundation, the Jerome Foundation, the McKnight Foundation, from Target, and in part from a grant provided by the Minnesota State Arts Board through an appropriation by the Minnesota State Legislature from the State's general fund and its arts and cultural heritage fund with money from the vote of the people of Minnesota on November 4, 2008, and a grant from the Wells Fargo Foundation of Minnesota. Support for this title was received from the National Endowment for the Arts, a federal agency. Coffee House also receives support from: several anonymous donors; Suzanne Allen; Elmer L. and Eleanor J. Andersen Foundation; Around Town Agency; Patricia Beithon; Bill Berkson; the E. Thomas Binger and Rebecca Rand Fund of the Minneapolis Foundation; the Patrick and Aimee Butler Family Foundation; the Buuck Family Foundation; Ruth Dayton; Dorsey & Whitney, LLP; Mary Ebert and Paul Stembler; Chris Fischbach and Katie Dublinski; Fredrikson & Byron, P.A.; Sally French; Anselm Hollo and Jane Dalrymple-Hollo; Jeffrey Hom; Carl and Heidi Horsch; Alex and Ada Katz; Stephen and Isabel Keating; Kenneth Kahn; the Kenneth Koch Literary Estate; Kathy and Dean Koutsky; the Lenfestey Family Foundation; Carol and Aaron Mack; Mary McDermid; Sjur Midness and Briar Andresen; the Nash Foundation; the Rehael Fund of the Minneapolis Foundation; Schwegman, Lundberg & Woessner, P.A.; Kiki Smith; Jeffrey Sugerman and Sarah Schultz; Patricia Tilton; the Archie D. & Bertha H. Walker Foundation; Stu Wilson and Mel Barker; the Woessner Freeman Family Foundation; Margaret and Angus Wurtele; and many other generous individual donors.

amazon.com

To you and our many readers across the country,
we send our thanks for your continuing support.

OUR SOMETIME SISTER
"Labiner, narrating in several distinct and haunting voices, proves herself a metafictional adept. She succeeds in crafting an ambitious, poignant and sharp-tongued novel filled with secrets and ghosts, jealousy and love."
—PUBLISHERS WEEKLY

MINIATURES
"A splendid, leisurely meditation on the meaning of fame, identity, and love . . ."
—KIRKUS REVIEWS (starred review)
• 2003 American Library Association
  Notable Book
• 2003 William Saroyan International Prize
  for Writing Shortlist

GERMAN FOR TRAVELERS
Alternating between the rise of Nazi Germany, 1960s and 1970s Detroit, and modern-day Berlin, this is a story about a girl whose dreams reveal the future, a family beset by ghosts, and the place that haunts them all.